I0655133

In the Shadows of My Mind

Andrew Massie

Savant Books and Publications
Honolulu, HI, USA
2017

Published in the USA by Savant Books and Publications
2630 Kapiolani Blvd #1601
Honolulu, HI 96826
http://www.savantbooksandpublications.com

Printed in the USA

Edited by Colleen O'Brien
Cover image © Pavel Losevsky | Dreamstime.com - White serious mask
and black mask
Cover by Daniel S. Janik

13 digit ISBN: 9780997247206

Dedication/Acknowledgement

For Lauren, Erik, and the Blue Cape Club.
Where would I be without you guys?

Prologue
Sunday, February 27, 2011

A funeral ends in the southern town of Hazelwood. An old woman has passed away, a member of the congregation. Though most people did not know her personally, they have come to pay their respects out of principle. The Methodist megachurch by the interstate, big enough to seat the entire town, slowly empties as the attendees disperse. They keep their eyes on the son of the departed, the most famous man to leave Hazelwood in a long time. They call him the Hero of Hazelwood, some earnestly, others ironically. Many know he was not born in Hazelwood. His family came fled the violence of neighboring Mastern when he was in high school. But at thirty, he is already more accomplished than his peers, so they claim him. He brings to the town an air of sophistication, of success, that it only hints at otherwise. They take pictures of and with him, and when they go home, they will tell their families and friends they saw him. The Hero of Hazelwood, in the flesh, standing beside his mother's casket. The image is mythical to them; they will carry it with them for years.

Among them is a boy of nineteen, another Hazelwood transplant. He has no business being at this funeral, did not know the deceased, even tangentially, but he came in his Sunday best. He observes quietly, respectfully, his hands folded in his lap. Were he more familiar to them, the men and women of Hazelwood might not even notice him. But they do, acknowledging his presence by ignoring it. Their silence toward him is so palpable, he might as well be alone in the cavernous room. As they begin to shuffle slowly out the door, he slips through the crowd like a mouse through a maze, finding each empty space to slide through until he reaches the end. Almost before anyone can comment, he is gone.

It had been an unusually cold winter, reaching below ten degrees at its worst. For the students who came from the north to attend university, it proved mild: a welcome retreat from the snow, from frozen roads, burst pipes, and the depression that grips with hands of gloom. For the southerners, it feels like death is resting in their chests. "Cold as a witch's tit," one resident remarks. "Mhm," their neighbor grunts noncommittally. They drive home, caught in the traffic they create, past dilapidated farm houses, rotting properties, confederate flags tattered by the winter wind. They remove their nice clothes and replace them with comfortable ones. Relieved of the day's duties, they return to their tattoos and piercings, tobacco and booze, their drugs and other escapes from reality. The richest among them gather for bourbon and barbecue. The poorest retreat to their couches and recliners, losing themselves in the television, attempting to enjoy the last few hours of peace before they must return to work.

The son of the deceased waits in the church, politely nodding as the townspeople drift by. His partner, his lover, stands beside him. The people of Hazelwood don't like her. They ask themselves why the Hero of Hazelwood ended up with her. She is not from Hazelwood, even if she did graduate from the university. Her skin has a suspect tint to it, and she dresses immodestly, showing off her strong, trained body. When she smiles, she beams arrogance and sexuality. At thirty one, she has no kids, no husband. They judge her and talk about her in hushed voices, hands covering their mouths. Who does she think she is? But then they remember, with the long memory of a small town, that he's always had bad taste in women. Remember his old flame, the Mincks girl? She's divorced you know, no children. She teaches that feminist drivel up at the university. And why is the Hero of Hazelwood so fond of these girls? What was wrong with their southern daughters, of whom they could name several eligible? He must be wrong in the head, they conclude. What else could it be?

The town goes home with the sun, and the man and his partner finish their duties at the church. They wait until the sanctuary is clear, the street empty, and then they fly between the walls of trees that line the interstate, away from the small town. The pines sway, dancing in the wind, and down the road, the sun falls behind the city of Mastern. The man carries sadness and anger in his heart. The woman carries anxiety in hers. Neither is much looking forward to the dinner they have to attend. But they are obliged. The Knights of Hazelwood have not met in more than ten years; it is due time for the Hero of Hazelwood to join them.

Part 1

The Whirlwind of Lovers

Andrew Massie

Chapter 1
The Knights of Hazelwood

Sunday, February 27, 2011

Stephen's grip on his steak knife tightened as he awaited what he figured would be an intentional slight from Matt toward Olivia. Nobody at the table noticed the way Stephen's knuckles tensed, the way he changed the angle of the blade, the way the serrated edges tore through the tender meat. Stephen himself didn't notice. I noticed.

At the time, I considered drawing his attention to it, making him aware of the way his knuckles arched just a little more than they should have. I decided against it, though. Calling his attention to his own subconscious would have taken his mind from the table of friends and the business at hand. I was especially concerned about Natalie. At that time, neither Stephen nor Natalie knew I existed. None of them knew I existed. But if anyone were to discover me, under the layers of Stephen's behaviors and thoughts, it would be Natalie.

Stephen had suspicions, but he had just chalked it up to his heavy case load, bureau politics and the usual everyday stresses. He had lived with me for years, but I had learned how to make myself a ghost, for the most part. Every now and then he would find his badge somewhere other than where he'd left it. Once in awhile, he would find the bottle of a beer that he hadn't drunk. Once, and only once, he woke up in bed with a girl he did not remember seducing. He would get headaches for no reason, massaging his temple with his right hand while he talked to his coworkers, or his waiter, or simply someone on the street. He could see the nervousness and apprehension it caused, but he was skilled in getting people to trust him, despite his quirks. Sometimes he would hear sounds or see images that didn't exist, that he knew couldn't exist. He could become angry for no reason, and in those times that he was angry, everyone near him said he wasn't himself. Still, despite all the evidence, his suspicion never once took form. Those vague feelings never once solidified into the phrase he was already familiar with. Dissociative Identity Disorder. Multiple personalities. These concepts enriched his understanding of the human mind, and he had been drawn to them since his time at the university. In theory and in practice, he was intimately familiar with them. But he never believed they had anything to do with him. His denial, his ability to rationalize, was strong.

"To success!" Matthew announced, raising his glass.

Stephen glanced around the table quickly as he raised his own small reservoir of wine. With the exception of Natalie, who was as observant as Stephen, he saw no sign that anyone else had caught the slip, and it made him feel a little better. At the same time, though, the thought took hold that at least one of them should stick up for Olivia. He drank his wine and forgot it, because it never occurred to him that he could be the one to do so. I didn't understand at that time why such a simple idea escaped him. He never stopped thinking about Olivia, and now, in her time of need, he was silent. But there were things happening in Stephen's mind that I could not know, did not see. Since his mother died, his thought process was more erratic, so I could not follow it the way I once had. I was invisible to him.

He was becoming a mystery to me.

Even as it didn't occur to Stephen that he could stick up for Olivia, neither did it occur to him that Matthew was slighting him most of all. Not because Stephen was unsuccessful; on the contrary, Stephen Lanford was the most successful person at the table. He was an honored veteran employee of the Federal Bureau of Investigation, having achieved Special Agent status after taking in three of the most publicly infamous serial killers in the last ten years, all thanks to his special skills as a natural-born psychological profiler. He was the cream of this small town named Hazelwood, the most important member of his graduating class, the most successful of the thirteen people who sat at that round table.

Natalie, his lover, sat to his right, while Olivia, the love of his life, sat only a few seats to his left. Matthew and Edna Graycraft sat almost directly across from Stephen and Natalie, turning the table into a battlefield. The old rivalry of their two factions hung in the air between them, unspoken yet tangible. To the right of the Graycrafts were Ryan and Kate Gathers, who had ridden Matthew's coattails into a comfortable business-class lifestyle that the couple was unprepared to live up to. That didn't stop them from trying, however. Between the Graycrafts and Natalie, Helen and James Dunn sat absorbed in their own conversation, not whispering but not heard by the rest of the table. The two of them had built a separate peace, remaining involved with the flustering dramatics of their old group, yet always careful never to be drawn into the tide of those other lives. Gilbert and Columbus sat to Stephen's left, filling in the seats between Stephen and Olivia. Dave Burns sat to Olivia's left, quietly resenting Matthew, tacitly supporting Stephen. David had brought a date, Sylvia, who sat to his left, acting as a buffer between him and the Gathers. But, as with many of David's dates, that was the last time any of us would see her. The Knights of Hazelwood were gathered around a table in an expensive restaurant in Mastern, and there they did verbal battle.

Natalie rubbed her bare leg against Stephen's pants, moving it back and forth slowly like a bow over a violin. The feeling soothed his nerves. He looked at her and caught the flash of her smile before she held her glass to her lips and drank. Her breasts rose and fell in irregular patterns as the sweet red liquid slipped inside her pink kiss. Stephen himself almost felt the bubbles forming in her bosom, the waves of pleasure flowing through her muscles, the tinge of desire being kindled in her heart. He felt his breathing deepen as he smiled at her.

On another night, he might have let himself slide into that intoxicating passion that befalls humanity in situations such as these: Wine flowing through the bloodstream, a beautiful partner full of life, energy and ambition, a twinkle in the eyes caught between each glance. Stephen suppressed that passion, much to my dismay. He would have gone with Natalie, gladly, would have taken her as his equal, as his partner, as his better half. She would have been good to him. But he saw Olivia in his eyesight's periphery, and he went back to swallowing pieces of overpriced steak.

Natalie caught that one, and her leg disappeared under her chair. Of course she was more sensitive to matters of Stephen and Olivia than she was to the way that Stephen cut his steak, but it still impressed me that she picked up on so subtle a glance.

It dawned on me that I underestimate her sometimes. She's never been as perceptive as Stephen: Stephen saw the way Kate lifted her chin toward Matt. He smelled the gentle lavender perfume she wore, heard the soft giggles she gave to every one of Matt's jokes and knew that she and Matt were having an affair. Stephen didn't figure that Ryan knew Kate was cheating on him, as he would every so often reach out and rub the small of Kate's back in the cut of the dress where the skin was bare. It was the touch of a man who loves his wife, the small token of a fool who does not know he's being cuckolded. But Stephen knew that Edna was aware of the affair. She folded her hands with deliberate actions that betrayed her ire and distaste for the man to her right. Every one of Edna's actions was precise, calculated. Matt noticed. Stephen caught all of this, but Natalie didn't seem to. I assumed she was too distracted by Stephen and the presence of Olivia.

"So tell me, Stephen," Edna leaned forward onto her elbows, giving Stephen a clear view of her cleavage as she prepared to verbally assault Matthew's ego, "was it harder catching Stringfield or writing the book about catching Stringfield?"

Stephen smiled, both out of courtesy for Edna's question and out of pleasure at the wince that flashed across Matthew's face. Natalie held her napkin to her mouth and covered the smile that came involuntarily.

"Well," Stephen started out, smiling lightly at Edna, "they both presented their own challenges, but when I almost had the account pinned down, it didn't fire a shotgun at me." Everyone laughed, although some of them more out of courtesy than out of genuine appreciation for the man and his quip. "But honestly, I enjoy being an agent more than a writer. Being an agent is what I'm good at. Writing is just a hobby."

"It sounds very exciting," Edna went on. "Getting to travel anywhere you want to, getting to see America, having grand adventures…"

Stephen felt Natalie stiffen, her spine straighten. Edna had apparently overstepped her boundary as far as Natalie was concerned. "Don't believe everything you see on the television," Natalie said. "You're essentially signing away your own agency when you become an agent. You don't get to choose where you go, where you stay, who you go after. It's a hard life. I wouldn't wish it on my worst enemy." She reached over and took Stephen's hand, running her thumb gently over his knuckles. "Of course, it helps when you have good company. But that's completely luck of the draw. I had to work with a lot of agents before they put me and Stephen back together."

Olivia's fork plunged through her steak and loudly scraped the surface of her plate.

"So, Olivia," Matt said, turning his eyes on the girl, "how is your semester going?"

Olivia shot a glance at Stephen and Natalie. There were several emotions reflected on her face, some of which even Stephen, who shared an intense history with her, couldn't identify. The main emotion he could see, painted in broad strokes, was regret. Once upon a time, all those years ago, Olivia was to be the best of the knights. She planned to travel the world, make a name for herself, go down in history. Suppose she had been able to leave Hazelwood like the rest of them, do something with her life, be a big success like all of them, rather than stay in the small college town and teach. Imagine she had gone home with Stephen that fateful night all those years ago, had made love to him, had married him. What would her life have been like all these years later? Then again, maybe she just wished she had chosen to take a bite of potato, rather than alert Matt to her discomfort with Natalie. In scraping her plate, she had given Matthew not only a new target but ammo with which to return fire on Stephen's party. Further still, maybe where I give Natalie too little credit, I give Olivia too much. Perhaps the past, perhaps the present, perhaps the future did not pass through her mind in the instant before she answered Matt's question. Maybe she was just uncomfortable in the way that people left behind are when confronted with capitalist success.

"It's great," she answered simply. "I'm using Stephen's book as an example of a non-fiction thriller. The students are tickled that anyone from Hazelwood is actually a celebrity." She smiled the quick, jerky smile they all remembered from her youth. "One of my more gifted students is considering following in Stephen's footsteps, going off to join the FBI once he graduates. He's an English Literature/Psychology double major. Absolutely brilliant…" Lowering her eyes to the candle in the center of the table, she finished, "…if I do say so myself."

What does she mean by that? Stephen wondered, his head tilting to one side, his mouth twisting slightly.

Kate yawned loudly, only half covering her mouth with the tips of her fingers.

"Tired, my dear?" Ryan asked.

"No, this conversation is just really boring," Kate told him, smiling at Matt for having done good by him.

Olivia gave a noncommittal smile. All night she had seemed distracted, as though she was living in a different world, her body simply floating through the events of the evening. When she was younger, she would have challenged Kate. Now, she simply ignored the insults slung in her direction. They passed through her as though she were a hologram. Natalie, though, covering her mouth with her napkin, muttered under her breath so that only Stephen could hear it, "Fucking Kate."

Stephen just nodded. The words built up inside him, attempting to wrench themselves violently from his mouth, attempting to put Matt and his regime in their place. But Stephen kept his teeth clenched firmly together and no words escaped.

His control impressed me. I often wondered where Stephen's anger stemmed from. It came and went in ebbs and flows, sometimes as regularly as the tides. Other times it would well up randomly, provoked by nothing and no one. It was worse when he didn't know it was coming. Then, it would slip out like fire through cracks in a building. But when he knew the fire was coming, when he knew the anger was about to build, he could seal it up, suffocate it in its kindling. Seated here while Kate and Matt attacked Olivia, he wanted a fight, but he chose instead to fold his hands in his lap and smile.

"So what is in store for you and Natalie?" Ryan asked, looking over at the couple.

Stephen announced, "We'll be in Hazelwood for the next week, squaring away my mother's affairs. After that, we'll be heading back to Virginia."

"Where are you staying?" Ryan asked.

"My father's old house," Stephen answered. "Once mom's affairs are settled, I'll put both houses up for sale. So if anyone wants a summer house in Hazelwood…"

This remark was met with genuine laughs, as a few of them thought about the absurdity of living in Hazelwood again.

James took a drink of water and said, "I think Helen and I will come over to Hazelwood for the spring festival. Do you think you might want to join us?"

Stephen had almost forgotten that James and Helen were sitting just a few feet from him. Stephen and Natalie looked at each other, reading each other's faces. Stephen smiled and nodded. "I'd like that, James. You guys give us a call when you get into town. I haven't been to the festival in…" he lifted his eyes as he followed the years back in his mind to the last time he'd stood in the town-square surrounded by the festivities of the spring festival.

"Ten years," Olivia finished for him. "We were twenty."

Natalie bit her lip as Stephen said, "Yes, that's exactly right."

"We should meet up and have dinner at the barn before the festival," James said. "It'll be just like old times."

"I'd like that, James," Stephen told him.

"It ought to be fun," Natalie said.

"Everything except the drive over there." Helen tilted her eyes at James and smiled. Everybody at the table laughed.

Natalie had fallen asleep by the time they pulled into the dirt driveway of Stephen's temporary abode. He looked up at his father's house, vacant since the old man's death in a car crash only a few years ago. He'd left it to Stephen, but Stephen had left it vacant in the meantime. His mother's house was north and west, past the university, hidden in the back roads and trees at the edge of town. A few days ago, she had died. That morning he had buried her. In less than a week, her house would be emptied, and soon after it would be sold. Then there would be nothing but his past tying Stephen to Hazelwood. He saw it as an easy out, a clean cut.

Turning to Natalie, he placed his hand on her bare shoulder, shaking her lightly. Due to intoxication or exhaustion, she didn't stir. Stephen opened the side door to the house, then walked around the car and opened her door, unbuckled her seat belt and lifted her up. He wrapped her arms around his neck, her hands draped loosely around his shoulders, before carrying her across the threshold of the house. She mumbled a little as he placed her in his bed, removed her heels and covered her with his comforter.

He closed up his car, locked up the house, pulled off his coat and shirts—dress and under—and sank down into the couch. The night closed in around him as he uncorked the bottle from the side table and let the liquid slide down easily. These were good times for me. The blue light and multicolored sparkles grew in his eyes as he let his neck rest on the leather cushion behind him and raised his feet onto the coffee table. Then I floated upward toward the surface of his consciousness and tasted the warm liquid drip down into my stomach, felt the alcohol permeate my bloodstream, felt my head start to pulse with the energy of the booze as he spiraled down, the darkness flooding around him, oblivion the destination.

I used the remote to tune the stereo to a smooth jazz station and settled down as the polyrhythmic cadence beat softly into the darkness. Art and life bled into each other as Copacetic Mingus' intentional dissonance became Stephen's dark lullaby. I allowed him to fall into a dream of Olivia. In hindsight, it was a bad idea, but I thought that he deserved it for having gone the entire night without attacking Matthew or damaging his relationship with Natalie. All of a sudden he was nineteen again, at home in the shadow of the university. He was sitting outside the student café, one hand lifting a cup of coffee to his mouth as the most beautiful girl he'd ever known ran across the grass from the student center toward him.

"Lover Boy!" she shouted as he rose to his feet, eager for her in his arms, "I'm doing it! I got into the program!"

It was the happiest Stephen had ever seen her, or would ever see her again. Her smile stretched across her face, her cheeks pink with excitement, her laugh strained with the effort of her run as she leapt up. He had caught her in his arms and spun her, kissing her lips. But now he felt a hand on his shoulder, shaking the muscles in his arm still sore from the journey south, the funeral, and the tension of the night. He remained halfway in that dream from which he would not have awakened if he had any choice in the matter, and he reached outward from the couch with desperate hands, groping at the air where he wished he could grasp the hand, the arm, maybe just a loose piece of clothing of the only girl he had ever loved.

"Stephen." A voice called to him from far away, a female voice, but not the voice of the girl that he wanted it to be, not the name that she would call him. "Stephen," the voice repeated, "there's a phone call for you…"

"What?" he asked, "Who?"

"You left your cell phone in the bedroom. It's Olivia," the voice efficiently explained. Her tone was matter of fact. "Take the phone," the voice ordered. Stephen reached through the darkness to where he could barely perceive the small rectangle of plastic and silicon, explored the area with his fingers, using them the way an ant uses its antenna, its feelers, until he grasped it in his palm and brought it to his ear.

"Hello?" Olivia's voice, sweet and subtle, emanated from the phone. "Lover Boy?"

Stephen's breath caught in his throat momentarily, and for a second he thought he had never awoken from his dream, that he was still held softly in the embrace of the past. Thoughts flooded into his mind in an explosion of energy as reality reeled with the upsetting interference.

"You there, Lover Boy?"

Stephen put his pointer and middle finger to his temple and pressed, attempting to calm the flurry of pops and splutters in his consciousness caused by the chemical catastrophe of sleep interrupted. He mumbled into the phone, still not one-hundred-percent certain that this was real, that it wasn't an illusion brought on by the expensive dinner and wine he had shared with the woman in the darkness above him. In all his fantasies of the moment when he would hear from his beloved again, when he would hear that sweet voice with its gentle cadence, when his memories would fly to his twentieth year of life, he always knew exactly what to say to win her back to his side, back into his life.

"I'm here, Olivia," he uttered, his voice so slurred he almost couldn't understand himself. "What time is it?"

"It's a little after three," Olivia answered. "Don't you still have that alarm clock next to your bed? The one with the inch-high blue numbers?"

Stephen shook his head in an attempt to quell his mind into a serviceable state so that he could converse with the girl he loved. "I do, I do," he answered her, "but I'm not in my bedroom."

"Oh." Olivia laughed. "Natalie didn't let you make it to the bed, huh?"

That sweet voice, full of wry benevolence and magnanimity, stung Stephen like a barbed whip.

"Lover Boy," she started, before he made an ass of himself trying to explain, "it's alright. Look, I need your help. Is your old promise still good?"

Stephen nodded his head, the way he had the last time she had asked the question, then realized he was on the phone. "Yeah, Lover Girl," he whispered. "Always. You know that."

In that moment, they were connected again, the bond of Stephen's promise powerful enough to hold them together through time as allies against a world that was out to get anybody it could.

"I'm at the university," she told him. "I'm sitting at the old tables. You remember, don't you? The ones outside the cafe?"

"Of course," he answered. Until the day he died, he would never forget those tables. And so he said, "I'll never forget those tables. How could I?"

"It's cold, Lover Boy," she told him. "I'll see you in ten."

The phone clicked, and she was gone, and the darkness drew in around him. "Bye, Lover Girl," he said into the dead phone.

From behind him in the darkness, the voice of a woman he'd forgotten was there said, "What kind of trouble is she in now?"

He jumped slightly, reaching for the gun which he usually kept in a chest holster at his left side. But he was not wearing the gun now, nor had he worn it for several weeks. Even if the gun had been where it had been for most of his adult life, his hand would never have made it to the holster, as he recognized Natalie's voice less than a second after he reacted. Natalie flipped the switch on the light and swung her leg over the back of the couch, straddling it momentarily, showing Stephen her silky thighs. She brought her other leg around and dropped easily into position beside him. She crossed her legs, and leaned her head over, placing it gently on his shoulder as though it were a pillow.

"Natalie," he muttered, not sure exactly what he was going to say, "Everyone needs help sometimes."

Natalie gave a bitter laugh. Her dark hair reflected red highlights in the lamplight, and her chest jumped and fell a few times with the heavy breath of her laugh. Stephen observed this out of the corner of his eye. "So, what? She's your princess and you're her knight in shining armor?"

He breathed in heavily, inhaling the incense of her perfume, overcome by the intoxicating scent. "She's family," he sighed.

Natalie fumed, her eyes angled sharply up at him, accusing him without speaking. Stephen knew that she must have heard his words to Olivia, and wished she would just verbalize her fears and deductions.

"She's going to get you into some real trouble one of these days," Natalie said, wrapping her hand around his. "Don't you see that she's poison?"

"Natalie, this is the first time I've seen her since college."

"She was trouble in college, too."

"You never really knew her back then."

Natalie scoffed. She pulled his head down and lifted hers and kissed him, the bristles of his unshaved face pricking her lips. "Go get your princess, then, Sir Stephen Lanford. I'm gonna put a pot of coffee on. How long do you think you'll be?"

Stephen shook his head. "I don't know. It depends on what happened this time. Could be thirty minutes, could be three hours."

"Well, there will be coffee when you get back," Natalie told him.

"If you're still awake, you'll make me a plate, huh?"

"Of course," she answered.

Stephen stood up. He took his undershirt from the back of the recliner, pulling it over his head and snugging into place.

"Stephen?" Natalie asked quietly.

"What's up?"

"You and I are family, too, right?"

Stephen pushed his shirt into the waistband of his dress pants and looked down at her. She was beautiful, her eyes alight with that divine intelligence of hers, her body made strong by her training, lithe and supple, her mouth furrowed in that way that Stephen found cute. I always thought he'd have been better off with her. I always wished he'd give up on Olivia and see the perfect girl in front of him as something more than a plaything to pass the time. He constantly saw her as a sexual object, not as the person she was behind the smile. "Natalie," he spoke her name slowly, intentionally, as he leaned down to kiss her, his lips pressing to hers, feeling the remnants of her lipstick like a ghost on her lips. He straightened up and smiled at her. "I love you. Go make breakfast and I'll be back before four."

"Alright," Natalie said. "Godspeed, Sir Stephen of Hazelwood."

I hated him for choosing Olivia again. Here Natalie was giving him yet another chance, and here he was leading her on, just like he always did.

Stephen found his socks and wrangled his boots on. He went to the door, pulled his coat from the rack, stopped, patted the chest pocket, then pulled out his badge. Flipping it open, he looked down at its familiar shape, the golden shield atop which sat an eagle, wings raised for flight. Opposite it, an identification card with his name, face and the words "FBI: Federal Bureau of Investigation." Stephen closed it, left it on the windowsill beside the door. Then he was out the door into the cold and darkness of Hazelwood on an early February night. He made his way down the sidewalk to the bookstore at the corner, where a streetlight cast a lonely circle, then up the steep hill to the dorm buildings, and from there east between the education hall and the student center to the cafe. Olivia Mincks was there, at the table where he had first met her, wrapped in a blanket and breathing out a warm mist from her smiling lips.

"You're late, Lover Boy," she said in her low, smoky voice.

"I have a brunette cooking French toast for me. I apologize for being a minute past the unrealistic deadline you set."

"The old you would have made it," she pushed. "The old Stephen would have made it in five."

"Thanks, Lover Girl. You know things change."

"Sometimes things change. Have a seat."

It only then occurred to Stephen that instead of taking her into his arms, he was still standing, looking down at the girl with the blanket draped over her shoulders like a shawl. His princess. His family. He went to sit down across from her, but she shook her head.

"Things do change, don't they? Why don't you sit next to me?"

Stephen walked around the table, looked down into her blue eyes, thought he might drown in that vast ocean reflected in them and swooned. I didn't think I'd ever understand the effect she had over him. His hand reached out reflexively and fell on her far shoulder, his arm around her back. The fleece blanket was soft and warm. She was snuggling into his body, her chest pressing against his in the intimacy afforded by the blanket. Stephen could feel her heart beating rapidly. He felt twenty again, as though the past ten years had disappeared like his fog of breath in the cold of the night.

She laughed. "There, that's better."

Stephen remained silent for a moment. As the smell of her wafted through the air, her hair tickled Stephen's nose. He reached up and scratched it.

"You know what they say," Olivia teased him. "When your nose is itching…"

"It means someone who loves you is thinking about you," Stephen finished.

Olivia represented so many things to Stephen—the old southern town he'd grown up in, beauty and truth and innocence untouchable by her erratic actions. But she also represented the loss and pain and shame that he felt from the days of his youth here in Hazelwood. She reminded him what it was to dream and what it was to see a dream go unfulfilled. To be with Olivia made Stephen feel alive, ashamed, hopeful, distrustful. I really wished then that I hadn't allowed him to dream about her. Maybe if I had stopped his dream, I could have saved him from the influence she had over him. A part of me knows that she had such a hold on him that nothing I did would make a difference, but the idea that somehow I was responsible for what he was doing overcame my mind. Without the dream, maybe she'd have been just another girl. With the dream, she was the princess of Hazelwood, and he, a Don Quixote, rushed to rescue her.

"It wasn't me," Olivia said, pressing his nose softly with the tip of her pointer finger.

Stephen kissed it, took it into his hand, pulled her to him, tasted strawberries on her lips. "Yes it was," he replied.

"I guess you caught me, then." Her smile went limp with desire; I could see in her breathing the arousal growing in her chest. He wanted to kiss her again, wanted to follow her back to her place, wanted to finish what he'd begun ten years ago, wanted to see and feel and taste the way her body had changed over the years. But she straightened up, held the blanket close, cleared her throat. "Stephen," she said, reclaiming the shroud of mystery that she wore like a second skin, "I need your help."

He smiled. "I want to help," he said.

She put her hand on his shoulder and pushed him back. "That's not what I mean. I'm serious," she said.

"So am I," he told her, sitting up, exhaling. "I want to help you. Whatever you need from me, you know I'm here for you."

He didn't know if he meant those words, but he knew she would believe them. She looked into his eyes, breathed in and out a few times. She pulled the blanket closer to her chest, tugging it from Stephen in a swiping motion and covering her entire body like a nun, creating a barrier, however thin and artificial. Her lips quivered, whether from the cold or from attempting to bring forth what she was having a hard time vocalizing.

She asked slowly, forming the words as though she did not know which one was going to crawl out of her mouth next. "Can you sit in on my classes this next week?"

Stephen pulled away and looked off toward the dorms, surprised by the anticlimactic request. "You want me to watch you teach?"

"I...um..." she stammered. "I've been..." She could not unleash those words. "I'm losing memories...saying things in class..." She trailed off, hating to admit that she needed help. "I think..." She started again. "I might be going..." She paused. "Crazy," she whispered.

Olivia had always been eccentric, unpredictable. Stephen had always thought it stemmed from her dissatisfaction with the roles that her parents and others had attempted to force on her. She wanted to break away from those old prescribed roles, but, in doing so, she oftentimes bounced from one extreme to another trying to shake the leash from her neck. To quit moving meant to settle, and for Olivia, that would be the greatest tragedy. Older, more conservative people might have thought she was crazy. But Stephen had always known better. She wasn't crazy; she'd only wanted to change the world.

"I'm sure you're not," Stephen finally told her. Olivia's words still hung there, despite his dismissal of them.

"Last week," she slowly explained, "I started a lecture in my class about Chomsky's theory of recursion. I got up in front of the class and introduced Chomsky, his background, his basic linguistic and psychological traits. Then I explained his theory of recursion. The students thought it was a joke."

"What do you mean?" Stephen asked. "What was the joke?"

"I already introduced Chomsky and recursion—two weeks before. I just didn't remember doing so."

Stephen put his hand around her waist. "Maybe the students were playing a joke on you," he offered. "Is this the first time this has happened?" he asked.

"In class, yeah. But I'll do the same thing in other situations, with other people, too: tell someone the same story multiple times; meet someone who already knows me and have no clue we've met before; find notes to myself that I don't remember having written."

Stephen touched her cheek, brought her head down on his shoulder. "Memory loss sucks, but it's not a sign of insanity."

"I've also…" She fumbled to talk, her tongue moving like a plank of wood. "I've been hearing and seeing things."

A light went on in Stephen's brain, and I knew what he was thinking. He had heard these symptoms before, had studied them extensively. They were some of the things that he had written about Stringfield only a few years ago. Erratic behavior, hallucinations, memory loss. Schizophrenia, Stephen thought. There were other explanations that fit the symptoms. Some forms of depression could fit. Addiction, as well. But with Stephen's fear of what he had seen develop in Stringfield, that explanation jumped to mind before any others.

"What kind of things?" he asked, settling back to look at her. "And for how long?"

She looked up at him, feeling his body moving away from her. The loss was visible on her face as she considered the question. "Shapes in the corner of my eye—a man, following me—I'll hear people talking while I lecture, but not see anything—or see someone leaving, but when I look over, nobody has moved. A few nights ago…" she took a deep breath and a hard swallow and said, "I thought there was a guy in my house."

"A guy? What did he look like?"

She shook her head hard and mouthed the words *I don't know*.

"What did you see?"

"A shadow," she answered, "no different than yours."

"It reminded you of me?"

She nodded. "I knew you were coming into town. I thought for a moment…"

Stephen opened his mouth to speak, but his words felt hollow in his mind. My words found their way out. "Have you ever seen anything more than a shadow? An actual person? Perhaps an animal or insect that wasn't there?" And Stephen would later wonder where they had come from, grateful that his psyche had provided words where he had none, relieved that those words were the right ones.

Olivia thought for a moment, then nodded. "The mosquitoes," she told us. "I see them flying, but I know they can't be there. I feel their needles prick my skin, but know there won't be any mosquitoes until spring. No bites ever form, and they don't die if I slap them."

"And people?"

She bit her lip, a minute movement, subtle, sexy, so much a part of his memory of her that Stephen felt his heart accelerate, his lungs swell in his chest. She shook her head no.

"Olivia," I said, wrestling control from Stephen again, "I need to know."

There was a bolt of electricity through her, from her thighs to her eyes, and something dark, angry, was momentarily illuminated. "There is a man. I've never seen his face. He might be the same as the shadow. He's tall and wears a stylish coat. He has brown hair, which is always disheveled. He looks familiar to me, somehow, but I can't explain it."

Silence fell for a couple of minutes until Stephen finally formulated his thoughts. It worried me how slowly he was thinking tonight. Even with the alcohol in his veins, he should be quicker than this. Somewhere buried under years of experience, he could still hear his father's voice saying, "You've got to be quicker boy. You've got to be quicker or you'll get the belt." He tried to be quick, tried to throw his thoughts together into something coherent. But he couldn't. I wondered if it was because of me. I'd been coming to the surface much more since his mother had died, and I was afraid that my actions were affecting him. As I was about to take over again, he opened his mouth. "You want me to watch you, and tell you whether you're crazy or not, but I've got to ask, what happens if it turns out that this guy is, well, real?"

Olivia shook her head, explaining without stating that she did not consider this a possibility. Stephen wrapped his arm around her shoulder and kissed her cheek tenderly. "Okay," he said.

"Okay?" she asked.

"I'd have done it if you'd just asked. I didn't need the hard sell," he playfully teased. "I'll sit in on your classes. But I can tell you right now, I don't think you're crazy."

Olivia looked into his eyes. I could see him reflected in those mirror-like pupils. "You don't?" she asked.

"Crazy people don't know they're hallucinating. They convince themselves that the things they're seeing are real. They think it's the rest of the world that is crazy for not seeing."

"But the hallucinations?" she asked nervously.

Stephen looked away for a moment, preparing himself to ask the question he didn't want to ask. "Are you taking drugs?"

Olivia shook her head vehemently. "You know I don't do that."

"Prescription narcotics? Codeine, Darvocet, Vicodin?"

She bit her lip again, a sure tell she had information she didn't want to share.

"You are," Stephen and I stated together.

"It's for the pain. From my shoulder."

"When did you start taking them?"

Olivia looked down into the blanket and said, "After John and I divorced."

Stephen wrapped his free arm around her and held her close to him in a tight hug. "That could be what's causing the problem. I'll keep up with you, though, just in case."

"Thank you," she told him. She kissed his lips again and stood. "You have to get back to Natalie, don't you?"

Stephen rose, too, and put his hand on her arm. "Don't do that," he said.

"Do what?" she asked, smiling. In this moment, Stephen hated her smile.

He released her arm, looked into her eyes, and said, "I want…"

But the rest would not come out. "I want…" said everything that he knew, everything that he was.

"Go home, Lover Boy," she answered. "I'll see you tomorrow, right?"

Stephen kissed her lips one last time. "Tomorrow, yeah. What time?"

"Meet me here about one. We can get dinner before class."

"Lunch," Stephen corrected. "Dinner means supper."

"No, supper means supper," Olivia corrected, happy to play the old game. She stepped backward a few paces, smiling wide. "Tomorrow, Lover Boy."

"Tomorrow," he repeated. And then she was gone, disappearing into the night as easily as a shadow fading into darkness. Stephen stood there watching the place where her form had dissolved, until the cold bit into his skin, until he couldn't feel the warmth in his cheeks, until his eyes began to hurt under the weight of the night chill. He walked back to the house, slowly.

Something unusual happened, though: We had made it back to the streetlight and its illuminated ring when he saw a figure walking down the other side of the street. I didn't recognize the form, but Stephen's hand shot out toward it and I heard our mouth shouting "John!"

The form slowed, its eyes focusing on us.

"John Spillers!"

The form crossed the street and shook Stephen's hand. His eyes were dark and tired, purple under them, and he had a thin layer of stubble across his face.

"Stephen Lanford, you old dog. I didn't know you were back in Hazelwood."

"I am now," Stephen said, slapping John's shoulder. "I actually just left Olivia down at the red tables."

John's smile turned south, and it made Stephen happy to see it. Not for the first time, I wished to myself that he wouldn't find joy in things like that. "Gosh," John stated, shaking off the comment. "I haven't seen Olivia in forever. What were you two doing down at the red tables?"

"Just catching up," Stephen said. "Listen, I've got to get back home. I've got this killer girl waiting for me, but you and I should grab lunch or something before I head back to Virginia."

"It's a deal," John said, smiling politely. "Just give me a call."

"Will do," Stephen said. "I'll get your number from James."

Stephen's mind had been snared by Olivia, and so he never questioned why John was walking around alone at night. It would have been a natural enough question for him. But Stephen was obsessive, and Olivia was, once again, his obsession. And so John's presence failed to elicit the question that I was silently asking myself from behind Stephen's tired eyes: What had John been doing tonight?

When we got back to the house, Natalie was in the kitchen, her kimono wrapped tightly around her as she poured the pancake mix onto the old skillet. Stephen came behind her and placed one hand on her waist, the other on her chin, and twisted her head so that he could steal a kiss as he ground his hard-on into her back. Natalie returned the kiss and arched her back a little, pressing back into him, but she pushed him away a moment later with the hand not holding her spatula.

"Stay back, good knight," she smiled playfully. "You'll make me burn your pancakes."

"And we wouldn't want that," he laughed.

"What did Olivia want?" Natalie asked, throwing her real smile over the serious subject, hoping to hide her anger, though at heart she knew it was a futile act. Stephen knew her, her anger, her jealousy.

"She wants me to sit in on her classes the next few days," he said easily, without a hint of deeper meaning. "She thinks it'll be good for the kids."

"So you'll get to meet that brilliant kid she was talking about at dinner?"

Stephen said yes and kissed Natalie's neck, the bristles of his beard tickling her skin, making her giggle. She flipped the last pancake onto its wet side and turned to face him.

"That's all?" she asked pointedly, the look of joy completely abandoning her face. "She pulled you out of bed at three in the morning for that?"

"That's it," he said.

She raised an eyebrow and tilted her head, her lips twisting uncomfortably.

"Olivia's been taking Vicodin," he admitted. "For her shoulder."

Natalie nodded, accepting that as Stephen's dark secret. She looked more accepting than she must have felt. "Thank you," she said and kissed his lips.

Chapter 2
Water

Monday, February 28, 2011

I had a bad dream. Or rather, Stephen had a bad dream. I should explain that even though I was living in the shadows of Stephen's mind, he was still as much a mystery to me as any person is. I could witness his actions, I could feel his emotions, and when he had a strong memory, I could experience it subjectively the way that he remembered it. My craft was influence, nudging his thoughts in certain directions, but I could not place a thought in his head without considerable effort. I couldn't choose what I remembered from his life, like pulling a book from a shelf, the way that some alters can. And I didn't slip into oblivion when he was awake, the way others did. Stephen and I were at once part and parcel, and yet completely separate entities.

Stephen had fallen asleep, finally, into a dark and uneventful night, a still and noiseless night. I waited until he and Natalie both were settled down, each one bathed in the other's sweat, before I allowed myself to relax, to sleep, to dream. I could have stayed awake, but our body only rests when both of us are asleep, so I had a responsibility to Stephen. Even if I hadn't, I probably would have slept that night anyway because all the effort I had exerted had drained me. Having no body, it wasn't very often that I needed to rest, but when I did, I did.

It's an odd sensation when you have two unique personalities in one body dreaming. There's an amount of crossfade between the two dreams that is certainly disconcerting, but even still there is something deeper, darker, something at a metaphysical level that wakes me if I'm in a dream, and keeps me awake once I'm out of it: If dreams from a physical level are completely random nerve firings in the brain—neurobiological mistakes resulting in the involuntary release of images, ideas, emotions and sensations along the cerebral cortex—then two personalities sharing the same brain should receive the same messages. But if the same shadows are being cast upon the wall in front of both me and Stephen, then how can his dreams be so different from mine? Could it be possible that my distinct consciousness could interpret the same random electrical storm in a way that was not only different than but also completely independent of Stephen's? And if it could, I wondered if there was really such a difference between him and me, control-wise. Could I have been the dominant personality and he the one behind the curtain, if only I had come first? I was getting stronger each day since I had been born from the confusion and panic of Stephen's confrontation with Stringfield. I wondered, would I soon be able to take control? Could I be the one in charge? And if I could, would I be ready for it?

These thoughts crossed my mind most nights, but tonight I was too tired to think them. Instead, we wrapped our arms around Natalie and held her until the light behind our eyes faded.

I still remember the dream to this day: I was standing in a small white room with no furniture. On the wall hung a painting that I recognized as Norman Rockwell's *Freedom from Want*. To my left was a large bay window, bending outward toward rolling hills and a swaying tree line darkened by night. Above my head swung a single bulb, lighting the room, casting shadows on the floor as it arced like a pendulum. There was no apparent door, and for a moment I was alone with myself and the dream-scape. Then, the light above my head began to flicker, the room blinking between light and darkness. I breathed in, feeling the air fill my lungs, and exhaled slowly. The flickering light went out. Darkness filled the room. I was blind.

Light slowly appeared at the right edge of the bay window. I watched it grow, flow inside, a reversal of the electric light emanating outside only a moment ago. But what grew was the dull orange light of a flame, not the harsh white of the bulb. There was a moment of stillness, the light neither growing nor moving. And then a flaming hand reached out, balled into a fist, and smashed the right window inward. Fire climbed the window frame, swaying like a serpent, until it got to the ceiling. The ceiling lit up, the flames hanging, dancing downward, and I cowered against its furor.

Hearing a sound to my right, I turned to see Natalie standing beside me, dressed all in black, Stephen's pistol clutched in her left hand. She raised it parallel to the floor and fired. The center window shattered. From the bottom of the window, water began to pour into the white room, a del-uge. Water rose above my knees. I turned to Natalie, but she had disap-peared. I had nowhere to run to, no way to escape. I was trapped.

The figure covered in flames pushed harder against the window, steam rising from its hand and forearm. The window cracked, spider webbed into broken images, memories flashing across every surface. For a moment, I had non-linear, polymorphic sight, like looking through the thousands of lenses of a fly's eye, and the images I was seeing were thou-sands of replications of the past—my past and Stephen's past. There was Olivia on the last night Stephen had seen her, her arm in a sling, her cheeks pale and wet with tears. There was Natalie, her hand in Matt's, looking back at Stephen across the crowded dance floor. Stephen's mother, father and a hundred other faces. Then the water flooded in, and I was swimming. I flailed my arms through the dark fluid, kicking against the invisible tides that pushed me back, trying to take hold of me, drag me down into the water.

I reached the surface after an eternity of swimming and found a dock with a path leading up to a cabin. In the dream, I recognized it, as Stephen did, as the dock that Olivia's uncle had built for his fishing cabin, where Stephen and Olivia had shared Thanksgiving dinner with her family back before I was born. My thoughts were lucid as I dragged myself up onto the shore. I was no longer trapped within my own dream but had by now intruded upon Stephen's dream. I didn't know whether he had circumvented my autonomy and drawn me into his consciousness, or whether I had accidentally slipped through his mental defenses. But somehow I had ended up in a place that I only recognized through him, and all I could do was move through the dreamscape until Stephen woke up, or I found my way out.

I walked the winding, muddy path up to the cabin, opened the door and looked inside to find a touching Thanksgiving dinner scene: Stephen helping Olivia's grandfather maneuver the long carving knife through a perfectly cooked Thanksgiving turkey, as Olivia, smiling, scooped stuffing onto her great aunt's plate.

I walked in and took a seat in the only empty chair, reserved for Olivia's older brother, William, who had gone missing before Stephen had ever met Olivia. From outside, the sound of thunder rolled along the sky and down through the open doorway behind us, and I thought I could hear a song on its mighty grumble, an ancient and terrible chant. I looked to the doorway and saw the same phantom from outside the white room standing at the threshold, looking in on us. The flames had been put out by the water, and now it appeared to be a shadow at the doorway. When I turned back, the turkey had become a young child of only a few months, and Stephen and the old man were busy sawing into it. I leapt up and threw my shoulder into the two, pushing them away, but the child never once cried as the knife bit into its skin, and I knew it must be dead already. As I reached out my hand to touch its scarred face, the image of the child destabilized and dissolved into dust. I picked the dust up into my palm, lifted it to my lips and blew it across the table toward the specter at the door, hoping to banish it back to my dream and away from Stephen's.

Then I felt a hand on my shoulder and looked up as Stephen grabbed me, and Olivia's grandfather laid a hand on my other shoulder. Then the entire family was jumping at me, crawling toward me across the table. The storm was in full swing, wind and rain pouring into the cabin. Catfish ate through the wooden table, coming for me. All I could do was stand and watch the world come for me while I observed the shadow standing in the doorway.

And then I was awake, and Stephen and I were at the gas-station off Main, pumping fuel into his car. That Stephen had awoken before I had was not unusual. Some days he woke before me, and some days I woke before him. But in just a fraction of a second I had been ripped from the cold illusions of the dream and thrown into the warm grip of sunlight, and the violent shift left me relieved but shaken. I worried that the dream represented Stephen's unconscious attempt to neutralize me, like an immune system attacking an infection. And if it did, then Stephen, somewhere in the tangle of his thoughts, must have become aware that something was wrong. Still, I didn't think he consciously knew that I was there, and as long as he was distracted by those people around him and the drama of their lives, I didn't think he would. I just had to bide my time until his defenses fell or figure out a way to combat them myself.

One of Stephen's old friends, Columbus, ran from the gas-station doors, a cup of coffee clasped in either hand. "Thanks again for giving me a ride on such short notice, man. You're a life saver."

"You're just lucky I'm here in Hazelwood to bail your butt out of trouble yet again," Stephen said with a laugh. The pump thumped hard to signal the end of the gas-flow, and Stephen returned the hose and climbed into the driver's side.

"Your high school is out in Fallburough, right?" Stephen asked.

"Yeah," Columbus told him. "Take the Wickvale exit and we can come in the back way. Less traffic." He passed a cup of coffee to Stephen and slid into the passenger seat. "I really would be screwed if it wasn't for you. I'm so glad you answered your phone this morning. I can't believe I forgot Gilbert had a meeting and needed the car," Columbus said and carefully sipped the steaming coffee.

"How are you two doing, by the way?" Stephen asked.

When Stephen had gone to the university all those years ago, when he and Olivia used to sit at the red tables, his arm wrapped around her waist and hers resting lightly on his shoulder, Gilbert and Columbus had been regulars at the red tables. In those days, the two boys fought non-stop about whatever subject came up.

"We're good. I mean, we don't talk as much as we used to, but we're doing fine. I guess it's just since he got this promotion, and he's always busy."

One day it had become so heated that Columbus had jumped the table and mashed a chili pie into Gilbert's face. Several of us had to pull the man off of his adversary, but Gilbert, taking advantage of Columbus' disadvantage, kneed the young geographer in the crotch. Columbus tore free of us and returned the favor before campus police intervened.

"I guess I'm kind of an idiot, actually. I pushed his boundaries really hard a few weeks ago, and things got kind of weird for a day or two, but we're good now. He's really excited about his job, and after this next big trip out of town, everything's going to go back to a state of semi-normality, so I think we're stronger for it, actually. This is a great opportunity for us both to get out of that stupid duplex and buy our own house, you know, settle down, once and for all."

Gradually, like the shifting continents that Columbus studied, the two of them shifted as well. Their relationship with each other changed. One day, Columbus complimented Gilbert's shirt. Another day, Gilbert bought Columbus lunch. The next day, weeks, possibly months later, Columbus sat next to Gilbert. Then there was comfort, then there was passion, and eventually there was love.

Columbus looked over at Stephen. "And how are you and the lovely Miss Natalie Newfield?" A teasing grin stretched across his face.

"We'll be fine once we get back to Virginia," Stephen told him. "She's jealous like hell of Olivia."

"I don't blame her. If Gilbert was running around with an old flame from college, I'd be jealous, too. But you're not going to do anything with Olivia, are you?"

"Nah," Stephen told him, shaking his head. "Anything that happened between the two of us is in the past, where it'll stay." Knowing it was a lie, the words seemed to hurt Stephen's tongue, cutting him like barbed wire as he vocalized them. He changed the subject. "I was wondering, did you know William?"

Olivia's lost brother had appeared in Stephen's dream, but it wasn't until he verbalized the question that I began to wonder why Stephen's mind had offered William as a thread to be followed. The seed must have been planted sometime during his chat with Olivia the night before, but what was it that had brought William to his mind? Was just Olivia's presence enough to remind him of the young man that he'd never met? It was a mystery that had never been solved, something terribly inviting to a mind like Stephen's. But so many years after the fact, even he must know that the chances of finding William were slim.

Columbus thought for a minute then nodded. "Yeah. Not well, though. I only met him a handful of times, but the LGBT community around Hazelwood is pretty small."

"I thought about him last night. You know, about how he'd gone missing. I never even got to meet him."

"He was a good kid," Columbus stated firmly. "The first time I met him was…let's see…the Future Teachers of America. That was before he'd come out to anyone. It was Christmas, our sophomore year of high school, and he had me as secret Santa. Now, he didn't really know anything about me, except for what I wore around school, so he got me one of those watch sets that come in the fancy box, and he wrapped it in this great silk scarf. The problem was," Columbus started chuckling, "the watch had a leather strap, but it connected at either side of the metal, rather than running under it, so when it got cold enough outside to wear the scarf, I couldn't wear the watch, 'cause the metal would get too cold. And when it got warm enough to wear the watch, it'd be too warm to wear the scarf. So I never wore both at the same time." He sighed. "I think I've still got that watch somewhere. The scarf is long gone, though."

Columbus tipped the bottom of his coffee cup up to get the last few swills at the very bottom, greedily devouring every last drop. Stephen maneuvered the car onto the interstate, picking up speed until he was comfortably cocooned inside a caravan of other cars.

"You'd have liked him. He was really good friends with Matt in high school, though, so things probably might have gone south after the whole casino night adventure, but you would have liked him back then. Who knows, throw William into the mix and maybe Matt would never have become the douchebag that he did."

"It's so weird how he just went missing. He wasn't messing around with anyone was he?"

"No, not that I'd heard of. I mean, it's always possible that the Hazelwood rumor mill could have missed it. William was kind of a loner, one of those private guys. To be honest, I kind of thought that he would run away eventually. He was miserable here in Hazelwood. Not that I can really blame him for that."

"Nobody could," Stephen agreed. "Was it a problem at school?"

"I think it was more his parents," Columbus answered. "They were very conservative, very American dream, very…" He spun his hand in the air, searching for the right adjective.

"Norman Rockwell," Stephen supplied. Olivia had told him about her parents' conservatism back when they were together. He'd thought that he could save her from their influence. Now that he was older, he realized he never could have, that some things can't be fixed from the outside. They were just another one of those tethers from which Olivia had been trying to escape, holding her in place with barbs that sunk in deeper the more she struggled to free herself.

"Yeah!" Columbus laughed, a goofy smirk hanging from his jaw. "I've got a freshman with a pair of those right now, actually. Those kinds of parents, I mean. His father thinks that anything less than an A is unacceptable, and every time Colin gets a B on a geography test, I get an angry phone call. I think his father has a personal grudge against me for not having married a woman by now, as if my 'bachelorhood' is somehow setting a bad example for his kid. I almost wonder if he thinks I'm some kind of Don Juan, tricking young girls into sleeping with me or something. The mom's not much better: She keeps offering to introduce me to one of the women from her prayer group. I don't know what they'd do if they found out I was gay."

"You don't tell your students?" Stephen asked.

"No, I do. The ones I trust, anyway. Most of them choose not to tell their parents for fear they'll get me fired."

"Does the faculty know?"

"Most of them. I think the ones that don't just assume I'm asexual."

"Man, how do you live like that?"

"Why do you think I live all the way out in Hazelwood?" Columbus asked. "I keep my professional and personal lives separate. Unlike some people."

Stephen immediately drew the conclusion that he was talking about Colin's father, or even Gilbert, but realized a second later that it was a jab meant for his side.

"And what's that supposed to mean?" Stephen asked.

"It means that you and your 'partner' have a good thing going for you. Even if you are mixing business and pleasure. Don't screw it up."

Stephen hit the exit and turned the car toward the high school. "Hey, I could leave you here and let you walk the rest of the way," Stephen teased.

"Yeah, you could," Columbus said, "But you won't. Anyway, if you really want to know about William Mincks, I think that I know someone who can help you. Will's best friend in high school was a girl named Allison. Allison Weston. She still lives in Hazelwood if you want to go talk to her."

"Any idea how I could get in touch with her?" Stephen asked.

"Well, you know how small Hazelwood is, and I'm sure a resourceful guy like you won't have any trouble finding her, but if you really need to be pointed in the right direction, why don't you look for her girlfriend,

Sandra Blanche. Sandra works for Ryan Gathers, so you should be able to find her, no problem."

"Thanks, man," Stephen said, pulling the car in front of the high school. "I really appreciate it."

"It's the least I could do," Columbus told him. "I still haven't forgotten how you helped me out back in college. And this whole giving me a ride thing. You're a pretty cool guy." He got out of the car, opened up the back door and grabbed his bag. "Keep your nose clean, kid. Don't do anything stupid with Natalie. You hurt her and I'll kick your ass."

"I wouldn't give Matt the satisfaction."

With a laugh, Columbus shouldered his bag and wandered off toward the school. Stephen pulled out his phone, pressed the numbers in, and held it up to his ear before navigating the car back toward the interstate.

"Dobbs!" he said when the ringing stopped, "It's Lanford."

There was a cough from the other end of the phone before Dobbs answered, "Let me guess, you want to extend your little vacation."

"Not at all, Dobbs. I'm gonna need to get into the database from an insecure location. I've found something of a pet project, and I just need access to the database."

Dobbs coughed again. "I don't know if I can authorize anything, Lanford. What's the project?"

Stephen breathed in deeply and told him, "A missing person."

Another cough; there was a sickness inside Dobbs that never went away. "You suspect foul play?" I always thought that the sickness may have been the job itself. It was as though he had internalized the business so thoroughly, telling people what they could and couldn't do, denying medical claims, denying paid leave, becoming the judge of right and wrong. He had seen a lot more of the world than Stephen and I had, had experienced the worst case scenario so many times it was killing him from the inside. His health and his social life suffered. No wife, no children, no family: just the job. Stephen often feared that the job would weigh on him eventually, too, or even Natalie. Law enforcement was meant to help people, but it showed him in no uncertain terms how bad the world could be as well.

"I wouldn't doubt if there was," Stephen answered.

Dobbs laughed and said, "Stephen, you know how I know when you're lying to me?"

Stephen sighed deeply and asked, "How's that, Dobbs?"

"I can hear your voice."

"Dobbs," Stephen said, swallowing his pride and anger in one hard gulp as he was often forced to do with his supervisor, "I'm one of the best criminal profilers you have. Doesn't that count for anything?"

"It counts for what I've given you. Stephen, do you understand what my job is?" Dobbs took a moment to clear his throat. "I am the one who maintains order in the universe when people like you think that they are above the law. You see, that's what we're supposed to do as peacekeepers: We're supposed to make sure that everything and everyone is in their right place, to make sure that society runs like a well-tuned machine, like a car or a computer. And when you start playing your hero act, when you start acting like the rules don't apply to you, when you start fucking with my system, it upsets the natural order of things. And when the natural order of things is upset, the world devolves into chaos and anarchy. Humanity can't govern itself, Stephen. You yourself are proof of that."

Stephen slammed his free hand into the steering wheel. His reaction was unexpected, even to him, and he felt the pain swell from his palm a moment afterward. I didn't know whether it was his mother's death or Olivia's presence, but he was becoming much angrier now than he had been before. "So this is all because I went over your head on the Stringfield case, is it?" His temple began to throb and I felt his control over the car begin to slip. Without alerting him, I took the steering wheel and began to steer for him, making sure he didn't swerve off into a ditch while the anger grew inside of him, deriving from his hand, radiating from his eyes.

"If you were in my position, maybe you would do things differently. But I've been doing this job for twenty years and if there's one thing I can tell you it's this: You're a good agent, Lanford, there's no denying that. But you wouldn't last long with my job."

Stephen began to breathe in and out slowly, channeling his training. "I don't want your job. I'm happy as an agent. But what are you afraid is going to happen, Dobbs? I just want to look up some information on a missing person."

"Two things: First scenario, you pull the same crap you pulled with Stringfield and go behind my back to make the arrest. Second scenario, you pull the same crap you pulled with Perrini, but somebody gets killed this time."

"And if I promise to share any information I come upon with the Bureau?"

Dobbs coughed out a loud laugh, and for a moment seemed to be choking on his own tongue. "As if I would or could trust your promise."

"And if your refusal to allow me to act causes the death of someone innocent?"

That one got him, Stephen could tell. Dobbs cleared his throat for a moment and asked, "The death of someone innocent?"

"William could still be alive," Stephen said. He used William's name for the first time, hoping that humanizing him might pressure Dobbs into action. He had no way of knowing if William was still alive, but until a body was produced, he could always argue that there was a chance. "If you're keeping me out of the loop, you're creating a circumstance by which he could be killed." Stephen let that set in for a moment, then added his coup de grâce: "Dobbs, what do you want?"

Dobbs sighed and breathed in deeply. For a few brief moments he said nothing. Then, "I just want you to use the information right, and I want you to follow protocol as you're using it."

"The protocol is there for a reason," Stephen agreed. He felt the breaking of Dobbs' defenses and wanted to position himself as best he could to take advantage of them. "I'll do my best."

Dobbs coughed loudly again and said, "Stephen, you know that I don't exactly trust you, right?" Stephen laughed and said yeah. "But I think I have a solution that can benefit you. I'm going to open up Newfield's account. If you want to follow your pet project, you'll have to do it with her help. Does that sit well with you?"

Stephen tried to tense the hand that I had control of, but didn't seem to notice that it wasn't responding to his intentions. People are willing to ignore so much of what's going on around them when they let their emotions get the better of them.

"If that's what you think is best, Dobbs," Stephen told him, knowing that he would not be able to get a better deal from this man. "I'll bring Natalie in on it. She'll act as my handler."

"I appreciate your understanding in this matter, Stephen."

"Thanks for your help, Dobbs," Stephen said before hanging up and throwing the phone at the passenger window. It bounced off with a loud crack and landed unbroken in the passenger seat.

Not knowing what to do now, both too angry at Dobbs and too energized to return home, Stephen went to his lawyer. There was really no reason to go there: His mom's affairs were settled as well as they could be, but there was something comforting in the efficiency of the man, Neilson, who could work and talk at the same time, conversing with any visitor who stopped by while typing out paperwork without a single pause in the clicking beneath his fingers. Somehow, the man seemed to have two different consciousnesses, one for typing legal paperwork, the other for speaking. It impressed and fascinated Stephen, who always liked to observe the strange phenomenon. He would never ask the man questions that were too difficult, because those might cause slight but noticeable pauses in the typing, which would destroy the illusion. When he was young he had once asked, "What exactly does a lawyer do?" That had made Neilson pause for at least a full minute. "Lawyers like me help people," he answered slowly. "We make sure that there's nothing that stands in the way between people and what they deserve. There are others that hurt people, just because they have the power to. But lawyers like me? We make sure that everyone gets exactly what they deserve."

So for the most part, Stephen and Neilson made small talk: "How are you enjoying being back in Hazelwood?"

"It's different from Virginia, certainly. How is business going?"

Near the end of the conversation, though, Neilson became a valuable asset in Stephen's search for William Mincks.

"Got any hard accounts?" Stephen asked, almost offhandedly, still watching Neilson mechanically type despite the words flowing through his mouth.

"I've got one very hard account. Sandra Blanche is suing Ryan Gathers for wrongful firing from his company."

It was such a sudden turn of events that Stephen almost didn't believe he had heard it correctly. Hell, I didn't believe I had either. Then we remembered what kind of town Hazelwood was. Stephen had been gone for so long, he had forgotten the way small towns work. Everybody is connected to everyone else, even if they don't know exactly how.

"I just ate dinner with Ryan last night," Stephen told Neilson, leaning forward onto the desk. "He didn't say anything about a lawsuit."

"Well, he's probably not too worried about it," Neilson answered, still typing. "I love Sandra to death, but I honestly don't think she's got much of a case here. Still, I'm gonna try to do her justice."

"What's the case?"

Neilson laughed. "You know that as her attorney I can't tell you that."

"What about as my friend?"

Neilson turned to face Stephen, abruptly interrupting his typing performance. "As your friend, Stephen, I can encourage you to stop by the Hazelwood Community and Arts Center tonight at seven. There's a showing there that might just interest you. Take Natalie with you. I'm sure you both can enjoy it." He chuckled under his breath in a way that made Stephen wonder what he was up to. "Besides, if they cut funding one more time, the HCAC might not be here the next time you come through," he said before returning to his typing. Recognizing that he had been dismissed, Stephen left the office, curious about the invitation.

Stephen called Natalie once he got to the car. "I'm taking you out to dinner and a showing," he told her.

"Ooh," Natalie cooed into the phone. "Hazelwood or Mastern?"

"Columbus wants to treat us to dinner, then there's some kind of exhibit at the HCAC. Neilson said we'd enjoy it."

"Aren't you old enough by now to know you should never trust a lawyer?" Natalie asked.

Stephen laughed. "I know you're right. But it would be rude not to go."

"Alright," she told him. "Call me when you're on the way home."

"I will," he promised.

He arrived at the red table at ten minutes to one. Stephen was perpetually early to events, derived from the punctuality training drilled into him all the way from pre-school to the Bureau, but he also wanted to arrive early for Olivia more than anything else. She was already waiting with a classic Italian sandwich for him from the cafe. She was eating a salad, picking through the leaves with her fork.

"You're late, Lover Boy," she said, smiling at him.

He felt good inside as he sat down at the table and opened the clear plastic container, looking down at the food in front of him. He didn't have the heart to tell her that he didn't eat Italian sandwiches anymore, that he now ate pulled pork, turkey, prime rib, even Reuben sandwiches, but he had lost his taste for Italian sandwiches after they'd broken up. Still, it was pleasantly nostalgic to be back here at the school, sitting at the old tables, eating the same thing he'd eaten all those years ago, looking at the girl he'd known and still loved.

"Actually, I'm early," he told her, taking up the sandwich and eating it quickly, greedily.

"Hungry?" she asked.

"Starving. I had to do a favor for Columbus, so I forgot to eat before running out of the house this morning."

The two of them were alone, despite the others who sat at the table. The others were nothing but trees whispering to each other in the ebb and flow of the wind. He joked; she did the same. She laughed and shook her head. He smiled wide, showing his teeth. There was a primal passion between them, anyone could see.

But because I could feel the inside of Stephen's mind, because I could hear his thoughts as clearly as if they were my own, because I knew his emotions better than he did, I alone could taste the bittersweet flavor that lingered on the back of his tongue in the wake of the tea and talk.

He was taken back to the past as he sat there. The first time he had ever sat at these tables with her, his hand wrapped around her shoulder, her hand in his lap, he had felt a connection between them that he had never felt for anybody before. When she had looked up at him and smiled, she had changed something within him, a setting in his brain that would lead him forever into the darkness of false hopes. On that day, so long ago, he acquired a thirst that remained unquenchable within him, a fire that raged no matter how much he attempted to smother or drown it.

"I love you," she had told him, and he had told her the same.

The last day that he had seen her there before he had gone to Virginia hung vividly in his mind's eye as well.

"Is your promise still good, Lover Boy?" she had asked.

He had nodded, not knowing what was in her head, not knowing what was going to happen next, what she was going to ask him. Though he tried to maintain his composure, he felt like a puppet, his strings the intangible chords of her words.

"Go to Virginia with Natalie. Live your life as if you had never met me."

"Olivia, I can't."

"You can. You will."

"Come home with me," he whispered, his hand on her cheek, his mouth to her temple. "Come home with me, lie down with me. We'll get out of this God-forsaken town together."

"I'm never going to make it out," she'd told him. "Stephen." She'd looked him in the eyes. "Let me go."

"Olivia…" Stephen could never articulate what he meant or knew or wanted when it came to Olivia, even then. "Please."

"There's something broken inside of me, Stephen," she'd told him. "Some mechanism inside of me that's defaulted, that wasn't installed when I came off the assembly line. I'm broken. I'm dysfunctional. I'm lost, and hopeless, and…and I don't even know what else. I'm broken. Broken like a kid's toy with a missing piece, like a computer with a faulty motherboard, like a house with a bad foundation. The doctors told me that my shoulder will never be the same; that the seizures aren't going to stop. And that's not even counting all the things that you can't see. I'm not functional, Stephen. Don't you get that?"

"I want…"

"It doesn't matter what you want. You're going to do what's best for you. You deserve someone who has similar goals in life as you do, someone who isn't selfish, someone who makes time for you, who will be there for you when you're having a bad day. You need someone who will give and not just take from you. That's not me."

He held her close, careful not to put pressure on her shoulder as he breathed in the scent of her hair, felt the electricity that radiated from her skin and the fire that burst forth within his breast as he frantically scavenged for some remnant of courage. He put his hands on her hips, looked down into her eyes and whispered, "Olivia, don't do that. Marry me."

And she had kissed his lips, and shook her head silently. "Do what?" she'd asked. And then she'd turned and walked away, disappearing like a specter.

Ten years ago, Stephen had said goodbye to Olivia for what he thought would be the last time. Now, he pretended that night had never happened. "So Haley and Cheyenne find out that Aaron is two-timing them," Olivia explained to Stephen as they walked into the Liberal Arts building, "and they both want to get back at him. They wait a couple of weeks until he has two important days in a row: He's got a job interview on Thursday and a class presentation on Friday, right? So Wednesday night he pulls out all of his clothes for the next day and lays them out on his kitchen table, then calls Haley over for the old ego boost."

Stephen opened the door to the classroom and gently ushered Olivia inside, nodding at her story. Her introduction to the parable was so complete that he thought he knew most of what was coming next: a right-hook from Haley, then a left hook from Cheyenne, possibly a knock-out from both of them. It was a familiar story, one that he had heard in different iterations, with different details everywhere he'd ever gone. He could picture the young player, an endearing smirk permanently fixed to his face as he spit game at every girl who walked into his line of sight; Haley the faithful girlfriend spurned, Cheyenne, the unknowing other woman; one probably blonde, the other brunette—their only distinguishing features.

"Aaron and Haley have sex, then Aaron falls asleep," Olivia continued. "When he wakes up in the morning, all he can find is a note from Haley telling him not to call her anymore. He's confused, 'cause the last thing he knew they were fine, but he doesn't have time to worry about it, because he's got an interview to get to."

Olivia sat on the desk at the front of the classroom, folding her legs and reclining on her elbows. It was a sexy pose, and it trapped Stephen in its snares without any resistance from him. Around Olivia, he was an animal doomed to throw itself into the same trap over and over.

"He shows up early, changes into his clothes, sits down in the office—and then starts yelling and stripping off his pants. He's beating his crotch like it's on fire. Turns out Haley had put chili powder in his pants while he was sleeping. So obviously he doesn't get the job, because now Matt thinks the boy is crazy and won't even hire him to work in the mail room. Aaron takes this as an isolated event and decides that since Haley is out, he's going to redouble his efforts with Cheyenne. So he takes her out to dinner, wines and dines her, then takes her back to his place. Aaron gets up in the morning to find a note from Cheyenne with the same words that Haley wrote him. So now he's terrified of what Cheyenne is going to do to him. He pulls out new clothes and inspects them, but just to be sure she doesn't sabotage his presentation, too, he goes out and buys new clothes. He heads to his presentation, and the whole time he's in class he's jumpy, looking over his shoulder like a man on the run. It gets to be his turn and he walks up to the podium, pulls out his note cards, and starts to recite this presentation he's memorized. From outside the window comes a sound like a pistol, and Aaron freaks out."

She mimicked his movements, jumping off of the desk and flailing her arms wildly. The students who had filed in laughed, enjoying the show. Olivia began to look around the room, inviting the students to join in on the story she was telling, welcoming them into the audience.

"He covers his head, jumps under the desk, not knowing what is going on. The teacher is yelling at him, trying to get him to calm down, but Aaron is temporarily deranged. He runs out of the classroom and out the door to see a parade of foot-racers running through the quad and a referee with a starting pistol. Now he's feeling like an idiot. He walks back inside, gets a pardon from the teacher and goes to read his note cards. They're all blank. Cheyenne has switched them. Aaron can't remember what he wrote, he can't remember what he was going to say, he can't even remember what his topic was. He comes out of the presentation with a poor but passing grade."

It was an interesting narrative, to be sure, I thought. It's not often in life that there's a clear-cut good guy or bad guy, so when stories like this are told, it reassures people that there's an order to the world, one where the good have the ability to bring justice down upon everyday villains. It reminded me of Stephen's book about how he had managed to catch Stringfield, very nearly single-handed. It had its clear-cut villain in Stringfield, and its clear-cut hero in Lanford.

"But now, he's pissed off," Olivia continued. "You see, Haley and Cheyenne were too busy worrying about how they were going to punish

Aaron to ever worry about the way it was going to affect Aaron psychologically. Of course these pranks were relatively harmless. He got a poor grade on one presentation out of five in the class, which was hardly a fatal injury. And there would have been other jobs out there besides the one at Cityscape, so that wasn't even really a problem. But Aaron couldn't see that at the time, because he was so mad at what those two bitches had done to him."

Stephen leaned forward over the desk, observing the way students listened to her. Most of them sat loosely, listening as they would to a story on public radio. The narrative captured their imaginations for a few minutes, planted ideas in their minds. As they took it with them, they would change until it was their own story, painted with their own experiences and beliefs. It was Stephen's story—smart as he was, he couldn't see Natalie or Olivia as anything other than symbols: the sex object and the one that got away.

"Aaron goes over to Haley's house first. He uses his knife to cut her brake lines. After all, that's fair, right? She embarrassed him socially, in the environment of someone who could possibly have hired him. Then he goes over to Cheyenne's apartment, using the spare key to get in. He punctures the gas line leading to the oven and flees the scene. Which, again, that's fair, right? She embarrassed him socially, in the environment of a teacher of higher learning. Luckily, neither of the girls was hurt. Haley knew enough about cars to maneuver her car to a standstill without injury, and Cheyenne smelled the gas as soon as she entered her apartment that night. But what if it hadn't been a gas leak? What if it had been poison in her leftovers? After all, who would suspect that?"

The students started to whisper to each other, discussing the awful fate that would have awaited Cheyenne.

"Even more disturbing, what if Aaron had been waiting for one of them with a knife?"

Many people in the class appeared to be disturbed by this last question. I guessed from their reactions that this was not a normal class day, that the shift to a narrative lesson was unexpected, and that many students were unsure how to react. But a boy in the second row followed along without so much as a question in his eye. He was handsome, with a knowing look plastered on his face at all times that contained both humility and hubris. I guessed from the tight movements of his body and the way that he listened that he was an adventurer, slightly brave and experientially stupid; he was a kid who knew the limits that existed in life, who'd been taught to fear the consequences of trespassing against those limitations, but who wanted to disregard them every chance he could, plunging into whatever he might find, dangerous or benign.

"Now, this story is alarming, but as far as a story, it shows a complete picture. You have the inciting incident with Aaron cheating, then the two girls taking revenge on Aaron for two-timing them, and you have the escalated reaction of Aaron on the girls for their actions against him. It's nice, neat and most of all, comprehensible within the tradition of violence against women. You can understand what the girls were attempting and what Aaron was attempting. But what about crimes that are neither simple nor neat?"

She paced back and forth in front of the desk, still looking at the audience, recalling information without pause.

"In 1888, Jack the Ripper murdered at least five prostitutes, beginning with Mary Ann Nichols. Annie Chapman, the second victim, had her uterus removed. Catherine Endows, the fourth, was missing her left kidney and part of her uterus. The final victim, Mary Kelly, was violently robbed of all her internal organs: Her face was slashed off, her throat had been severed down to the spine and her abdomen was emptied. Jack the Ripper took her heart."

The students looked appalled.

"This isn't a clean story. It's not a neat story. It's a challenging, difficult story, without inciting incident, without a justifiable reaction. But it's a compelling story. It's a detective mystery, and a psychological thriller, and a horror, and, in a way, it's a tragedy. Remember the delineation of literature from Aristotle: History states what happens, philosophy states what should happen, but only literature melds events and philosophy together into allegorical importance."

She reached into her purse and produced a copy of Stephen's book.

"Now, life isn't neat, and it isn't easy, and it's a lot more complicated than fiction, however involved the story is. Non-fiction can be just as compelling and just as important as fiction, especially when told creatively. Creative, or narrative-nonfiction, is the art of using literary techniques to tell a factually accurate story. In this way, it imitates historical fiction, showing both historical fact and philosophical importance, as in the case of Truman Capote's *In Cold Blood*; but in autobiographical cases, such as Dave Eggers' *A Heartbreaking Work of Staggering Genius*, it also has the advantage of being a lived experience."

Olivia took the book and flipped through it until she found the passage that she was looking for.

"In Stephen Lanford's *Plagued by What We Know*, we find a non-fiction thriller, an autobiographical novel. It's a mystery, and a psychological puzzle, and a horror story, and, in a way, it's a tragedy. It's not a clean story, or a neat one, and it's certainly a challenging, difficult story. It's a compelling story for all those reasons, the kind that would make Aristotle proud."

Her eyes dropped down to the page she held between the pads of her forefinger and thumb. For a second she frowned, and swept the page with her hand, then she read.

"'Many of us were confused by the Avalon City murders. They seemed to be random, motivated by nothing more rational than the flow of the wind. I felt that the first murder, Lilly Price, was the one to focus on, but I quickly became discouraged when I began to look at her life. Lilly was clean: She was the city's favorite daughter, the homecoming queen, a civil volunteer, valedictorian. Her boyfriend, Bartholomew, was loving, passive and well-adjusted. They had argued, but never once had anyone heard him raise his voice or seen him raise his hand to her. She had a good life, filled with friends and family, full of love and happiness. And she had earned it herself, working her way through school, fighting against the troubles of the world toward her goal of a perfect life. It seemed as if the killer, like a child smashing a ceramic angel beneath his shoes, had chosen her because she was perfect. Many times I had to ask myself how someone so warped could exist. When he had murdered Lilly, he was not just destroying a life; he was destroying beauty itself.'"

She turned the pages of the book with the tips of her fingers, shuffling it with the talent of a card-player. Sweeping the page with her fingers again, she swallowed to clear her mouth and looked back up at the class.

"Much like Chillingworth from The Scarlet Letter, Stringfield made it his mission in life to destroy the things that others found beautiful. Stringfield killed girls that he found sexually attractive, girls that displayed brilliance or excellence, girls who made the world a better place. Or as Lanford states in his book, 'He was a demon masquerading as a man.'"

She looked up at the class and opened her mouth to speak, but as her voice rose to her lips, a light went out behind her eyes. This demon, the invisible entity that clutched her and blew out the candle that animated her, was different but just as dangerous as Stringfield. One minute Olivia was standing, ready to teach the students an important lesson using Stephen's book, the next she was on the floor, convulsing.

Stephen was on his feet, bounding down the aisle with the stride of a trained runner, but he wasn't the first to reach her. The boy from the second row had hopped the desk with great agility and dived down to her side. Then the two of them and I were around her, looking down into her wide vacant eyes.

As subtly as he could, Stephen unsnapped her bra as he and the young man gently rolled her onto her side. Pulling off his over-shirt, the young man rolled it into a ball and pushed it under her head. The way the two of them worked together was almost professional, almost mechanically precise. Stephen handed the young man his cell phone and the boy made the call without hesitation. A few minutes later two men came in, put her on a stretcher and carried her toward the door.

"Don't leave until I get in there with you," Stephen told them. One of the medics turned and nodded to him but spiraled his finger in the air signaling for him to make it quick. "Thanks for your help," Stephen continued, turning to the young man. "Olivia's spoken about you. She said you were brilliant."

The young man's eyes sparked with pride. "You didn't disappoint either." Holding out his hand to Stephen, he repeated Olivia's words. "Absolutely brilliant."

"What's your name?" Stephen asked, taking the boy's hand.

"Allen," he said. "Allen Silverman."

We nodded, pumped his hand once, then turned and ran to the door.

Chapter 3
Poker

Monday, February 28, 2011

The setting sun blinded Stephen as he pulled into the parking lot at Burns'. He closed and opened his eyes rapidly a few times, trying to blink out the sunspots that attacked him as he folded the visor down. He knew he was late and that Natalie was worried about him. But he sat in the car for a moment, thinking about Olivia, weak and fragile in the back of the ambulance. He rubbed his temple gently as the music from the radio pulsed through him. He recognized the tune as a Beatles song, but it was a jazz cover, so the words were absent. For some reason his mind could not focus long enough for him to conjure the name of it. He pushed into his temple a little bit harder, trying to force himself to remember.

Gently, I whispered it to him.

"Let it be," he muttered under his breath, before shutting off the car and heading into the restaurant.

Dave Burns, owner and operator, called to him when he made it inside the doors. Gilbert and Columbus sat on one side of the table, from which they could see Stephen enter. Natalie faced away from him, and Dave stood at the end of the table, apparently keeping them entertained until Stephen got there.

"Well if it isn't Mr. Successful himself," Dave shouted, coming around to take Stephen's hand and hugging him with a pat on the back.

"Look who's talking, Mr. Entrepreneur," Stephen laughed, pointing at the restaurant around him. "A nice little place you have here."

It was a sophisticated, chic place, full of curves and ingenious flourishes of color. It almost seemed too rich for a town like Hazelwood. As he looked up, Stephen noticed a dining balcony and, on the east and west ends, high windows through which light must pour almost all day long.

"This old place?" Burns scoffed. "This is just the prototype. Hopefully it'll bring Hazelwood some much needed cash flow. In the spring I'm going to open one up in Mastern twice as integrative and just as stylish. Matt tried to block my bid on the land, but I was able to get a helping hand from the planning commissioner."

Stephen slapped him genially on the shoulder. "You're a credit to the old gang, my friend."

Burns said seriously, "Don't forget, Matt used to be our friend once upon a time." Then he laughed, "But it just goes to show, money can't buy everything, now can it?"

"Absolutely right," Stephen agreed before stepping over to Natalie.

He pulled his chair out a few inches, leaned over and kissed her cheek. "Sorry I'm late," he whispered.

Natalie's smile was pursed, but she kissed his cheek in return. She put her hand on the back of his head and rubbed the spot where his spine met his skull. "Can't you stop being a hero for just one day?" She asked it as a joke, and the others laughed lightly, but Stephen felt the tinge of accusation the question carried with it.

"Maybe someday," he predicted vaguely, before taking his seat.

Gilbert nodded at him and said, "We're even now, right?"

Stephen's face must have betrayed his confusion, because Gilbert continued, "You gave my boyfriend a ride this morning, I gave your girlfriend a ride tonight. Even."

Stephen laughed. "I guess that's as fair as it can be. I'd prefer if I was the one giving my girlfriend a ride, though."

"And I'd prefer to give Columbus a ride," Gilbert said, patting his companion's head affectionately and ruffling his dark brown hair. Stephen smiled at them before turning his smile to Natalie, which she reluctantly returned.

"Is that a new dress?"

"I thought you were the observant one," she joked. "Yeah, Helen and I walked down to the Hub earlier and this was on sale. Do you like it?"

He did. It was white and black, the colors contrasting each other strikingly as they wrapped around her body in elegant ribbons. It made him want to hold her, to peel the ribbons away one by one until all that remained was her. He tried to imagine what Olivia would look like in the dress, but he couldn't. Olivia liked darker, more homogenous clothes. The white streak, striking on Natalie, would look conspicuous on Olivia.

"I do," he answered honestly.

Natalie smiled sexily, raised an eyebrow at him and touched his knee under the table.

Stephen's smile was real enough now as he turned back to the table to see Gilbert and Columbus mimicking the two of them, their heads tilted lovingly, peering into each other's eyes. Stephen laughed happily, and the table followed.

Burns waited on the table himself. Stephen enjoyed being in his company again. David, Stephen and Matt had been the original group, the Three Musketeers, until the group had grown into the collective, then finally collapsed. Stephen had forgotten that he and Matt were once friends.

Not just friends, but best friends.

Stephen remembered the day he punched Matt. The night of the car crash. Such a long night, so many years ago. It was the night that I was conceived, though only I could know that. It would still be a number of years before I sprang out of Stephen's consciousness fully formed, but that was the night the seed of my birth was sown in Stephen's psyche.

Olivia had been gone for about three months, the international teaching program taking her far away from this place, to countries and schools that Stephen might never set foot in. After the school year was finished, she would receive her degree and teaching certificate, while everyone else in her class was walking across the stage in the basketball stadium. Three months ago, Stephen had driven her to the airport in Hedgemill, watched her fly off to Chicago to start training. Now, he was sitting at the red tables, as he often did, attempting to read his assignment, a story about a man with two families. One wife was timid and not much fun. Another was fun and liberal, but not much of a homemaker. He thought to himself what a terrible person the man was, leading the two girls on without any regard for them. The man was selfish and didn't deserve either of them, Stephen thought, hoping that the man would end up alone.

Alone, he reflected, closing the book, just as he was.

Matt and Natalie walked up, Matt's arm around Natalie's waist.

"Hey, Stephen," Matt greeted cordially.

"Why the long face?" Natalie asked, just a hint of concern in her voice.

Stephen waved halfheartedly, raising only a couple fingers. "Just doing homework."

"Speaking of," Matt turned to Natalie, "I've got to get to the lab and print my business report." He kissed her lips and looked to Stephen. "You'll take care of her for me, won't you, Stephen?"

Stephen gave a half-smile and nodded.

"That's a buddy," Matt said. "Be back in fifteen."

When he was out of sight, Natalie slid down on the bench next to Stephen. She placed one palm on his shoulder, folded the other on top of it and rested her chin along the ridge of her fingers.

"What's wrong, Eeyore," she asked, her warm breath on his ear.

Stephen inhaled deeply and said with a single hissing exhalation, "You still haven't told him, have you?"

Natalie, rather than being scared and jumping back, as he'd expected her to do, kissed his cheek lovingly.

"First, you don't tell me that you're dating him; now, you won't even tell him you cheated on him with me."

Natalie nodded, seeming to understand the trouble this had caused in Stephen's mind, but completely unrepentant, as though she held absolutely no responsibility for her own actions.

"Don't you have anything to say for yourself?" he asked, "An excuse, an explanation, an apology—anything?"

She kissed his cheek again, saying nothing.

"Natalie, if you want to be with me, be with me. Stop playing games."

"I can't be with you," she stated, with that matter-of-fact voice she was just then starting to develop. "I'm with Matt."

Stephen raised the elbow opposite Natalie onto the table and rested his forehead in his palm. "Then why?" he asked.

"For someone so smart, you sure can be awfully stupid," she told him. Shrugging, she kissed his cheek again, then nuzzled her nose into his neck. "If I wasn't with Matt, I would be with you. You're better than him." Her lips were painful to Stephen, hot on his skin.

Stephen spat the words "In bed?"

"In everything," she answered. "You're smarter, stronger, a better person all around. And yes," she seemed to purr the words into Stephen's ear, "you're better in bed, too." She leaned up and nibbled lightly at his ear with the tips of her teeth.

"Then why are you with him?" Stephen asked.

Natalie smiled wryly. "'Cause even though I fell in love with you freshman year, you never noticed. All those times I tried to get you alone, all those times I tried to tell you how I felt, all those times I tried to show you what was in my heart, you never noticed."

Stephen shook his head. He hadn't noticed, to be sure, but her words were an accusation. If you had only noticed back then, these things would never have happened, she said without saying.

She went on, seeming to ignore Stephen. "Until she left, you could never see me behind Olivia. I waited and waited, and waited some more for you to see that she was no good for you. And when I eventually realized that you were never going to figure that out, Matt was there for me. He deserves a chance. If things don't work out with him, then you'll get your chance. That's as fair as it can be."

Stephen observed her out of the corner of his eye. He felt tired and angry all of a sudden. There were words and ideas bubbling up like bile in his throat. But he breathed in and out, channeling his training. Still, when he opened his mouth and spoke, the barbs stung her. "Maybe you won't get yours," he suggested.

She frowned at him, then forced herself to smile and jumped up from the table. "Matt!" she shouted, wrapping her arms around his neck and kissing him with a dozen little pecks.

"You coming to Vegas Night tonight?" Matt asked Stephen.

"Yeah," Stephen answered. "Edna and I."

Matt put his arm around Natalie. "We'll see you there."

They were gone, and, again, Stephen was alone. A sharp winter chill cut through his shirt, causing gooseflesh to sprout over his arms in patches as he gasped and fought to recover his breath. His eyes watered and his nose began to run. A violent emotion overtook him, and he suddenly wanted to tear the table apart piece by piece, to rip the metal frame into a hundred little chunks that all the king's horses and all the king's men could never put back together again.

Breathe in, he thought, remembering the voice of his therapist. Breathe in, breathe out, and just let the emotion flow through you. But it wasn't flowing; it had stagnated in his head, breeding and amplifying feelings of anger, isolation and fear. "You've got to be quicker or you'll get the belt," he heard his father saying in the back of his mind. "You never noticed," he heard Natalie saying. He saw Olivia at the airport, hair tied back, rolling suitcase under one hand, waving to him for what he thought was the last time. He was angry at all of them, but he was even angrier at himself.

He thought of going to his apartment, crawling into bed and sleeping forever. But it wouldn't do, and he knew it was an unhealthy solution. He thought of going to see his mother, but she would worry at him until he snapped at her, too, then he would feel guilty for that on top of everything else. He even thought about going to his father, but the scene of their last fight played vividly in his mind and he forgot the suggestion almost as soon as it had entered his head. It was he and he alone who would be left to deal with the emotions. Not for the first time, he marveled to himself about how this town, his own home, and his head were such efficient breeding grounds for apathy and depression.

But as soon as he started to push the idea around his mind, Dave was coming over the hill, running toward him.

"Stephen!" he yelled angrily.

Stephen was on his feet and ready for a fight before he had time to wonder to himself why Dave was angry. A holdover of all the times his father had called his name in anger, Stephen had taken it for granted that since Dave had called his name, it was he who Dave was angry at.

But when Dave reached the red table, he demanded of Stephen, "Have you seen Matt?"

"Yeah, a few minutes ago. He and Natalie went to get ready for Vegas Night."

"I'm gonna kill him!" Dave declared.

Stephen stepped in front of Dave and put his hands on the angry man's shoulders, holding him firmly in place. "What's gotten into you?" he asked, staring into Dave's eyes, which were wide and red. "Why?"

"That bastard undercut my business proposal. He knew I was gonna quote from fourteen thousand, so he went even lower, quoting at twelve. It's the same sneaky shit that his father pulls."

Stephen shook his head, incredulous. "There's got to be a mistake. Matt wouldn't do that."

Dave pulled a stack of letters out of his back pocket and tossed them on the table. "He would and he did. I should have known better than to be friends with that snake. He's just like his old man: a no good, dirty, greedy capitalist."

Stephen opened one and read it. Sure enough, it was all there in black and white. Stephen recognized Matt's signature at the bottom of the page.

"One of my friends at the company thought it unusual that Matt knew my quoting offer before they did. If he hadn't sent these to me, I would never have known. Matt's been doing this for months."

Though Matt was not the reason for his anger, he provided Stephen with a target more satisfying than the table. "Dave, do me a favor and wait until tonight. You're going to Vegas Night, right?"

Dave nodded twice.

"Don't kill Matt. Hit him where it hurts. Embarrass him, expose him before his peers."

"How do I do that?"

"Follow my lead. I've got a plan."

Dave was still filled with fire, ready to strike out at Matt. But he trusted Stephen and was prepared to follow him. So as Stephen explained what to do, and how Matt was going to react, Dave gradually came around. Rather than go off and get in a fight with Matt, the two of them would draw Matt out together.

Once each trimester, the university transformed the student center into a Las Vegas casino. In the fall, they reproduced Caesar's Palace, in the winter the Luxor, and in the spring, Excalibur. Great roman columns stood along the walls, gaudy streamers tied between them in ribbons of color. Plaster statues of gods and goddesses stood at points around the room, and the ceiling was painted to look as though it was open to the sky, and it was a bright summer day outside.

Stephen, Dave and Edna found Matt, Natalie and Ryan sitting at a poker table decorated to look like it was carved from marble. A sophomore girl wearing the black and white uniform of a Vegas poker dealer greeted them. The newcomers sat down across the table from their counterparts, and everyone greeted each other.

Stephen had nodded at Natalie as he pulled Edna's chair out for her. Natalie could tell something was happening from the look on Stephen's face, but what it was Stephen doubted she could guess. Stephen sat with Edna at his left and Dave at his right; Matt with Natalie at his right and Ryan to his left.

"You look nice, Stephen," Natalie complimented, admiring his suit. "You really cleaned up tonight."

"You look stunning," Stephen returned, admiring her dress. "I wish I could enjoy it."

Edna looked between them, knowing that something was being exchanged but confused as to what. Matt also caught the look and the comment. He reached out and touched Natalie's back, petting her through her dress. Dave smiled, knowing that he and Stephen were in this together, knowing that soon Matt would get what was coming to him.

The pot was filled and the cards laid out. Ryan and Natalie folded. So did Edna.

"Out of curiosity," Matt began, looking between Stephen and Dave, "why can't you enjoy it?"

Stephen smiled and showed his hand. Dave had high pair, so the pot went to him. The dealer raked in the cards and shuffled.

"Because I'm here with Edna, of course," Stephen answered. Everyone was dealt again, bet, and then folded, except Stephen and Natalie, who held their hands.

Natalie looked at Matt's face, a questioning glance full of curious annoyance. "What did you do?" she asked.

"What did he do?" Edna asked Stephen and Dave.

Stephen and Dave glanced at each other, then turned back to Matt. "Go ahead," Dave said. "Tell us what you did."

"I don't know what you're talking about," Matt said. His left hand came up and nervously fiddled with his tie.

"You're lying," Natalie told him.

"What?"

"You're playing with your clothes," she explained. "You do that when you're nervous and lying." They showed their cards. Natalie had a full house; the pot went to her.

The cards were dealt again, the dealer now very nervous, hesitating between hands as though the students might take her hands off.

"He's been reading Dave's business proposals," Stephen said casually, glancing at his cards.

"Is that true?" Natalie asked indignantly.

"Maybe," Matt answered nervously. "Maybe I saw one or two. But what does that matter?"

Natalie looked to Dave, her eyes apologizing. "I didn't know."

"He's been using my own proposals to undercut me," Dave explained, looking around the group. "It eats into his initial profit margins, but he's been making contacts at companies and using contracts that should have gone to me."

"That's not true," Matt tried to lie, biting his lip. "You know I wouldn't do anything like that."

Natalie looked to Stephen, who nodded.

"And even if it was," Matt continued, "that's just business. We live in a capitalist society, a war of all against all. The only way to get anywhere in the business world is to be the better predator, to use every advantage you have to overcome the people who are competing against you. All of you should understand that. Stephen, you're the best predator I know academically. Natalie, you're the queen of social warfare. Dave, you can write an airtight business proposal that will lock out any newcomer. If I were to do what you're accusing me of, that wouldn't be a personal assault against you. It'd just be business."

"What a bastard you are," Natalie stated. "Not one of us would have sold you out for anything. Academics, social drama, business, anything. We would all take care of you, we'd all protect you, and not a single one of us would have stabbed you in the back. If you want to play Judas, take your silver and go do it somewhere else. But don't ever accuse us of being as weak and petty as you."

Stephen flushed. The pot went to him.

Matt's face turned red, and he sank his teeth into his lips until he drew blood. "I don't want to hear anything else out of you, you little whore!" he hissed at Natalie.

Stephen rose to his feet, and so did Dave. They had pushed Matt as hard as they could, and he had reacted to their provocations. But they had meant for him to come after them. Turning his anger toward Natalie was such a cowardly act, their anger was renewed. They were ready for blood.

Matt grabbed Natalie's wrist to pull her up. Natalie tried to yank her arm away, but Matt was too strong. He grabbed her around her waist and threw her toward the door, while Stephen and Dave attempted to pursue him, blocked by milling students. Matt pushed Natalie through the crowd, throwing students out of the way, until he was at the emergency exit in the corner. Stephen and Dave were slowed, trying not to hurt anyone as they followed in Matt's wake. Matt pulled Natalie out the door and was across the street before Stephen and Dave caught up to him, Dave a step ahead of Stephen. Matt turned and struck Dave with the back of his hand, sending him sprawling to the sidewalk.

"Weak little rodent," Matt spat at him.

Natalie hit at Matt, but she was nowhere near as strong as she would become later, and Matt held her as easily as a hawk holds a field mouse between its talons. But while she could not free herself, her strikes were able to distract Matt for a few precious seconds. With a solid hit square across the jaw, Stephen struck Matt for the first time. On reflex, Matt re-leased Natalie to retaliate, but Dave, still on the ground, knocked Matt's legs out from under him in one sweeping kick.

Stephen scooped Natalie up, her arms around his neck, his under her knees and shoulder.

Dave, who had not yet gotten his hit in, was up on his feet. He grabbed Matt by the collar and pulled, buttons ripping from their home and falling to the ground like spare change. He pulled Matt's tie taut, as if it were a noose, reared back with his fist and punched the traitor in his already bleeding nose.

Ryan followed them outside, but he wasn't going to join in, even to help his buddy, Matt. Edna had come too, but she seemed fixated on Stephen and Natalie; she did not appear to notice that Matt was laid out, his nose and lip bleeding.

"Hey!" One of the school cops shouted at them, crossing the busy street cautiously. It was a younger woman, very strong looking with bright, intelligent eyes. "Are you the young woman who was assaulted?" the cop asked. Natalie nodded. "And the assailant?" Natalie, Stephen and Dave pointed at the man on the ground.

"It looks like he's suffered a pretty bad fall," she said.

"Probably from fleeing the scene," Stephen offered.

"That would be my guess," the woman said. "You three get out of here. I'll deal with him."

"What's your name?" Stephen asked her, moving backward with Natalie in his arms.

"Ariadne Stahl," the cop told him.

"Thank you!" Stephen shouted, and then he was running up the hill with Natalie in his arms. Dave kept pace with him, running at his side all the way to the baseball field. There, Stephen put Natalie down in the grass and let her run barefoot with them from one side of the diamond to the other, and then they were almost skipping across the street to Stephen's apartment building. They finally collapsed on the stairs, laughing hysterically, unable to breathe, falling into each other. Stephen and Natalie sat on the steps while Dave supported himself against the rail. The cold wind howled through the open walkway, cooling the group as they slowly returned to normal. Dave, with a sputtering laugh, said, "God I love living in a small town." And then they were laughing again, gasping for air against the cold and themselves.

"I'm going," Dave finally said after they'd stopped laughing. He stuck his hand out to Stephen. "Thank you."

Stephen gripped Dave's hand firmly. "It was my pleasure."

Dave shook his head vigorously. "If it wasn't for you, I probably would have killed him. Instead, I got to embarrass him." He laughed again, "Which is much better for everyone."

Stephen shook Dave's hand with a strong pump. "Good night," he said, and then Dave was gone.

Natalie put her head on Stephen's shoulder, kissing his cheek, his neck, nibbling at his ear. "I'll race you to your apartment," she whispered in his ear, stimulating his nerve endings into electricity.

He smiled at her, then was at the top of the flight of stairs. "Come on, slowpoke." And she was beside him. "Speak for yourself," she said. And they were through the door and in his bed, rolling around, kissing and shedding clothes. She got on top of him, then the tables turned and he was atop her, then they were on their sides, baring their teeth at each other in a feral celebration neither could explain. And then it was over, and she was snuggled up against his chest, moaning softly.

There was a knock at the front door.

"Don't answer it," Natalie told him.

"What if it's Dave?" Stephen asked.

"He left an hour ago. I'm sure he's in bed by now."

The knock came again.

"Let me just see who it is," Stephen said.

"But I'm comfy," Natalie complained.

Stephen kissed her forehead. The knock came a third time, and Natalie lifted off the bed so he could move. "Be quick. If I get cold, you're gonna answer for it."

Stephen laughed, said "Yes ma'am," and walked down his hallway, wrapping a blanket around his waist. When he opened the door, he gasped and his face turned white, the warmth of his recent carnal adventure failing in the cold fall night.

"Hey, Lover Boy," Olivia said, smiling at him.

That was the night I was conceived, out of rage and joy and confusion, out of the fight that followed with Olivia and the accident. The night that Stephen's mind first felt stretched to the point of breaking. If I'd been born that night, my life and Stephen's would have been so different. But either I was not ready yet to be born, or Stephen's mind was not ready to release me. Time and memory shifted, returning Stephen to the present, sitting in Dave's restaurant, talking with his friends.

"So what happened with Olivia today?" Gilbert asked somewhere between the main course and dessert.

"She had a grand mal seizure," Stephen told him. "But she's all right. Her star student and I were there at the time."

Natalie exhaled so sharply that Stephen thought she had gasped, but Gilbert and Columbus failed to notice.

"Does she have a history of seizures?" Gilbert asked.

Stephen nodded. "She was in the international teaching program when the first one hit. She was at Larkin Community College in Dublin when she seized going up a flight of stairs. They were concrete stairs, and she tore up her shoulder something fierce."

Natalie gently touched his elbow.

"So she's going to be okay?" Gilbert asked.

"The doctor said she's fine now. He's going to keep her overnight and she'll be released in the morning."

Dave set the dessert on the table. It was a cake as elegant and smooth as silk.

"What do you think?" Dave asked. "It's my own creation. I adapted it from an old family recipe. It starts off just like any other cake, but then I take it in a whole new direction. Nobody has ever attempted anything like this before. Try it."

Stephen took a bite, overcome with the bittersweet of dark chocolate mousse.

"It's delectable," Natalie said. She gave Dave a hug before taking another bite.

Stephen raised his fork and said, "My compliments to the chef."

"You see," Dave said, "this is how you run a business: a good building in a good location, a relationship with your customers and, most important of all, an excellent product." He took a bite of his own piece, kissed his fingers and laughed. "And that's why I've got a building in Mastern, despite Matt's attempt to sabotage it."

"I'll toast to that," Columbus said, raising his own fork full of cake into the air. Everyone else followed suit and the laughter and jokes recommenced, like in the old days at the red tables.

"So where are you guys going now?" Dave asked.

"We were invited to the exhibit at the arts center tonight," Natalie told him.

Columbus and Gilbert exchanged glances, then shared a small laugh. "Do you know what the exhibit is?" Columbus asked.

Natalie and Stephen shook their heads.

Columbus smiled. "This is going to be fun," he said, looking around the table. "Well, if everyone's finished, let's go." They said good-bye to Dave and as a group walked up North Main to the Arts Center, connected cunningly to the Hazelwood Library, both of which were lit. Small groups of people wandered between the library and the center. The sign advertised the "controversial" works of Sandra Blanche.

"What have you gotten me into?" Natalie jokingly asked, jabbing Stephen in the rib with her elbow.

"I don't know," he admitted honestly. He put his arm around her and together they followed Columbus and Gilbert into the building.

The Arts Center was divided into three rooms. In the first was a forest motif: Hanging from the walls were vast draperies of beads and boughs woven into netting, forming scenes of witch revelries and fairy palavers, young lovers caught together in trees, eternally reaching for each other but never managing to make their fingers meet. At the very center of the room was an ivory carving of Daphne being transformed into a tree to escape the lust of Apollo, her bright hair waving in the wind as her fingers and feet morphed from human to plant while bark grew over her skin.

"This is controversial?" asked Natalie.

"Just wait," Gilbert said.

The second room was a depiction of Hades and the Greek underworld. A frightening depiction of Cerberus, the three-headed dog, stood in the middle of the room, a black marble predator with three sets of snarling razor-sharp teeth bared at all who entered. Around his neck hung a mane of snakes, and his tail was serpentine. On the left head was carved the word "Past." On the middle was the word "Present." On the last the word "Future."

Cerberus guarded the walls upon which were depicted countless examples of humans doomed to suffer for eternity, each of them sexless shadows who had passed from this Earth. Stephen felt a cold chill as he observed the shadows caught together in a dark whirlwind of ineluctable pain. But it wasn't just their misery that made it so terrible. It was their lack of contact, each shadow separated from the rest by only a few small millimeters, never to feel the physical body of those around it.

Natalie grabbed Stephen's arm tightly. He took her hand and snaked his free arm around her waist.

"One more room," Columbus nudged them through double doors.

In the center of this last room stood a marble Apollo, his hand out-stretched toward the door, presumably toward Daphne in the center of the first room, hoping forever to take her as his, even in her transformation. For a moment, Stephen was struck by the ornate appropriateness of the three statues in the progression from one room to another. It was breath-taking, really. Then he discovered the controversy.

The room they were in was the peak of Mount Olympus surrounded by Greek columns that supported a canopy of stars, in which were written the stories of Chiron, Leo and Orion. But there were no gods here on Olympus—only goddesses. Two goddesses were placed between each col-umn, and each goddess couple was in the process of making love.

While it was shocking enough to encounter a picture of Artemis standing behind Persephone, one hand on Persephone's breast, the other between her legs, what made it more shocking was that the pictures were not paintings, as the shadows in Hades had been, but digitally altered pho-tographs of real women.

Stephen examined the photo of Artemis and Persephone: Artemis wore a quiver of arrows on her back, her veil intricately detailed with crescent-shaped moons. Her most captivating, bright green eyes popped brilliantly against her dark skin. Persephone held six pomegranate seeds in one hand, while the other wrapped behind her to massage Artemis' neck. Her legs were tattooed with black snowflakes, which faded at her thighs.

"It's beautiful," Natalie breathed from beside him.

"Thank you," said a female voice with a heavy New Orleans accent. "I spent a lot of time working on it."

When Stephen turned he was face to face with an androgynous girl with short brunette hair and green eyes like Artemis. "Sandra Blanche?" he asked.

"Charmed," she said, offering him her hand. "And you are?" He squeezed her fingers, which were light and delicate, and wondered at how this small girl had created such detailed and ambitious work.

"Stephen Lanford," he told her.

"I didn't expect a writer of your status to appear tonight." She offered her hand to Natalie, and when Natalie took it, Blanche smiled a wide, appreciative smile. "You are very beautiful yourself," she said, looking the FBI agent up and down. "I would love to use you as a model..." She smiled inquiringly.

Natalie blushed. "Thank you, but I'm not a...I'm straight."

Sandra laughed. "So is Artemis," she said with a nod at the photo.

Natalie looked to Stephen for support, and he put his arm around her shoulder and smiled amusedly. "Your work is inspired," he told the artist.

"Have you seen the main panel yet?" she asked. Without waiting for an answer, she took hold of Stephen's wrist and led the couple to the far end of the room. In the center panel, at the very end of the artistic journey, their final destination was a picture of Athena kneeling down between Hera's thighs as Hera sat on a golden throne. One of Hera's hands was rested on the back of Athena's head, while the other one held a bright red apple, seeming to offer it to the viewer.

Athena's face could be seen only in profile, but still Stephen recognized it. "You're Athena," Stephen remarked.

"Yes," she said smiling, a wicked spark behind her eyes. "And my girlfriend is Hera. This truly is my paradise."

Stephen studied the face and said, "Is that Allison?"

Sandra seemed surprised. "Yes it is. You know her?"

Stephen lied with a nod. "I went to school with her. She was good friends with William Mincks."

Stephen heard Columbus cough. It startled him, as he'd forgotten Columbus and Gilbert were there.

Sandra smiled at him. "Will you be in Mastern tomorrow, by chance?" she asked.

"I can be," he answered. "Why?"

"I'll be having lunch with her," she told him. "At the Gardens. You know where they are?" Stephen said he did. "You four should come. You will be my guests."

"We would be honored," Natalie said.

"I can't," Columbus said, "I've got work."

"Me, too," Gilbert stated with a sigh of disappointment.

Sandra frowned. "I can add your names to the guest list, in absentia," she offered. "It won't be the same as having you there, of course. But you would be there in spirit at the very least."

"That would be great," they agreed.

The four were about to leave when they heard a familiar voice coming through the double doors. "What are you doing here?"

As he turned, Stephen was shocked to catch sight of Ryan Gathers standing in the doorway.

"Admiring the artwork," Stephen told him blankly. "And you?"

Ryan shook his head, a scowl of disgust plastered across his face. "I suppose I shouldn't be surprised that someone as licentious as yourself would consider this pretentious pornography 'art,' but I thought even you had enough intelligence to recognize mediocrity when you saw it. I guess that simple spectacle will capture the lowest minds."

Stephen felt the old anger fill him like the wrath of Achilles. He struggled to remember his training, breathing silently through his nose. I did all I could to keep him calm, but his anger was too great for me. Sandra stepped between the two of them, but Stephen retorted mildly, "You know, I've always found people who are afraid of sexuality to be either hopelessly repressed or woefully ignorant."

"Mr. Gathers," Blanche interrupted, "I assume my lawyer has contacted you."

Neilson beckoned from behind Ryan. He said, "I believe that's why he's here, Sandra."

"It is indeed," Ryan agreed. "I gave you the option to choose your job or this exhibit, and you made your choice. I cannot have a woman represent my company who thinks that this..." he jerked his hand violently at the picture of Artemis and Persephone "...is art. I urge you to drop your lawsuit civilly."

"And if I don't?" Blanche asked.

"Then I'll counter-sue for defamation of character," Ryan answered defiantly. "The reputation of my company is at stake."

Blanche appeared to be considering it, rolling her eyes toward the stars on the ceiling, her lips furrowing sternly before she smiled, shook her head and said, "I'll see you in court, Mr. Gathers."

Ryan, overcome at her insolence, rushed at her, but Columbus and Gilbert stepped between them. Wanting to destroy something but cut off from the source of his wrath, Ryan drew his keys from his pocket and thrust them like a blade into the breast of Persephone. He then dragged the key down her body, cutting both her and Artemis down the center. A woman in a tailored black skirt and a black jacket came up behind him and snapped his arm to his back, ending his reign of destruction, forcing him to the ground and handcuffing him.

"You are under arrest," she stated, "for destruction of private property, as well as for causing a public disturbance. You have the right to remain silent."

"Bitch," he spat at her.

"Anything you say can and will be used against you in the court of law."

"Whore!" he shouted.

"You have the right to an attorney," she informed him, forcing him to his feet.

"What's your name?" he demanded of her. "I want to know your name!"

"Ariadne Stahl," she answered, ushering him out. "It'll be on your police report if you need it spelled out for you." She turned her head back. "I'll see you tomorrow, Sandra! Call me if you need anything else."

Sandra walked slowly over to the tattered picture and lovingly pulled it from the wall. "You," she pointed at Stephen. "You will help me out?"

Stephen nodded. "Just a moment," she said, and walked out of the room, returning a moment later with an identical, unharmed picture. With Stephen holding it straight and Sandra tacking it in place against the wall, the Olympus columns were filled again. Artemis and Persephone were as loving and blissful as ever, as though nothing had ever happened.

"Why do you have an extra?" Stephen asked.

"I have extras of all of these. You can never be too careful when men are opposed to you."

"I'm sorry about Ryan," Stephen told her.

"Don't be," she answered. "Remember my exhibit. Sometimes you have to go through hell to reach Heaven." She paused and looked in his eyes, as if trying to read something in them, or perhaps trying to tell him something without words. "Have you ever read *The Divine Comedy*?"

He nodded.

"It's my greatest inspiration," she stated. She placed her fingers to her lips, kissed the tips, then transferred the kiss to Stephen's mouth. Stephen didn't stop her. "Though he was a moral absolutist, Dante understood that love can save anybody, no matter how far they've fallen."

Stephen placed his own fingers to his lips and returned the kiss in the same manner. "I think I know what you mean," he told her.

I was confused by the scene. I saw all the players, heard all of their words, could guess at their motivations. But my mind was unable to formulate all the pieces into anything coherent. What had Ryan hoped to accomplish with his outburst, and why had Blanche kissed Stephen, and why had Natalie been silent when he had kissed Blanche back? I knew that I was very young compared to Stephen, but I wondered if more experience would help me to understand what had transpired that night. Stephen was able to read people and to a lesser extent, so was I. But he seemed to understand what had happened, while I was still trying to mold dry sand into shape. He and Natalie didn't say much on the way home, while all I wanted to talk about was the art, the stabbing, the kiss. What was I missing?

Even though the kiss had been transferred on Sandra's fingers, Stephen still felt it on his lips late that night when he and Natalie pulled into the driveway of the house. He still felt it when his mouth dropped open in surprise as he saw Allen sitting on the concrete porch.

Allen met them at the side door as Stephen and Natalie crawled out of their seats.

"Natalie, this is Allen, Olivia's pupil." Natalie took the young man's hand. "Allen, this is my girlfriend, Natalie." Allen smiled and shook her hand. "What are you doing here?" Stephen asked.

"I wanted to talk to you about Ms. Mincks," the young man said. "She said I could talk to you after class today, but what with everything that happened..." His voice trailed off and he shrugged. "So I thought I would meet you here. I was beginning to think you'd never get home. That porch isn't really comfortable."

Stephen laughed at the young man's comment, remembering the days of his youth, sitting on that hard concrete after school, waiting for his mom to get home and unlock the front door so he could take his afternoon snack and finish up his homework. He remembered high school, sitting on the porch with his friends and watching fireflies float through the air, feathers of spark. Just one of those little sparks could light his imagination like nothing else in the world. He remembered when he was Allen's age, lying on that porch next to Olivia and watching the stars spin through the sky.

"Come on in," he said, ushering Allen into the side door.

Natalie kissed Stephen's cheek and told him she was going to change, leaving Stephen and Allen alone. Stephen sat down in the recliner and offered Allen the couch. "How old are you, Allen?"

"Nineteen," the young man told him. "Why?"

Stephen produced the bottle of dark liquid from the side table and uncorked it. He tilted it sideways, hanging it by its neck, and offered it to the youth in front of him.

"What is it?" Allen asked, taking it from him.

"Whiskey," Stephen answered. He took a couple of glasses from the side table and put them down on the coffee table. "Go ahead and pour." Allen poured about two inches of liquid into each glass and handed the bottle back to Stephen. "Actually, the technical term for it is moonshine. My own father made this particular bottle the year I was born. It's the last one the old man ever made. He was an alcoholic, but he kept this one safe. Left it to me, along with the house. Found it in his old hiding spot when we came back for his funeral. The last Lanford original."

Allen raised the glass and tapped it lightly against Stephen's. "I'm honored. What are we toasting to?"

Stephen thought for a moment. Would it be a toast to the university and the mascots that neither Allen nor Stephen cared about? Would it be a toast to good health and good fortune for both of them? What did the two of them have in common? Olivia and the university, he thought. And neither of those things felt right. Finally, a Jonson quote occurred to him that he thought the boy would appreciate.

"To the old, long life and treasure. To the young, all health and pleasure."

"I'll drink to that," Allen said, taking a sip of the liquid. He looked for a moment like he was going to spit it out, then he swallowed hard and put the glass back on the table, his eyes wide and watering. Stephen tilted his head back and took the liquid all at once.

"How did you find out where I lived?" Stephen asked idly.

Allen laughed. "It's a small town. I just asked the right people and they pointed me here. It's hard for anyone to disappear in a small town."

Stephen thought about his search for William and how William had left town to disappear. There must be something, he thought, a clue to his whereabouts, something to point me in the right direction. I know it's there, he told himself. But the alcohol had already climbed into his brain, and it was hard for him to think too hard on the subject.

"Can I ask you a question?" Allen asked.

Stephen nodded.

"I've been reading your book, and I don't exactly understand something. You see, you say that you caught Stringfield because you divined that he wanted to destroy beauty, and by getting into his head you were able to understand what he found beautiful, which is how you eventually ended up catching him." Allen cleared his throat and took another tiny sip of his whiskey. "But the picture of his third victim doesn't look like the description you gave of his definition of beauty. The other girls, Lilly especially, were too good to be true: blonde, socially competent, upper-middle-class girls. But Constance was different; she was a red-head, had social issues, was working class. Stringfield wouldn't have found her beautiful in the same way that he did the other girls. She was a major outlier for your theory. I was wondering what you made of that, because you don't address it in the book."

Stephen poured himself another glass and sipped it, letting himself taste it this time. "What motivated Stringfield wasn't exactly his need to destroy beauty. Stringfield had a pathology of what can informally be called infornography."

"Infornography?" Allen asked. "I've never heard of it before."

"That's because it's not an accepted theory. It actually comes from the science-fiction novels of Darryl Phoenix. Olivia said one of her more gifted students was planning to follow my footsteps, to sign up with the bureau. I'm assuming that's you?"

Allen nodded, seeming embarrassed that his teacher had been bragging about him outside of class.

"Once you get to the bureau you'll hear more about it, if you still choose to go that route." Stephen sipped his whiskey. "Infornography is a pathological need to acquire data. It's an obsession with information. For Stringfield, this obsession with learning new information manifested itself when he read some books. Let's see, what were they?" He thought for a moment and let his head roll back, feeling the alcohol cloud fill his brain. "*The Wizard of Oz* by L. Frank Baum, *Valis* by Philip K. Dick, and even *O Coward Conscience* by Darryl Phoenix. He—Stringfield—became obsessed with the idea that the world was an illusion and that he had to find the secret to unveiling the reality behind this plane of perception. His mission then became to throw back the curtain that hid the true world, which is what he was trying to do with his murders of the first two girls. They represented for him the illusion: They were classically beautiful, idealistic and they helped to maintain a world that was, in effect, imprisoning everyone with its non-reality."

Stephen finished his second glass and covered his mouth as he burped lightly into his fist. "Constance was a nanny. She was teaching children to believe that the world they lived in was the real world, which is what drew Stringfield to her. When he killed her, he was doing it so that she could never teach anyone else that the world they see around them is real."

Allen nodded. "You never said anything about this in the book."

Stephen nodded back. "I had to edit it out to comply with the FBI regulations. Now the title, Plagued by What We Know, doesn't make sense, either, but publishers didn't seem to care."

Stephen thought about pouring himself another glass, but decided against it. His vision was already starting to shift.

"How did you figure out that he was…?"

"An infornographer?" Stephen asked, smiling. "Because I'm one, too."

Allen finished his glass.

"It's just that I manage mine," Stephen told him. "Natalie sees to that, more often than not."

"You have an obsession with information?" Allen asked him.

"When I work I do. When I was on the Stringfield case, I completely lost sight of the world around me because I was trying to make sense of the crimes. I stopped eating unless Natalie told me to, stopped showering unless Natalie told me to, missed appointments left and right because I simply forgot about them. When I was on the Perrini case, I almost got a reporter killed. Perrini followed me to the reporter's house while I was reading through his investigative articles. The killer pulled a knife on him, got a good cut on his chest before the reporter fought him off. Of course if he had never followed me, who knows if we would have ever discovered that he was a cab driver, which eventually led us to solving the case, but my superior officers never forgave me for going to see the reporter behind their backs."

Allen nodded, listening intently. "Is Olivia an infornographer?" he asked hesitantly.

Stephen laughed. "No. She's smart, but she's hardly obsessed with information."

Allen leaned in and asked, "Is that the first time you've ever seen her seize?"

"No." He coughed and leaned in himself, speaking quietly to the youth. "I've seen her seize twice before."

"I heard that she screwed up her shoulder by seizing a long time ago."

"That's what we tell people," Stephen told him.

"But it's not true?"

"No," Stephen answered grimly.

"What happened, if you don't mind my asking?"

Stephen coughed again, put the bottle of whiskey into the side table and closed it. "I did it," he quietly confessed. He sat in silence for a long while as the boy looked at the glass in his hand. "It was an accident."

"How did you...?" the boy's voice faltered weakly.

"Hold on," Stephen told him. He stood up, tipsily stumbling as he walked through the house to the bedroom. Natalie was lying on the bed in her peach-colored kimono, her eyes closed, her breathing heavy and regular. Her breasts rose and fell in steady rhythm while her lips and eyes twitched lightly. She was deep in her REM cycle, and Stephen was sure she would not wake up, even if he crawled into bed next to her and fell asleep himself.

"There was a car accident," Stephen told Allen when he had re-claimed his seat. "I was angry with Olivia. I was yelling at her."

In his mind's eye he saw himself driving down the old highway, his hands clutching the wheel tight as his eyes were on Olivia.

"She and I had broken up. She went off with the international teaching program, and I had started a relationship with Natalie. Then one day she just showed back up, out of nowhere."

He remembered the rosy color of her blouse hugging her chest as she reached for the handhold above her window.

"I told her I couldn't be with her, because I was with Natalie, but she said she wanted me back."

He remembered his voice, angry and impatient. "I can't," he'd told her. "I'm with Natalie now."

"I was taking her to her mother's house, up at the edge of the farm-lands, when she started to fight with me."

He remembered the smell of Natalie, even though he had left her in his apartment.

"She said to me, 'I guess I was always right about you. You're all talk. You've always been all talk, and no backbone.' And I said to her, 'I guess I was always right about you. You've got no conscience whatsoever.' And I didn't see the red light."

He remembered seeing the truck screaming toward the window like a missile, the yellow headlights slamming into Olivia's door, the way she fell limp across the stick shift as the car slid around on the road like a top, and how her body was like a tattered rag doll when the car finally slowed to a halt. He dissociated for the first time in those slow seconds, saw everything happening but felt unable to move, unable to change his fate as the car spun on the road. His mind felt disconnected from his body, his car like a distant country viewed through a spyglass. Olivia looked into his eyes, but she seemed to be on the other side of a river, and he knew that he could not reach her, no matter how he tried.

"Along with the seizures, the accident crushed something inside her. Her confidence was shattered; she couldn't lift simple objects, couldn't walk right. It was tragic. She became trapped in this town by what had happened to her. It's a shame, really. She was always the one with the most potential."

Tears streamed down Stephen's cheeks.

"I don't understand. Why did you lie?"

"I don't know. Because I was embarrassed. Because I didn't want anyone to know that it was my fault."

"You feel responsible?" Allen asked. His hands were on his knees and he was arched over the table, listening intently to Stephen.

"I am responsible," Stephen said. "It was my fault. I destroyed her life, I destroyed her future. I destroyed her and everything about her that once made her beautiful. It was all my fault." He wiped his cheeks and told the young boy again, sighing out listlessly as he spoke the words, "It was all my fault."

Chapter 4
Silver and Gold

Tuesday, March 1, 2011

I woke up before Stephen did. It wasn't very often that it happened this way, so I decided to enjoy the sunlight by myself for a while. Stephen never enjoyed the sunlight; he was always moving too fast to appreciate anything. I always loved the way the sun painted the walls golden for only that short time in the morning. Nothing ever shown as brightly, and I never saw anything so clearly as then.

I remember the first time I saw sunlight. I had been conceived in Stephen's consciousness on the night that Stephen hit Matt, on the night of the car crash, but I was not born until some years later. It was approaching night and the setting sun washed over the warehouse with a silver twilight. I opened my eyes and saw those beams of silver falling through the dirty windows.

It was a violent birth. For a few moments I was both myself and Stephen simultaneously, my consciousness attempting to forcibly rip itself from his, the material binding us together reluctant to snap. My head hurt. When I put my fingers to my temple it hurt worse, and when I looked, my fingertips were stained red. I thought to myself, *I'm still alive*. Natalie would be mad that I had put myself in this position, but at least I was still alive.

Then I thought, *Who's Natalie? What's going on?*

That's when the dissonance started. Suddenly, I was in two places at the same time: I was in a field, what I felt to be paradise, with long grass rising like great oaks above my head, and that silver radiance hypnotizing me; I was also in a warehouse, and I had just been grazed by a bullet from the pistol of a man named Stringfield. I was two people: I was Stephen Lanford, a young profiler brashly pursuing a dangerous man through the warehouse where he had destroyed at least five lives, five beautiful examples of life; I was also a man without a name, seeing sunlight for the first time as bullets pounded into the metal sheet that separated me from that monster. I heard the bullets spitting and the casings clinking as they failed to break through that metal sheet; I heard a river bubbling and spitting as it flowed along rocky, porous stones. Blood poured from my—from our—ear.

Get up, Stephen thought. *You have to go after Stringfield. You have to stop him from hurting anyone else. You have to fix this.*

Who is Stringfield? I thought. *Why is he shooting at me? Stay here. Let him go. I can't fix this.*

This is it, he thought. *This is what you've been training for all your life. You can be a hero. You can make the world a better place. Get out from behind this useless machine. Take down Stringfield. Remove the cancer from the body. You can do this. Take him dead if you have to, but don't let him hurt anyone else. Lilly. Constance. All the rest. This is all for them.*

Lilly, I remembered. Constance, I remembered. Natalie, I remembered. Dobbs had warned me not to go after the Avalon City Murderer myself but like a fool I had rushed in without a plan, and here I was, pinned down and being fired upon. Some hero. Some difference I could make.

No, Stephen thought. *You can do this. You can catch him. You're a hero. You can make a difference.*

Who am I? I thought. *I'm not an agent, I'm not a hero, I'm just some kid lying in a field.*

What field? Stephen thought. *We're in a warehouse and the shooting has stopped but I still hear him. We can still catch him.*

We can still catch him, I thought. *Stringfield.*

I ran toward the sound of gunfire, up the metal stairs that seemed to buckle under every step that fell, across the banister that should have crumbled with rust years ago, and jumped. I saw Stringfield's eyes grow wide; I saw his gun lift to meet me; I saw the muzzle flash. And then I was on top of him, hitting him again and again until the gun was across the floor and his face was a stain of red and purple.

That was my first experience in life: an act of violence. It wasn't one I would have picked for myself. And yet here I was, dislocating a man's shoulder in the name of justice, cuffing his hands behind his back so that he could never hurt another human being so long as he lived. This was my feat and my fault. I had foolishly rushed in without contacting Dobbs, I had allowed myself to confront a dangerous man without back-up, and I had messed up the arrest in an amazingly inexperienced way. And yet none of it was my fault, since I had not even existed when all of these decisions were formed in the back of Stephen's mind.

I felt a pain in my thigh where the heated barrel of the gun had burned me. Police sirens grew slowly in the periphery of my mind while Stringfield and I were both clothed in silver twilight streaming through a skylight that one of his stray bullets had shattered above us.

"I guess you caught me," he had whispered against the splatter of blood that had grown on his lips.

"Yeah," I had muttered, breathing heavily. "I caught you."

"Do me a favor," he had said. "Show people what is real. Show them what is true. Don't let the illusion win." He coughed hard, blowing a bubble of red spit into a crimson puddle on the floor. "Do you understand me?"

"Yeah," I'd told him, finally regaining my breath. "I understand."

Natalie stirred in the bed, breaking the flow of my memories. As Stephen slept on, I rolled over and ran my hand through her hair. I heard her moan lightly. My fingers massaged her back as I moved closer to her, pulling her body against mine. She smiled and moaned louder, snuggling up against me. I kissed her forehead, then the tip of her nose, and finally her soft pink lips.

"I love you," she whispered, kissing my chin.

"I love you, too," I whispered.

She nuzzled her nose into the crease of my neck and fell back asleep, smiling sweetly as I held her. I took her hand in mine and ran the tips of my nails up and down her fingers, from the base of her palm to the very ends of her fingertips, which I momentarily pressed my own fingers to before dragging my nails back down to her palm. I could feel her breathing change, hear the involuntary murmurs escaping her throat, but she never stirred. Just continued to dream.

I didn't think in all the world there could be anything more sublime than that moment for me. The sun pouring in the window making everything golden; she, asleep, snuggling up against me, cooing as I played with her fingers; all existence represented by the two of us, everything else irrelevant; the entire universe at peace around and within us. If there was nothing else, there would be this moment, and that would be enough for me. It might have to be.

I felt Stephen's consciousness stir. He rose to the surface and kissed

Natalie, waking her up.

"I don't want to get up," she sighed, kissing his ear. "I'm comfy."

"We've got to go to Mastern," Stephen told her. "Sandra is expecting us at the Gardens."

With a little bit of coaxing, Stephen was able to get Natalie out of bed, showered, dressed, coffeed, and in the car. However, only a few minutes after pulling onto the interstate, Natalie drifted back to sleep, leaving Stephen alone with his thoughts. Engaging the cruise control, Stephen looked over at Natalie, scanning the lines of her face, noting the way her chestnut hair fell across her neck in thin ribbons, red strands reflecting in the morning sun, crowning her. She smiled at something from her dream.

I thought about how beautiful she was, about the smell of her hair tickling my nostrils, about the feeling of my mouth on hers, about the sight of her that morning and the intoxicating emotions that came along with that memory. Stephen thought about Olivia.

"Natalie," Stephen said, putting a hand on Natalie's knee, "Time to wake up."

"Wah?" She jerked awake.

"Bad dream?" He asked.

"Yeah. I saw…" Her green eyes met mine and she blinked a few times, before shaking her head and saying, "Nothing, it was just a silly…" She clenched her fists and relaxed them a few times and said, "I thought. Oh, well…" She put her hand to her nose and laughed. "Whatever. Never mind. Come on, let's go," she finished.

She was acting like it didn't bother her, but her dream, and the fact that she wouldn't tell us what she'd seen, disturbed me. Stephen was too caught up in his own quest to notice Natalie or her silly dreams. If she were to be struck down by a thunderbolt beside him, I doubt if it would distract Stephen from his mission. I knew that I was being dramatic, but

Stephen would sacrifice Natalie any day if it brought him one step closer to Olivia. So Natalie's upsetting dream, to him, was insignificant.

We left the car in the parking lot and went together into Gardens. There were stands with people giving away hot dogs and cocoa, a platform where a small acoustic band played sing-along songs, streamers falling from every tree with silver stars that shone in the late winter daylight and hundreds of people wandering the park.

"What is this?" Natalie asked, looking around.

Stephen shook his head. "I didn't know anything about this."

"It's beautiful, isn't it?" A voice spoke from behind us. When we turned, Stephen was face to face with Athena.

"Come, Achilles," Athena said, taking Stephen's hand, then Natalie's, calling her Briseis. "Come hold communion with us."

Sandra Blanche led them to a picnic blanket between two trees, where a group of people sat on a quilt, circling a basket full of bread and fruit. Stephen recognized Allison Weston, Ariadne Stahl, Neilson and a man he had never expected to see, science fiction author Darryl Phoenix. Darryl wore large mirrored sunglasses under which Stephen could not see the man's eyes, but he noticed how the man stared at him as the three took their places in the circle.

"Stephen Lanford," Darryl said, licking his lips and extending his hand. "I wasn't anticipating the pleasure of having a fellow writer here."

"Darryl Phoenix," Stephen said, enthusiastically shaking the man's firm hand. "Honestly, I didn't foresee either of us being here today." Darryl's mouth twisted into a strange smile, a knowing one with a hint of amusement. Stephen sat down and looked at Neilson. "I hope I'm not paying you for your time here."

"Not yet, but if you were, you'd be getting your money's worth."

Natalie sat next to Stephen and asked Sandra, "What's going on here?

All these people?"

"I just told you," Sandra laughed. "This is our communion." She took a piece of bread from the basket and handed it to Stephen. "Our group holds a get-together at least once a week. This week, we were granted permission to use the Gardens on Tuesday and Thursday."

"Your group?" Natalie asked.

"The arts community," Stephen concluded, looking around.

Technically, the Gardens were the Mastern city park, taken over by the Mastern art community and left to the care of the university before Stephen had ever set foot in that institution's hallowed halls. Partnerships between the university in Hazelwood and the city of Mastern were commonplace; people and properties traded between them like blood between heart and hand. The Gardens were one of those partnerships, owned by Mastern, managed by Hazelwood, and currently left to the care of Sandra and her group. Over the last several years it had been nurtured from an unkempt jungle of foliage and social debris into a series of beautiful gardens designed to relax the spirit and enrich the soul. The arts community had brought the park to life, and today it seemed that the Gardens had brought the arts community to life as well.

"I knew from the first moment I saw you that you two were with us," Sandra said. "You and your friends as well." Stephen tore a handful from the loaf of bread and passed it to Natalie, thanking Sandra for inviting them. "When you said you knew Allison, I knew."

Allison, sitting with her feet in front of her, leaned forward and hugged her knees to her chest. "I don't recognize you."

Stephen took a bite of bread and swallowed it. Looking Allison in the eyes and smiling, he said, "We both went to high school in Hazelwood. I think we had math together…with Miss Benton, if I remember correctly."

She smiled back and said, "I guess. Did you sit near the middle of the class?"

"Gosh, it's been so long since that class," he muttered, looking up and to the right. "I think I sat next to Mary…I can't remember her last name." Stephen had chosen the name Mary because he knew that it was the most common female name in America. There was always a possibility that Allison had not had a Mary in her high school math classes, but he could always talk his way out of it by blaming it on a bad memory and moving onto another name. Elizabeth or Sarah, maybe. That was one of the great things about lying; the farther back into the past you ventured, the easier it was.

"Judson," Allison provided for him, completing the ruse for Stephen. She relaxed, and Stephen knew that he had earned her confidence with the lie, had broken inside her defenses. It might take some work, but he could at least speak openly with Allison now, as an old high school friend. "I hated Mary back then," Allison reminisced. "She was always spreading rumors about how I would have sex with any guy who bought me alcohol. Joke's on her." She laughed and laid her head across Sandra's shoulder. "I hear she's running around with John Spillers now."

"Olivia's ex-husband?" Natalie asked, leaning forward.

"That's the one."

Stephen remembered seeing John the other night. He remembered that he had been so preoccupied with digging the knife into John that he hadn't bothered to ask what the man was doing wandering around at three in the morning. Stephen cursed himself but swallowed his anger. He heard his father's voice saying, "Don't give me that look, boy!" and then his therapist telling him to breathe. I pushed his mind away from those memories gently, pointing him back to the task at hand. He asked Allison, "You used to be friends with Olivia's brother, didn't you?"

"Up until he disappeared." She put her head down into her knees, but

Stephen could tell she was sucking on her lips.

"You know where he is, don't you?" Natalie asked.

Allison shook her head, checking the left side of her eyes. "No." It was spoken with the quickness and inelegance of an unexpected lie, and both Natalie and Stephen knew that she actually did know. "He just..." She looked up at them and tried a little harder to convince them, "He just disappeared."

"The case is still open on William," Ariadne said. "There haven't been any clues or breaks in the case since the last time he was seen all those years ago. The trail's gone cold."

Darryl took a silver cigarette case from his jacket pocket and produced one cigarette for himself and one for Allison. Allison took it without speaking, and Darryl sparked both to life with a lighter he seemed to conjure from nowhere.

"Isn't that a nightmare?" Darryl asked the two FBI agents. "To one day awaken and discover that someone that you once loved has gone missing? No note, no clues, no closure. Just poof!" He blew a line of smoke in front of his face and fanned it away with his free hand. "And he's there no more."

"Truly," Stephen agreed.

"Of course, it comes from a deeper fear than just social attachment, I think." Darryl waved his hands in front of him when he spoke, his fingers dancing in the air to illustrate his point. "You see, humanity exists in three states: the past, the present and the future. All of us exist in each simultaneously. We possess within ourselves each of our past moments, as well as each of our future moments." He held up three fingers together.

"It is like the thread of the fates," Sandra stated.

"And when a person goes missing, or is killed, then there are two states in which they just simply cease to be." Darryl dropped his ring and middle finger, leaving only his pointer finger still raised. "Each future moment that this person contained within them, each drive to work, each first kiss, each lazy dinner spent with company, all wiped out in a single instant." He blew another trail of smoke and wiped it out, as though erasing the future state of his cigarette. "And the present state also disappears. The person is no longer there to remind us of them, to make us happy when we have a bad day, or to keep us in line when we start to venture past the boundaries of social acceptance. And when we see that, we imagine how quickly our own existence could be erased, how quickly we can vanish. That's what truly scares us, I think."

Stephen smiled. "I can kind of see what you mean, yeah."

"We should not be scared of this, though," Darryl went on, taking Stephen's agreement as a cue to continue, "because even though a person has ceased to be with us physically, it does not mean they are not still influencing us." He took his cigarette, burnt down to nothing, and stamped it out on the ground in front of him. "You see, I had a boyfriend once who told me that he had cheated on me with one of my friends. I later found out he had been lying in an attempt to hurt me. He had succeeded, to be sure. Since then, every boyfriend or girlfriend I've ever had, I've had to ask myself time and time again, 'Are they cheating when I'm not around?' So even though I have not seen this boy for..." He scanned the cloudy horizon, searching for the number, then stated, "ten or so years, he has had a profound influence on my personal life, you see?" he asked, looking to Natalie and Stephen for support.

Natalie nodded, a look of quiet contemplation on her face. Stephen nodded as well.

"Let me give you a happier example," Darryl said. "When I was young, I was always in trouble with my parents. It seemed like everything I did was wrong. My father would criticize everything I did, from the way

I washed the dishes to the way I vacuumed the carpet. I never seemed to know what I was doing. I always tried pointing out to him that other children I knew didn't do the dishes or vacuum the carpet, weren't responsible for cooking themselves lunch or taking care of the wood floors, but he would always stare down at me with those wolf-like eyes of his and scare me into submission.

"One time, he criticized the rice I made myself for lunch. I had let it sit too long, and it became sticky. I tried to defend myself, stating that nobody had ever taught me how to make rice, that I was mostly guessing on what to do. He yelled at me. 'Why are you always so sensitive? Why are you always so defensive? ' He stormed off in a huff, stomping the floor, leaving me to my thoughts, my rice, and the knowledge that after lunch I would have to clean fresh scuff marks from the entire first floor.

"I had, however, a friend at that time, one whose parents would let me crash at her place whenever I wanted to. I probably spent more nights on her couch than I did in my own bed. This irritated both of my parents immensely, my mother because she wanted me within her domestic cloud so she could appear to be a diligent and thoughtful parent, my father because I was outside the limits of his control and oversight. But if it wasn't for my young friend, I doubt if I should have any concept of geniality or love."

Allison put her hand on Darryl's shoulder tenderly, smiling at him. She loved him, Stephen could tell. Loved him in a different way than she loved Sandra, but still loved him. Perhaps she saw both Sandra and Darryl as great minds in a world of dull and lifeless people. Maybe that was what attracted her to such artists. Or maybe she saw deeper than that, saw past the artist and the wounded dear to something that Stephen couldn't see. Maybe she loved him not because of his greatness, but because of his humanity.

"Her influence continues to influence me to this day," Darryl stated, rubbing his cheek against Allison's hand. "In every relationship I have lives a little piece of her."

There was a moment of silence before Ariadne began to speak.

"I never liked my mother. My father left when I was young, so she was all I had, but she never listened when I told her things, so I eventually just gave up. My first boyfriend was a jerk. When he wouldn't take no for an answer, I kneed him in the balls and walked home. I wanted to talk to my mom about it, but she talked over me when I tried to bring it up. I guess she thought that if she didn't hear my problems, I didn't have any. Whenever I got mad at her, she would take on this disapproving, holier-than-thou tone and speak down to me. I was retarded, I couldn't do any-thing right, who was I to judge her?"

She rubbed her eyes with her forefinger and thumb.

"She used to smoke all the time. I always wanted her to stop, but she never would. A few years ago, she finally developed Chronic Obstructive Pulmonary Disease, which developed into a full-blown heart failure. She didn't listen to the doctors who told her to stop smoking. Even though we were never really close, it still hurt me when she died. Whenever anything important happens in my life, I still hear her disappointed voice.

"When I got promoted to detective, I was so excited for myself. I told every single one of my friends that I'd finally achieved my dreams. But who I really wanted to tell was my mother."

Sandra smiled. "I remember the call. She sounded so pleased with herself, and we were all so happy for her."

"My boyfriend at the time was prouder than anyone else. When I saw him there in the audience, his eyes full of love and pride, I felt an elation I'd never felt before. It was unreal. But still, I heard my mother's disap-proving growl in the back of my head. Even though I've worked hard to achieve everything I've ever wanted in life, I still feel empty when I re-member her."

Sandra reached out and took Ariadne's hand, running her thumb over her friend's knuckles.

"If it weren't for Allison and Sandra…" Ariadne trailed off.

More silence ensued. Stephen looked at Natalie, who was rubbing tears from her eyes. "What's wrong?" I asked.

She took a deep breath, a few teardrops rolling down her cheek. "When I was a little girl, I always tried to get my daddy to pay attention to me. He was so busy with his class loads, he never had time for me. I re-member one day, I snuck into his study just so I could watch him work over his shoulder. He'd go through paper after paper, marking through cer-tain sentences, underlining others. He would circle words or passages and write comments in the margins. I sat there for a long time, just watching him work, but he never knew I was there.

"After my mother found out he was sleeping with one of his students, she left him. I wanted to live with him, thinking that maybe, maybe he would pay attention to me if my mom wasn't there to take care of me for him. But my mom wanted full custody, and he didn't bother to fight against her. I think he was actually a little relieved that he didn't have to take care of us anymore.

"He…" Her voice trembled. "He took his own life my senior year of high school. Mom and I were both shocked. But she tried not to show it. I remember at his funeral, she didn't cry. But when we got home that night, she locked her door and cried for hours. I could hear her. When she came out, she pretended like nothing had happened, like dad hadn't died, like she hadn't just cried until she didn't have any tears left. Even at eighteen, all I could think about was how pathetic she must be to pretend she didn't have any emotions. I knew that she knew that I knew. But she still pretended."

After all the years Natalie and Stephen had been together, Natalie had never talked about her father or mother openly like this. I bypassed Stephen's consciousness, reached over and put my arm around her, pulling her to me.

"I never cried," she muttered. Her eyes grew red. Fresh tears burst forth. She put her face to my shoulder and wept, soaking my shirt through. For all that we had ever seen, neither Stephen nor I had ever known this side of Natalie. I felt like maybe this could be a turning point for him, that maybe now Stephen would see Natalie. He did feel bad about it, I could sense. But it was Stephen. I didn't know what he would do, even after seeing Natalie this way. But I knew that he would never give up on Olivia.

"I remember the last time I saw my father," Sandra spoke up now. "It was the day that he found my girlfriend at the house." A small laugh escaped her, before her smile contracted into a wrinkled brow. "We weren't even doing anything wrong at the time, just kissing. She was like cotton candy, soft and sweet. My father came home early from work and found us in my bed, kissing. He threw a fit. After dragging my friend out of the apartment without even the decency of letting us say goodbye, he told me he was going to kill me. I was terrified of him.

"I tried to get out the front door, but he blocked the way. I tried to go down the fire-escape through the kitchen, but he went around through the living room and grabbed a knife from the counter. 'Go to your room,' he told me. So I ran to my room and locked the door.

"He started pounding on the door, even more enraged now that he couldn't get to me. He kept rattling the handle, yelling at me like a klaxon. I was so scared, and I didn't know what to do, so I went to the window. It was a three story drop straight down." She reached down and began to massage her ankle, the memory dredging up the old pain. "It was the only way."

A faint growl of thunder rumbled in the distance. Neilson's phone went off. He talked into it for a few minutes, then flipped it shut and turned to Sandra. "Matthew Graycraft just bailed Ryan Gathers out of jail."

"We expected that," Sandra said.

"But he pulled his attorney from representing Gathers. Gathers is on his own now."

"Why would he pull his support from Gathers?" Ariadne asked.

"Isn't that just the selfish way Matt works?" Allison responded. "As long as it's just us against Gathers we stand a chance."

"I still don't like it," Ariadne said. "What if Matt is going to pull something sneaky out of his hat?"

Sandra was silent, looking from face to face.

Natalie seemed to be almost catatonic against Stephen's shoulder. He figured she'd fallen asleep. But I felt her breathing against me. I heard her sobs whenever the flow of sorrow flooded back up. I felt her fingers clutching at his arm like a lifeline. She was deep in the water, deep in a bottle of memories she had uncorked. I rubbed her back, consoling her, but made no effort to pull her away from me. I just wanted her to cry until she didn't need to anymore, no matter how long it took. I just wanted her to get it out of her system.

But the more she cried, the weaker her grip became. I became afraid she was draining herself, using all of the strength she had to hold on. I kissed her forehead and put my hand on the back of her head, holding her so that she knew I had a grip on her, that I wasn't going to let her drown. I felt her grip fall away. She kissed my cheek, whispered, "Thank you," dried her eyes and returned to the circle.

Stephen nodded, then turned back to the group. "It's because of what

Ryan did last night," he said. Everyone looked at him. "When Ryan destroyed Sandra's artwork, it went from being a case of a disgruntled ex-employee against the guy who fired her to a case of Ryan Gathers against a struggling artist. When Ryan blew up, he changed the narrative."

It seemed to be a good enough answer for everybody. Except Stephen didn't actually believe it. It wasn't Matt's style to shrink from public opinion; he believed he was smarter than anybody else, so what did their opinions matter? But it wasn't Matt's style to leave Ryan to fend for himself, either. Perhaps they had fallen out over something; perhaps Ryan had asked Matt to pull his lawyer; maybe it really was a trick, like Ariadne suggested. Stephen didn't know. But I thought I had a guess.

"We have to go see him," I whispered to Stephen. "We have to go talk to Matt."

"What?" Stephen asked.

"I said it's your turn," Sandra told him. "To share."

Stephen cleared his throat. "Go ahead, Stephen," she whispered.

Thoughts of Olivia filled Stephen's head so full that he almost seemed to forget he had parents. But once the memory was dragged from the depths of his mind, he could not help but share. Somehow, the pain is always sharper when we share the things that hurt us the most. But for some reason, we still do it.

"My parents split when I was young. I was five when…"

Rain began to fall on us. Stephen stopped and looked upward, holding out his hand to catch a few of the drops in his palm. Natalie stood up and held her arms out, letting the rain shower her. Sandra and Allison stood, joined hands and began to dance. Ariadne sat back, crossing her legs in front of her. Darryl lit himself a new cigarette, shielding his lighter and cigarette from the rain. Neilson opened his briefcase and produced an umbrella, which he opened and held above his head.

Ariadne held her head back, running her fingers through her wet hair. Neilson watched her, smiling to himself. She opened her eyes and smiled back at him. Neilson jerked his head, silently offering her a place under the umbrella. She laughed, then crawled under the umbrella and pressed herself against him. He lowered the umbrella so that they were out of our sight for a few seconds, then raised it again. His arm was around Ariadne's shoulder, her cheek against his chest.

Rising from his seat in the grass, Stephen stepped behind Natalie and wrapped his arms around her waist. Her arms wrapped up into a pretzel, her hands falling on the scruff of his neck. He put his fingers on her chin and turned her face so that he could kiss her.

"Can we go back to Hazelwood and crawl back into bed now?" Natalie asked, kissing his cheek.

"I need to stop somewhere first," Stephen said, kissing her lips. I wanted to stop him from kissing her, but I couldn't. "But that will definitely be our destination." He smiled at her, and she smiled back at him, and the rain fell on us.

As they started to leave, Sandra looked to Stephen. "I'm sorry you didn't get to tell your story, Achilles. Some other time?"

"Of course," Stephen said. "There are other stories besides mine that need to be told anyway."

Sandra smiled and let the couple retreat to the warmth of the car.

Drained from the conversation, from the rain, or from the events of the past few days, Stephen's consciousness began to fade into that waking dreamscape, his body a train without a conductor, moving without a ruling will. He was on cruise control, and it was easy for me to slip into his place without him knowing, without Natalie realizing. One second it was him, the next it was me.

"No more sunlight," I muttered under my breath as the car started down the road to Cityscape Productions, Matthew Graycraft's corporation.

"Not today, anyway," Natalie said. She still had the soft features of arousal written on her face, but I needed to talk to Matthew before I could let Stephen take advantage of her. Her hand slipped out and took my free hand, and I felt a shot of compound guilt and joy. It was the first time she had ever held my hand, and even though I knew she thought I was Stephen at the time, it didn't stop the bliss from growing inside me.

I parked in the alley behind Cityscape and turned to her. "I'll be back in ten or fifteen minutes. If you want to go grab us something to eat, there's money in the glove box."

She smiled and nodded. "I have money. You're going to talk to Matt about why he pulled his lawyers from Ryan's defense case, aren't you?"

I nodded. She leaned across the car and put a hand on the back of my head, her fingers ruffling my hair. "I guess I can't blame you for playing the hero this time. Nobody deserves a hero more than Sandra."

I looked into her eyes, seeing the rods and cones, the divine intelligence, the beauty and the incorrigible faith. I ran my fingers through her hair, gently pulled her toward me, and kissed her. Her lips sent another shot through my body like lightning through my bones. "You do," I whispered to her. "You deserve everything I can give you."

The playful mirth that crossed her face was the most beautiful sight I had ever seen. After everything that Stephen had put her through, that happiness inside her shone more brightly than I could ever have anticipated. "I love you," she said.

"I love you, too," I returned. "I'll be back as soon as I can, alright?"

I could tell that she was holding something of herself back as she nodded and let me go. "I'll be waiting," she said simply.

I opened the door into the cold shower of spring rain. Standing there for a moment, I thought about giving up on it, pretending I didn't need to see Matt after all, going home and coming back some other time. But then I shook my head. If I was going to be better than Stephen, I couldn't start off by shirking our responsibility to Sandra. I would be back in only a few minutes, and, if I could hold onto control for just a while longer, then Natalie and I could be alone together.

I pulled open the glass door and entered the lobby of Cityscape Productions, looking around as I went. There was a podium at the end of the entrance hall, a blonde secretary sitting behind it, smiling with false joy as I attempted to shake myself dry before stepping onto the marble floor. "Welcome to Cityscape Productions. How can I help you today?"

"Matt Graycraft," I said.

"I'm sorry, sir, Mr. Graycraft is only available by appointment during business hours."

I smiled, ingratiating myself with her. "I'm an old friend of his, and I happen to know that he goes on his lunch hour..." I pulled out my cell phone and checked the time "...in about five minutes. I'm sure he'd be very grateful to you if you made an exception just this once."

She didn't seem to be prepared for the words that came out of my mouth. I'm not sure I was actually prepared for the words. But she looked like she was considering.

"Those are lovely earrings," I said, still smiling. "Your boyfriend get them for you?"

She blushed. "Oh no, I don't have a..." She cut herself off and looked at me with surprise and bewilderment. "Are you Stephen Lanford?" she asked.

I grimaced. "Guilty," I said.

"Of course, I'll give Matt a call right away." She lifted a corded telephone from the podium and said, "Matt? Stephen's here. Yes, I'll send him up." She returned the phone to its cradle. "Matt told me you would show up and would know just how to gain my confidence. If I hadn't been on the lookout for you I probably would never have caught it." She walked around the podium and asked, "How did you do that?"

"Sorry," I answered. "A magician never reveals his secrets."

"Come on, let me know," she pressed.

I took a deep breath. I hated Stephen's mind and the way it worked, efficiently dissecting every person he came in contact with. It was cruel, the way he cut into the heart of people. But she had asked. "The impression of the ring on your finger, but no more ring. The smell of your dogs mixed up in your expensive perfume. The magazines sticking out of your purse. You're on the hunt."

I pushed the office button and said, "Of course I didn't really need any of that. I saw the way you looked at me from the moment I walked in the door." The doors of the elevator closed, separating me from the girl. Stephen had forgotten about her by the time we reached the top floor. I hadn't.

Matthew's office was a large open room, abstract paintings in wild colors hanging from three walls, the far wall all window from which Matt could see the entire eastern side of Mastern. When this had been Matt's father's office, Mr. Graycraft had once pointed to the window and asked Stephen if he could see Hazelwood way off in the distance. When young Stephen had shaken his head and replied that he couldn't, Mr. Graycraft had declared that one day Hazelwood would be large enough to see. All these years later, and the old guy's prophecy still had not been fulfilled.

Matt stood up from his desk. He wore a look of exasperated belligerence masked with his usual false and prideful smile. "You just caught me. I'm about to go to lunch."

"I know," I said. "I just needed to talk to you about something real quick, two minutes tops, and then I can let you go."

Matt's eyes flashed to the elevator, then to the window, then to his watch, then back to me. "Alright, what is it?"

"The Sandra Blanche case."

Matt's eyes clouded. "I'm not involved in that. If you want to know anything about that, try talking to Ryan."

"I want to know why you pulled your lawyers from the case."

Matt was taken aback. "How did you know?"

"Neilson told me."

Matt shook his head and sat down behind his desk. Waving his hand at the chair opposite him, he ordered, "Come. Sit."

Taking a bottle and two glasses from the bottom drawer of his desk, he poured two measures and handed one to me. "This scotch was bottled December 8, 1980. It was the day that John Lennon was shot, both in photograph by Annie Leibovits, then later to death by Mark David Chapman. A little after five in the afternoon, Chapman approached Lennon with a copy of *Double Fantasy* which Lennon autographed. A fan, Paul Goresh, snapped a picture of Lennon and Chapman together. About six hours later, John and Ono were entering their home when Chapman shot John five times with hollow-point bullets. John never had a chance.

"Scottish distiller, Anderson MacCutcheon, had twelve bottles worth of this scotch in his cask. When he heard about Lennon's death, he took the case he had just bottled and gave them away, all but this one, which he saved for his unborn son. He remarked of the scotch that it was probably the best a human being had ever crafted, although it could never bring Lennon back."

Matthew drank the scotch like it was a glass of water, finishing it in a few seconds. I took a drink from my own glass and wiped my lips.

"Thank you for sharing," I told him.

"With the money I spent on this bottle of scotch, I could have bought your contract from the federal government if I were so inclined and sold you to a Mexican drug cartel as an enforcer; I could have bought the Hazelwood Town Hall and burned it to the ground; I could have done countless things with the money I spent on this single bottle of scotch; but instead I bought myself a slow poison."

About three-quarters of the bottle had already been consumed.

"Matt," I said, leaning onto my knees, "don't pretend to be a wounded healer, just because you're wounded. You're a lot better off than most of us."

"You asked," Matt responded. He cracked his neck to one side, then the other, then fixed his gaze on me.

"Was it because of you and Kate?" I asked.

He exhaled hard. "Of course you would know," he muttered. "Ryan sees me every day, sees Kate every night, and he doesn't have a clue that I'm the one screwing her. You're in town three days and you know. I bet Natalie does, too."

I nodded. He poured himself another measure and drained the glass again.

"Yes," he finally answered. "Well, partly. It's for Kate, for Ryan, even for Edna in a way." He shook his head. "I just don't…" He rubbed his neck. "I don't know what I'm doing. I know at one point I was a good person…" He raised his eyes to look at me. "I had friends. I cared about you, and Dave, and Natalie, but somewhere along the line, everything went wrong."

I nodded. "You betrayed Dave."

"Yeah…" He laughed a single bitter, regretful laugh. "Yeah, I remember." He sighed and shook his head. "Dave wasn't the first. And he wasn't the last. I've been working my way up the ladder one poor fool at a time since I was in grade school. Whatever it takes, Dad always said." He sighed. "You know, my old man was the reason your old man never made it. You know that right?"

I shook my head.

"Yeah," Matt said. His voice was starting to increase in pitch, without increasing in volume. It's a sad habit of a man on the edge of cracking like glass under pressure. "My dad had yours on payroll for years, feeding him just enough money to keep your dad in booze. But he told me one time that if your old man ever came to know his potential, there would be no limit to the things he could achieve. He would be the greatest threat to my dad's company, to my company, if he only understood how smart he was."

"Why are you telling me this?" I asked.

"Because my dad put his hand on your dad's head and held him down while he himself climbed the ladder, and I've been doing the same thing all my life. Ryan Gathers is my best friend, and I've been doing the same thing to him that my dad did to yours. And all the time I'm sleeping with Kate, leaving Edna alone at home to cry herself to sleep. And that's why I pulled my lawyers from Ryan's team. Because I…" He laughed a demented cackle that rebounded off the walls with the force of an icepick to the eardrum. "I am a bastard."

I finished my scotch and set the glass on his desk. "It's a little funny, in a sick kind of way. I came here to tell you that I thought you'd finally done the right thing for once, pulling your support from Ryan. And I guess you did, really. In the most asshole way possible."

Matt stood up and ushered me to the elevator door. "Why, Stephen," he said, fitting a false smile onto his broken ego, "I think that's the sweetest thing you've ever said to me." When I was safely inside the elevator doors, he muttered, "I despise you, Stephen Lanford."

"The feeling's mutual," I said, pressing the button for the first floor.

Matthew's secretary was gone when the doors reopened. I stepped out into the reception area and looked around. It felt so empty; yet suffocating at the same time. My steps echoed along the marble floor. When I finally made my way outside into the steady drizzle of rain, it was a relief.

Natalie smiled at me as I climbed into the passenger seat. "You find what you needed?" she asked.

"Yeah," I said, and then my lips were on hers, and I was kissing her as hard as my lips could bear, my fingers unbuttoning her jeans and slipping between her panties and her bare skin. She grabbed my wrist, but let me continue for a few seconds before pulling my hand away.

"The back seat," she whispered. She crawled catlike over the armrest and twisted in the seat, then lifted a finger and beckoned me. I was less graceful in joining her, but soon we were kissing like teenagers, and I was undressing her and she was undressing me. This was the first time that I'd ever been the one kissing Natalie, the first time I was the one to make her smile like that. For a few moments, I felt like the hero, like the knight, but my body betrayed me.

Try as I could, it knew I was not its rightful owner, and it refused to heed my wishes. So as much as I wanted to be the one that Natalie held in those moments, I had to give Stephen control again. I should have known better than to try and compete with him.

A few minutes later the windows were fogged, and Natalie was screaming his name while I lay silent.

Chapter 5
Night

Tuesday, March 1, 2011

The rain stopped a little after six, so John and Stephen bought sandwiches from a Papa Burn's stand on the corner of Main and Madison and walked down through the historic district. Stephen devoured his sandwich; early in the day, Natalie had bought a small box of donuts from one of the old breakfast shops in Mastern for them to share, but after the exercise of the morning, those carbs had been burned at least twice over.

Natalie was at home sleeping now. I wanted to sleep next to her for a while, but Stephen wanted to talk to John about why he had been wandering the streets of Hazelwood the other morning. As always, he won.

The two men turned left onto Park and wandered between the iron gates of Sunset's patio, dropping the paper that had wrapped their sandwiches into a trashcan before finding a seat at one of the round metal tables.

"When was the last time you were here?" John asked, raising a hand to signal the cocktail waitress.

Stephen wiped his mouth and thought for a moment. "My twenty-first birthday," he said.

John nodded, a look of embarrassed regret appearing on his face. "That's right, the night of the fight." The waitress looked up and saw John waving. Recognizing him, she smiled and waved excitedly. She was very pretty. "Did you ever know Mary Judson when you were here before?"

Stephen started to shake his head no, then remembered the lies he had told earlier that day. "I had a class with her in high school. With Miss Benton, if I remember correctly. Why?"

John smiled wide and rose to his feet. "Mary!" he shouted, holding out his arms.

Mary flew through the door and leapt up into John's arms. John caught her and kissed her lips, lifting her into the air so that her toes dangled inches above the ground. "What are you doing here?" she asked him, hugging him tight. "I thought I wasn't gonna get to see you today."

He set her back down and kissed her one more time before holding his arm out to Stephen, who rose to his feet and offered his hand.

"This is my old college buddy, Stephen Lanford."

"The famous writer." Mary held out her hand, gripping his firmly between her thumb and forefinger. "Very pleased to meet you." She had dirty blonde hair that curled around in corkscrews and a smile that contained a hint of violence in it. Her face, chest and hips were plump in the way that Southern girls grow, her cheeks rosy, her lips pink. She seemed dangerous to me. Stephen didn't say anything, though.

"Actually, you two have already met," John said. "Stephen says you two had Miss Benton's class together in high school."

"I'm sorry," she told him. "I don't remember you."

"I was friends with Allison Weston," Stephen offered.

Mary's face grew red, her eyes narrowing, shooting hatred at Stephen. "Allison Weston. That little whore stole my first boyfriend from me because I wouldn't sleep with him and she would. And she was always sucking up to Miss Benton for extra points." She shook her head. "I hated that class. I hated Miss Benton, I hated Allison Weston, and I still hate math." She took a deep breath and closed her eyes for a few passing moments. "I know it's a long time to hold a grudge, but I always hated her after she took William away from me."

"William Mincks?" Stephen asked.

Mary nodded, biting her tongue between her canines. "He was my first love."

"I, uh, I'm sorry. I didn't know," Stephen said. I looked between Mary and John.

"Mary and I have a lot in common," John explained. "Mary! Stephen hasn't been to the Sunset in almost ten years. Think we can get a few free drinks?"

"I think I could hook you up." She forgot her anger and winked at John. "Rum and Coke?" John nodded. "And Stephen, I bet you're a…" She looked him up and down. "Jagerbomb kind of guy."

Stephen shook his head. "How about a Jack and Coke?"

"Done." She left to fetch the drinks, shaking her hips wide as she walked.

John watched her ass until it disappeared behind the bar, then said, "Dating the owner of a bar has its perks."

"She seems nice," Stephen lied.

John shook his head. "Maybe not nice, but she's a lot easier to read than Olivia was. It was always drama with her, and I never knew what was going on in her head. With Mary, it's…I always know what she's thinking. When she's happy she smiles, when she's sad she frowns, when she's angry she fumes, when she's horny she crawls into my lap and kisses me. There's no wondering whether she's angry or not when she just stops talking in the middle of a thought, or what she's thinking about when she sits silently looking out the window, or if she's happy when you do something good but she doesn't smile."

Mary reappeared a second later with a tray, one drink for each of them balanced in the center. She placed it on the metal table and began to sip on a Long Island.

"It's been refreshing," John said, moving his chair closer to hers and placing his arm around the chair back. Mary gave him a quick, peckish kiss, smiling lovingly at him.

"So why has it been so long since you've been to Sunset?" Mary asked Stephen without looking at him.

Stephen drank, then swirled the liquid around in his glass and admitted with a put-on embarrassed smile, "Your predecessor kind of banned me."

John started chuckling lightly, covering his mouth with his fist.

"What's so funny?" Mary asked, looking back and forth between the two.

"There was a fight," John told her, a wide smile spread across his face. "It was one of the best things I'd ever seen, honestly."

"A fight? In my bar?" Mary asked, rubbing John's leg.

"You would have loved it, actually," John said. "Do you know Ryan Gathers?" She nodded. "Ryan was harassing this gay guy, Columbus…"

It was after the night of the accident, after the knights of Hazelwood had schismed, when Olivia no longer spoke to Stephen and Natalie hated Matt. The night of Stephen's twenty-first birthday, he and a group of red table members went out to Sunset to celebrate. The nice thing about Sunset was that unlike the other Hazelwood bars, you could still sit around if you weren't yet legal to drink. Columbus and Gilbert were there, Gilbert's wrist encircled by a neon orange wristband to denote that he was only twenty. John was there, sitting at the table with everyone else. He was quiet, though, and it was easy to forget him. James and Helen were inside, playing darts and trading inside jokes. Edna had her feet up on the table and was sipping from a flavored Smirnoff, while Dave, drinking from his pint of Guinness, fruitlessly flirted with her. Natalie was there, sipping Sangria and chatting happily.

Everyone in the group had decided to buy Stephen a drink, which was a good idea in theory, but as the night went on, all those different alcohols began to mix inside of him. A few hours after he'd begun drinking, he patted Columbus' shoulder. "Hey man, can you do me a favor?" he'd asked, slurring his words.

"No problem," Columbus said.

"Can you get me…glass a water?"

"I got you, man," Columbus said. He finished off the last of his martini and stood up, marching confidently through the doors toward the bar.

Natalie took Stephen by the chin and started kissing him. His lips were numb, his cheeks were warm, his reactions sluggish, but those kisses dragged him from the depths of drunken stupor to the shallow shore of consciousness. "Happy birthday, baby," she whispered in his ear, before nibbling at it lightly.

"I love you," he told her for the first time.

"I love you, too," she said, running her nails along his back, smiling sweetly.

That's about the time the shouts started erupting from inside. Gilbert was the first one around the corner, Dave the second. Stephen was the last one, but he was quickly guided to the front of the group, an unofficial leader of the red table faction. "What's going on here?" Stephen asked, slightly slurring his inquiry.

Ryan Gathers was at the head of the other faction. "Well, if it isn't the birthday bastard?" he asked, clapping Stephen roughly on the shoulder. "I was just having a chat with your friend here." Stephen looked left at Ryan, who was surrounded by a group of his friends, then right at Columbus, who had been pushed up against the bar. Columbus' shirt was wet, and there was a broken glass on the bar beside him. "Isn't that right?" Ryan snapped his fingers a few times, as though thinking up the name. "Columbus?"

Columbus looked at Stephen, then to the bartender. "Can I just get another water, please?" he asked with a tone of agitation.

The bartender looked at Columbus, then at Stephen, finally at Ryan. "If you try any more funny business, you're all out of here for the night," he said, looking at Ryan but speaking generally to all three of them. He reached down and got another glass, filling it with water.

The second the bottom of the glass touched the bar, Ryan's hand shot out and struck it, sending it shattering against the wood counter top and splashing Columbus with water again.

"That's it!" the bartender said, reaching out to grab Ryan's arm. "Y'all are out of here, we're clos..." One of Ryan's friends took care of the bartender with a left hook. The rest of the bar quickly dissolved into chaos as punches were thrown, glasses broken and the sound of knuckles striking skin filled the bar. Somebody started singing, and then they were all drinking and singing and throwing punches in a spectacle of violent fun.

Stephen stumbled through the fight, muttering verses of song between dodges and punches until he was covered in beer and not a little blood dripped from a cut in his eyebrow. He grabbed the man who had punched the bartender and pulled his arm, bringing the boy to him. When he was close enough, Stephen lifted his fist and brought it forward into the man's nose. Blood dripped out of the boy's nostrils as he fell backward into the crowd.

As Stephen turned away from him, another of Ryan's friends drove his fist into Stephen's gut, causing Stephen to lean forward and heave. Though he felt like he was going to lose his birthday presents, he was able to hold on but just barely. He stood, grabbed his antagonist's shoulder and kicked his knee, bringing him down to the floor, before bringing his elbow down on the man's head, leaving him prostrate.

"Stephen!" He turned toward the cry and saw Columbus being dragged by three boys out the patio door. Each of the boys was from Ryan's faction, but Stephen did not see Ryan with them. "Help!" Columbus called, struggling to free himself as he was dragged from sight. Stephen clambered through the crowd out the doors into the night air after his captive friend.

One of the three who had been holding Columbus ran forward and threw a punch that connected with Stephen's shoulder with all the force of a hammer. Stephen fell against the door frame, lifting his fists in front of him for protection as the man brought his fist back for another punch. But the second punch never came. Natalie grabbed the man's elbow and spun him around to face her, then grabbed him by the back of his neck and kneed him in the balls. The man's eyes rolled back in his head as his body folded to the ground.

"Natalie," Stephen sputtered incredulously. Natalie smiled back in answer.

"Stephen!" Columbus yelled from outside the iron gates of the patio. Stephen and Natalie both turned and ran after him. The next thing they saw, the two remaining men who held him tossed Columbus out into the street, rolling him out away from the curb until he was sprawled out and helpless in the middle of the road. Natalie ran, Stephen ran, Columbus attempted to stand. Stephen saw the headlights of the car first and started running as fast as he could. Natalie grabbed one of the two jerks who had tossed Columbus and punched him. Columbus stumbled trying to run back to the curb. The car slammed on its breaks, but it was crossing Park too fast to stop without hitting Columbus. Columbus braced for impact.

Stephen pushed Columbus to the side of the road, semi-tackling him as they both collapsed into the grass beside the railroad tracks. The car passed by harmlessly, not even bothering to stop. That was when Stephen's stomach finally decided that it had had enough. He spun away from Columbus and vomited into the grass.

Columbus patted him on the back. "Feel better, buddy?" he asked. Stephen nodded, his sick moment passed. "Thanks," Columbus said. "I owe you one." He put his arm around Stephen's shoulder and squeezed him tightly before helping him to his feet and back across the road.

Natalie had the third guy on the ground, wrapping his arm around his back. Her knee was on his spine as she pushed his face into the concrete of the curb. "Natalie," Stephen said, putting a hand on her shoulder, "You can get up now. The police will be here any minute."

"One second," she said. She unhanded the guy and stood, then slipped her foot from her shoe and stepped on the back of his neck. "If you ever try something like that again—if you ever try to hurt my friend, or anyone else like that ever again—I will personally see to it that you never father children, you understand me?"

"'Es!" The guy screamed from his concrete pillow.

"Natalie, we've got to go," Columbus hurried her.

Natalie nodded, jumping away from her victim quickly in case he decided to come up swinging. But the guy rolled onto his side and cradled his twisted arm, not even paying attention to the group of three.

"I like being strong," Natalie told Stephen, smiling confidently. She slipped her shoe back on quickly. "I feel like I can take on Matt if he ever decides to flip out again."

"Where's Gilbert?" Columbus asked. His eyes shot back to the iron gates, searching for a sign of his lover. A second later he was running toward the bar, Stephen and Natalie right behind him. They arrived seconds before Ryan from the opposite direction. Like a rat attempting to escape a sinking ship after creating the fatal leak in its belly, Ryan was trying to flee from the bar fight he had created. Natalie caught him by the wrist and twisted, shoving him against the gates in a fluid swipe that her sensei would be proud of.

"Let go of me, you bitch!" he shouted.

"Alright," she said. She drove her elbow down into his shoulder and kicked out the back of his knees, sending him sprawling to the ground with a loud thud. "I'm going to keep him company until the cops get here," she told Stephen. "You and Columbus find…"

"Gilbert!" Columbus shouted, taking his lover in his arms in a tight hug that seemed ready to crush Gilbert's ribs.

"Columbus!" Gilbert shouted, returning the hug. "I punched a redneck in the face! It was awesome."

"Guys," Stephen said. "I hate to interrupt, but…" The sound of police sirens approaching began to ring in their ears. "Police," he finished, jerking his head toward the door.

Gilbert and Columbus looked at each other, then, in unison, scrambled out the iron gates and across the train tracks. Stephen wrapped his arm around Natalie's waist and jerked his head again. She nodded and began to run. Her hand found Stephen's, and then they were running along the train tracks and back to Stephen's apartment just like a night several months prior. Another memory that hadn't passed through Stephen's mind in years. I enjoyed the story as John told it, seeing it pass across Stephen's consciousness.

"Ryan was arrested for inciting a fight, but the charges didn't hold." John tapped his glass on the table. "He was up for release before they even got to the police station because of Mr. Graycraft's political sway."

"That's crazy," Mary said, finishing her Long Island. "And Darren banned you because of that? Why you?"

Stephen shook his head. "We all got banned: Columbus and Gilbert, James and Helen, Dave and Edna, Natalie, me, Ryan and all his friends; even John-boy here got it."

"John never told me that," she said, sharpening the word "that" into an accusation and raising an eyebrow in John's direction.

"I'm not the first person to lie for love," John joked, leaning forward.

Mary leaned forward, too, inches from his face and playfully said, "Do it again and we'll see how much love you're getting."

Stephen coughed into his fist. "Hey, Mary, can I get a glass of water, if you don't mind?"

Mary said "Sure, hon," and stood. She walked a few steps, then turned around. "Do you really want water, or do you just want me to go away so you can get some guy-talk in with my boy?" Stephen tried to smile. "That's what I thought," she said. "You've got five minutes." She held up her fingers and counted from her pinkie to her thumb, then turned and walked to the bar, swinging those hips.

"Refreshing," John repeated, watching her walk.

"So why did you and Olivia split up? I never got the story."

John sighed, breathing in hard. "Things just kind of, uh, fell apart. A divorce seemed like the obvious solution. Like I said, everything with her was all drama. You know she cheated on me?"

"What?"

"Yeah. Honestly, that was the final straw in the whole thing. I mighta stayed with her if it was just the aggravation with her job. I could even stay with her if I had to hear her complain about her shoulder and her condition every day. Hell, I'd stay with her despite the fact that she shrank me down to the size of a mouse and stepped on me every chance she got. But when she cheated on me with that Silverman kid..." He shook his head and finished off the last of his rum and Coke. Swallowing hard he said, "That was the last straw."

Stephen gagged on his drink, spitting it into his napkin as he covered his mouth.

"Yeah," John said. "Allen fucking Silverman. Can't believe it, can you?" Stephen shook his head, still covering his mouth with the napkin. "Yeah. He's actually a pretty cool guy, but after the whole affair thing I could hardly look at him. He was here the other night, though."

"The night I saw you?" Stephen asked.

"Yeah. He came here and we sat around and talked for a while. Mostly with me, but he's cool with Mary, too. She went home early, but he and I were out here until probably three in the morning or so. He says he's worried about Olivia, wants to know what my advice was for dealing with her when she starts getting depressed."

Stephen rubbed his eyes. "What did you tell him?"

"I told him that if I knew that, she and I wouldn't have gotten a divorce."

Stephen nodded and let the conversation shift. John began to talk about his life since the divorce, about working on the oil field and being on call every day of the week, about how he was making good money, but how it made him mad that no matter how many hours a week he worked he always made the same salary. He told Stephen about how he and Mary had hooked up at a party one night, and how they had "perfect chemistry." He told Stephen about how much he preferred Mary to Olivia. But Stephen knew that John was hurting inside, that he regretted how things turned out, even if John didn't know it himself.

As cautious as Stephen was toward Mary, she and John really did seem to be in tune. She told him about how fun John was and about how she felt a lot safer having him at the bar whenever he made it around. She said that it was nice having a father figure for her little girl. She didn't seem to be aware of John's lingering feelings for Olivia. She saw John as he wanted to be seen, rather than as he really was, but John was happy with that. At least, Stephen thought he was.

Stephen enjoyed the company and the time away from Natalie. Since they'd been in Hazelwood, they'd been around each other constantly, and he felt like they needed space. But now that he had a new target in his mind, he had to pursue it, so his interest in the conversation waned. His old obsession was beginning to awaken in his mind, the puzzle pieces circling around his head, forming together and breaking apart as he thought more and more about what was going on around him. His temple pulsed, his head throbbed in a steady ache, his feet tapped impatiently. He checked his watch and told John that he had to get home.

John smiled and shook his old friend's hand. "It was good catching up, man."

Mary smiled and gave him a friendly hug. "It was good seeing you again. Don't make it so long next time." Stephen laughed and said he wouldn't and then left to chase the clue that he'd just been presented with. I could feel that he hoped it wasn't true. I knew that he hoped it was John-boy overreacting to a complicated situation that he couldn't understand. But I could also tell that somewhere deep in his consciousness, Stephen knew it to be true. In fact, I think he was even a little angry at himself for not seeing the intimate connection between Allen and Olivia sooner.

He made his way west along the train tracks, knocking rocks and pebbles down the slope as he went. He and this path had a long history, beginning when he was a child. He had walked it for years. He let his muscle memory take over and tried to clear his mind. It began to rain again, but lightly, a mist descending on the town. He let his head fall back and held his arms out, the water collecting on his skin, his hair, his clothes.

It was a short walk to Steeple Valley, the townhouses where Olivia lived. To get there, Stephen had to pass the crossroads at Marilyn Street and Jackson Avenue. He could have turned south, and walked through the university grounds to his house, could have crawled back into bed with Natalie, could have spent the rest of the night in peace and solace. Instead he kept west into the valley.

A large stone fence ran around the townhouses like a barricade, the tops of the houses rising above the wall like the towers of a castle. Stephen entered the gates and walked to Olivia's townhouse. He knocked on the door with the bottom of his fist and waited. It did not surprise him that Allen opened the door.

"Stephen! What are you doing here?"

Stephen's face was numb and his lips dry. "Can I talk to Olivia?"

Allen moved aside, and Stephen stepped across the threshold. The door closed behind them, and he walked through the house in a dreamlike daze, following behind Allen as the young man led him up the stairs and to the bedroom where Olivia lay in bed.

"Stephen!" she smiled, sliding from the bed. "What are you doing here?"

"I wanted to talk to you," he said. "Alone, if you don't mind."

Olivia smiled at Allen and said, "Why don't you go make a pot of coffee for us all. Stephen and I won't be very long."

Allen grimaced. "No problem," he muttered and closed the door.

There was a thick silence in the room as Olivia tried to read Stephen's stolid face. I don't know what she saw there, but she can't have liked it, as her lips sank and her eyes grew dark.

"Feeling better?" Stephen asked.

"Yeah," she said. He nodded. She glared at him. "Lover Boy. Don't do that."

He smiled as wide as his mouth would let him. "Do what?" he asked.

She stared at him for a long time, reading the lines of his face, the curves of his eyes, the color of his cheeks. Then she turned away, walked over and lifted the window, letting cool air flood into the stuffy room. "Open the door," she commanded.

Stephen obeyed, throwing the door open with a force that should have scared Olivia. She just stared at him, frowning. "Allen!" she shouted in a cheerful voice. "We're done, whenever you want to bring us the coffee."

"Alright!" he called from the bottom of the stairs. "It'll be just a minute."

Stephen shook his head. "Can I ask one thing?"

"Make it quick," Olivia said.

"Why?"

She sat down on the bed and looked up at Stephen, swallowing hard. "He reminds me of you."

He wanted a drink, something strong. He wanted to lie down in bed and forget the world.

"Why didn't you tell me?" he asked.

Her lip trembled. "Why would I?"

Allen entered with two mugs of coffee, handing one to each of them. He then sat down on the bed next to Olivia. Stephen went to take a drink of the coffee, then shook his head again. He handed his mug to Allen. "I've got to go."

"Stephen, wait." Olivia stood, but Stephen was out the door, down the stairs and through the front door before Allen caught him by the shoulder.

"Come on, man," Allen said. "Just relax." It was almost seven and the sun was beginning to set in the west, casting a strip of gold across Allen's face as the tower of other townhouses broke the light.

"I'm fine," Stephen lied.

Allen stood with his hand on Stephen's shoulder for a second, studying his elder's face. Then he released Stephen and reached to his pocket. He pulled out a metal cigarette case and flipped it open. "You're not fine." Allen pulled two cigarettes from the case and slid it into his back pocket. "Here," he said, shoving one of the cigarettes into Stephen's palm.

Stephen looked at it and realized that it wasn't a regular cigarette, but a homemade one. He sniffed it and discovered that it wasn't filled with tobacco either. "Allen, I can't take this."

"Yeah, you can," Allen said, flipping open a silver Zippo lighter. He lit his cigarette and placed it to his lips, offering Stephen the lighter. "To the old, long life and treasure. To the young, all health and pleasure," he repeated Stephen's toast from the previous night.

Stephen felt as though it had been ten years since then. He looked down at the cigarette, brought it to his mouth, lit it and inhaled.

"Do they test you when you try to go for the FBI?" Allen asked.

"A piss test," Stephen answered. "At Quantico. You can't get caught while you're employed, or they'll strip you of everything: your job, your pension, your ability to be employed by the government. But as long as you clean up before that first test and don't keep a habit, you're okay."

"Aren't you still employed?"

"They won't test me anytime soon. My mom just died."

Allen's eyes were beginning to glaze over, the THC already affecting his brain. "I guess I should probably stop soon. It's just a lot easier to pass my classes when I'm not stressed out all the time. I mean, I only work part time, but four classes on top of work is hell. The Dean actually told me it was nearly impossible."

"You should give it up, and soon," Stephen told him. "It might take awhile to break a habit like that." Then his brain changed gears. "I got enough in student aid and scholarships to not have to worry about working. It helped me out a lot."

"Were you from a low-income family?" Allen asked.

Stephen nodded his head. "Low enough."

Allen studied him for a few seconds. He smacked Stephen on the shoulder and said, "You're alright, old man."

"You're a punk," Stephen said, inhaling the last of the cigarette, holding it for a few seconds, then exhaling the smoke noiselessly. "But I guess you're alright, too." He stamped the spent casing under his heel.

Olivia came downstairs and stood in the doorway. Allen looked back at her and tossed his own casing into the road.

"You going home?" Olivia asked.

"Yeah," Stephen said. "I was just chatting with Allen here."

Olivia nodded, then looked at Allen. Allen looked from her to Stephen, then back. "I'll catch you some other time, alright, man?

"Definitely," Stephen told him. Allen disappeared behind Olivia.

"Lover Boy," she whispered. Stephen stood silent. "Please," she whispered.

"What do you want from me?" he asked.

"I want…" Her lips stopped moving.

Stephen nodded. "Good night, Olivia."

She swallowed hard and said, "Good night, Lover Boy."

Stephen walked west along Jackson until he reached his old apartments. He stopped and thought about all the good times back when he was young and took it for granted that he and Olivia would be together forever. Memories of all the times they'd shared passed through his head: all the smiles, all the love, all the laughter—the good, the bad.

He walked through the baseball field, his feet sinking into the spongy grass and moist earth. He crossed the train tracks onto school grounds, tracing a path between the English and architecture buildings, up alongside the student center, zigzagging through the quad. He stopped for a few seconds to admire the school fountain, a large pool with the figure of Athena in the center of it. As he gazed into the eyes of Athena, the eyes of Athena gazed back into his own. In that moment, he realized that he was a fool. He knew that he was Don Quixote, chasing a princess and true love that had never existed. The knowledge knocked the air from his lungs.

He made his way through the quad and around the student center to the red table. He slumped down and put his face into his hands, pressing his palms into his eyes as though with his bare hands he could erase the knowledge of what he finally knew.

It had been one thing when she had gone with John: He was a shitty replacement for Stephen, and Stephen knew that the quiet loser would not last forever. But Allen… Allen was everything that Olivia wanted, without all the things she didn't. He was Stephen without the complications of the past they shared. Stephen could have been happy for them, but he wasn't. Instead he was filled with rage and jealousy.

His impotent possessiveness frightened me. He had missed his chance with her long ago, had moved away, as she'd asked him to. He had a job, a partner, a life. He had no future with Olivia. Time had moved forward, but his obsession, his entitlement, kept him viciously tied to the past. He had no right to blame Allen or Olivia. But still he did.

He thrust his fists down onto the table top, feeling the pain in his knuckles. With a rush of serotonin to his brain, Stephen felt his headache begin to waver and break. Between the weed and the pain in his hands, the pain in his head was almost gone.

Stephen remembered the first time he met Olivia. He was walking to his new apartment from his dad's house late one night, crossing through the university grounds to his apartment, when he saw a Hazelwood policeman talking to a girl by the red table.

"I'm just going home," she angrily explained to the cop. "I don't see why you're giving me such a hard time for…"

"There's a curfew, young lady, and you're not supposed to be out here by yourself."

"The curfew doesn't start till eleven, and it's not eleven yet."

The cop's eyes grew wide and he asked, "Are you talking back to me, miss?"

"Hey, Candace!" Stephen shouted, walking up next to her. "I told you to wait for me back at the house."

"Who…" Olivia began to speak, but Stephen cut her off quickly.

"Hey, officer, is there a problem here?"

The cop looked him up and down. "Do you know this girl?" he asked.

"Yeah, this is my sister, Candace," Stephen said, putting his arm around Olivia's shoulder. "I was going to walk her back to her apartment but she left before me."

Olivia fumed for a few seconds, then exhaled her anger. "Sorry, Quentin," she told Stephen. "I guess you were right this time. I just got tired of waiting." She slipped her arm around Stephen's waist and pulled him close. "See, officer, I'm not by myself. So can we please go?"

The cop looked from Stephen to Olivia and back to Stephen. "Keep an eye on her," the cop told Stephen and walked off toward the dorm buildings.

Stephen looked down at Olivia and smiled. Olivia elbowed Stephen in the ribs and leapt away from him. "I didn't need your help," she growled.

"Hey, hey, now," Stephen said, holding his hands in the air. "I was just trying to keep you out of trouble."

Olivia sighed and shook her head. "Yeah, I know, I'm sorry." She held her hand out. "I'm Olivia."

"Stephen," he said.

"It's just… I'm nineteen, and I've been running around Hazelwood by myself since I was old enough to cross the street without holding my mom's hand, and this freaking curfew is just…" She sighed. "I can't even talk right now."

"Sorry," Stephen said. "I have that effect on women."

She laughed. "Really?"

"It's working, isn't it?" He winked at her and laughed.

She rolled her eyes and laughed back. "Alright, Mr. Smart-Ass."

Stephen felt a connection with the girl, something he hadn't felt ever before. It was an odd mixture of fear and attraction. She was smart, he knew, and strong-willed, and probably ambitious. And the way she looked at him made his heart skip.

"So what are you doing out here this late at night?" she asked him.

"I'm just walking back to my apartment," he answered. "It's one of the new ones, right over the train track."

"Oh, I live in the same ones!" she exclaimed. "I'm in the building right off Withers."

"I'm in the one across Jackson," he told her. "Come on, I'll walk you home. Since you're on the way and everything."

"Aww, is big brother gonna protect me from the scary evil monsters?"

"If by scary evil monsters you mean Hazelwood police, then, yeah, as a matter of fact I am. Got a problem with it?"

"Oh, no, of course not," she said, grabbing his wrist and leading him toward her apartment. Her fingers were warm, her grip strong. He was taken aback by how quick she was to grab him, only having known him a few seconds. "I've been in a lot of trouble with campus police, actually, so it'll be nice to have someone here to keep them off my case."

"A lot of trouble, huh?"

"Mostly just trivial things, but yeah. Let's see, I got picked up last week for falling asleep in the library until someone found me at three in the morning; they apparently thought I was trying to steal one of their new computers or something. A few weeks ago one of them tried to tell me that my jeans were inappropriate because they had holes in them, and they insisted that I go home and change, whether it made me late for class or not. I got pulled over for speeding about a month ago, but that was a complete crock. He said I was going twelve miles faster than I actually was."

Stephen slipped his fingers between hers, then pulled her back next to him and looked her in the eyes. "Are you trying to get into trouble?" he asked curiously.

"What are you, a psych major? Don't be silly. Why would I try to get in trouble?" She scoffed and continued to pull him along, this time hanging back beside him.

"I don't know. Why would you?"

She glanced at him, apparently trying to read him. Finding that she couldn't, she glanced at her watch instead. "I hope my roommate didn't lock the door. I forgot my key again."

"Again?"

"Don't judge me," she snapped. "I've got a lot on my mind. I've got an interview with the people at the international teaching program on Saturday, and I'm trying to get all my stuff together between all my classes and work."

"All your classes?"

"Are you just going to keep repeating everything I say?"

"Well, you're speaking so fast, I just want to make sure I'm hearing you right."

She scoffed again. "Yeah, all my classes. I'm in five classes right now so I can graduate a year early and get into this program. I'll get to travel all over the world—the UK, all over Europe, China, Korea, Japan—teaching English lit. Can you imagine that? Getting paid to travel all over the world?"

Stephen smiled at her. "I'd be happy to just travel around America, to be honest. There's so much to explore beyond these town limits."

"Exactly!" Olivia agreed.

They crossed the bridge along Withers Street and casually made their way to the apartment complex. They climbed the stairs, Olivia in front. "Are you staring at my ass?" She asked when they reached the third level up.

"Would you blame me if I was?" Stephen asked in return.

She rolled her eyes. "I knew I should have made you walk up first."

"Are you saying you want to stare at my ass?"

"You're a bit of a dork, aren't you?"

"Something tells me that you like dorks, so, yes."

Olivia shook her head once again, smiling wide. "Come on, Stephen. Fourth door." She ran along the corridor, her hair blowing behind her, and grabbed the door handle, turning it back and forth several times, shaking it in agitation. "God is dead," she groaned. "I guess I'm locked out."

"Where's your roommate?" Stephen asked.

"You ask a lot of questions," Olivia informed him. "She's with her boyfriend."

"Well hey, I'm like right across the street. You can stay the night at my place if you want."

Olivia laughed. "I just met you, Lover Boy."

"Come on, you aren't safe hanging out here all night."

"Oh, and I'll be safe with a strange boy I just met?"

Stephen smiled and nodded. "You're safer with me than with anyone else."

Olivia seemed to consider it for a second. She took Stephen's hand and held it up in the air, placed her free hand on his hip and pushed him up against the metal rail that separated the two of them from a free-fall to the grassy earth below. The rail pressed up against the small of Stephen's back as Olivia stood on the tips of her toes and looked him in the eyes. "You're interesting, Lover Boy," she said.

"You are, too," he told her.

Her hand slithered around his head to the back of his neck and pulled him closer. Leaning up, she placed her lips to his and tentatively kissed him. He kissed her back, wrapping his arm around her waist. She pulled away.

"Come home with me," Stephen said.

She shook her head. "I'll go back to my mom's house. I'll sleep in my old bed tonight and get in touch with my roomie in the morning."

Stephen blinked, trying to understand. "I'm sorry. I thought…"

"No, no. You've got nothing to be sorry for. Just not tonight, Lover Boy." She smiled and kissed him more confidently.

"When can I see you again?" he asked.

"Tomorrow, if you want. Meet me down at the red table where we first saw each other. Twelve noon; don't be late."

He nodded. "What about now?"

"Go home, Lover Boy."

"Alright," Stephen said.

Olivia jumped up and kissed him again, then stepped away, pressing her back up against the door of her apartment. "You're just gonna leave, just like that?" Stephen said he was. "You're the real thing, aren't you?" she asked. "Make me a promise, Lover Boy."

"What kind of promise?"

Stephen moved closer to her, put a hand on her hip, another on her cheek, leaned forward and kissed her deeply. Her kiss was sweet and intoxicating, her hand on his body strong and comforting. He was happy, then. He felt real for the first time in his entire life.

"Promise me that if I ever need you to do something for me, you'll do it."

"I promise."

The door opened and the two nearly fell inside, Stephen catching Olivia under her ass and pulling her up to stand next to him. Helen stood there looking at the two. "Hey, Olivia," she said.

"Helen. Hey. This is…"

"Stephen Lanford," Helen finished for her. "He's friends with James."

"Hey, Helen." Stephen waved awkwardly.

"I thought you'd left already," Olivia said.

"You just caught me, actually," Helen said, stepping outside. "Lucky you, huh?"

Olivia laughed, her face red. "Yeah, I guess."

"Stephen, why don't you walk me to my car?"

Stephen accepted and smiled at Olivia. "Good night, Olivia."

Olivia smiled back at him. "See you tomorrow, Lover Boy."

As they walked down the steps, Helen asked Stephen, "You know she's trouble, right?"

Stephen said that he had already figured that out.

"You know she'll only take from you, use you up until you're nothing but a casing of your former self."

"Well, damn, Helen, why don't you tell me how you really feel about her?"

"I just want to make sure you know what you're getting yourself into."

Stephen looked her in the eyes. "I don't care what I'm getting myself into. It's my mistake to make. Thanks."

All those years ago. All that time passed. So many wasted years. Stephen thought that he'd understood, thought that he could handle everything that was going to happen to him. He couldn't. He hadn't.

A sound came from the corner of the cafe, and Stephen looked up. There was a man standing there, wearing a stylish coat and a pair of horn-rimmed glasses. He looked familiar, but Stephen couldn't tell who he was. The man saw Stephen looking at him and ducked behind the wall of the cafe.

Stephen jumped to his feet and followed, but when he reached the place where the man had disappeared, he saw nothing. It was as though the man had never been there at all. Stephen had seen him, hadn't he? He didn't even know anymore. Perhaps Olivia's madness was infecting him, or perhaps it was his madness that had infected her, or perhaps they had always been mad, and the symptoms had just taken awhile to manifest. Who even knew anymore?

Stephen circled the building, searching for any trace of the guy, but there were too many tracks from students coming and going. It had to be the person Olivia had seen. Was he stalking Stephen now? Stephen couldn't think straight. A man. A coat. John. Olivia. Allen. Natalie. Everything.

A fool. A damnable fool. That's all he was. He walked to the bookstore. The streetlight at the corner cast a solitary light in deep darkness.

There he stood, looking up into the bulb, his eyes hurting even more than they had before. He turned around to see the coat moving away from him. Whoever it was had followed him to the corner, watching him, and now was slinking away. Perhaps he was going to Olivia's. Stephen headed back her way.

Then he stopped. What did he care anymore? Natalie was probably waiting for him. Olivia wasn't. It was time for him to move on.

Natalie was sitting on the couch reading when Stephen entered. She placed her book on the coffee table, then stood and moved toward him. "What's wrong?" she asked. Stephen didn't speak. He put his hands on her hips and pulled her to him. She wrapped her arms around his neck and pulled his head to her shoulder. "What's wrong, Stephen?"

He shook his head and picked her up around her waist, holding her body to his. He walked through the house to the bedroom and laid her down on the bed, then crawled onto the sheets next to her and placed his head to her breast. He could hear her heartbeat thumping against his head.

There was silence. The clock ticked, seconds passed. And then it was after midnight, and Stephen's phone was ringing. Natalie gently guided Stephen's head to the pillow and picked up the phone, flipping it open. "Hello? Ariadne? Yeah, I…" Her eyes grew wide and she placed a hand over her lips. "Oh gosh. How?" Her breathing grew agitated. "Well he's here, but…"

"What's wrong, Natalie?" Stephen asked.

Natalie eyed him up and down. "Here, Ariadne, I'll let you tell him." She handed him the phone, then slid off the bed and ran to the bathroom, closing the door behind her.

"Ariadne? How'd you get this number?"

"It was in Olivia Mincks' phone. Allen asked me to call you."

"What do you mean, asked you to call me?"

Ariadne inhaled deeply, sighed and said, "Stephen, I know you were friends with Olivia, so I don't know exactly how to tell you this but, Stephen, Olivia's…"

Stephen cut her off, "No! No, she can't be, I just saw her a few hours ago."

"Allen found her an hour and a half ago."

Stephen's stomach heaved, and he ran through the house, stumbling into the kitchen just in time to lean over the sink. He raised the lever and water poured through the faucet to flush his chunder down the drain as rain beat against the windows. And then he was on the floor, his head against the counter, and tears were running down his face.

Part 2

Distant Music

Chapter 6
Submerged

Wednesday, March 2, 2011

Stephen stepped into the bathroom slowly, maneuvering his way between the police documenting the scene for their report. Ariadne stepped behind him as a camera flashed a few times, filling the room with a burst like lightning. Stephen rubbed his eyes.

"You gonna be okay?" Ariadne asked.

Stephen went to speak, then closed his mouth. He couldn't answer honestly and didn't feel capable of lying just then. I answered, "I'll be alright."

Olivia was in the deep old-style bathtub, submerged under two feet of water, her eyes still open. From the depths of the water, they looked up at Stephen and Ariadne. She looked as though she were resting comfortably in bed.

"Where uh…" I swallowed the bile that had risen to my throat. "Where's Allen?"

Ariadne took Stephen's wrist and tried to pull him from the bathroom, but he was stuck. Those blue eyes. He thought he might drown in them. He felt tears at the back of his eyes, desperate to drop.

See you tomorrow, Lover Boy, Olivia had said.

"He went to get coffee," Ariadne answered. "Mostly, I think he just wanted to clear his head."

"And you let him go?" I asked.

"Why wouldn't I?" Ariadne asked. It was clear that she didn't consider him a suspect or at least expected him to return. There were dark shadows underlining her eyes. The whites were riddled with red, her dark brown pupils dull. Frizzing out as though it hadn't been combed, her hair formed a mane around her face, making her look predatory, something neither Stephen nor I had seen in her before. "What are you doing here?"

Ariadne's lips drew back into a sad excuse for a smile, as though she were about to tell a terrible lie. But as she spoke, she looked up at me, her voice steady, her body language open. "I've been investigating the William Mincks case for Allison ever since I made detective," she admitted. "When Allen's call came into the Hazelwood dispatch, one of my buddies over here thought it prudent to contact me." Her eye twitched, as though she'd just told a lie, but the rest of her body was calm and still, as though she hadn't. Why would she lie, anyway?

"The dispatch called you?" I repeated.

"Yes," she said, her gaze steady this time. Her words were true, but something behind them was false. Something I didn't recognize yet.

"And Allen was the one who found her?" I asked. I could hear my voice changing, becoming deeper and more commanding. I was investigating; I was interrogating. Stephen was in shock.

"That's what he said," she answered slowly, as though responding to my tone. "He left around nine at her request, walked to the cafe at the corner of Main and ate a piece of chocolate cake, walked by the Sunset to say hello to John and Mary, then went to his apartment, where he discovered he'd left his keys here. By then it was almost eleven. When he came, the front door was locked and there wasn't an answer, so he broke in through the kitchen window and wandered through the house searching for Olivia. He found her like this at approximately eleven twenty."

I closed my eyes and tried to remember all the details she'd just given me. They swam through my mind with the ease of a bread-ball through molasses, breaking apart and reforming in new patterns, new shapes, more tainted and impure the more I thought about them.

"I'm going to push to be lead investigator on this one," Ariadne said.

"If it doesn't cause too much trouble, can you ask for me to be added onto the investigation as a consultant?" I asked.

She put her hand on my shoulder and squeezed lightly. "Of course," she said.

"Thank you."

Stephen's mind was racing with possibilities. He was already drawing up lists of suspects. Allen was his prime suspect. The boy was bold and overconfident, but he was young, and youth often meant uncontrollable emotion. But there was also John-boy, the spurned ex-husband. Except that Allen had said that he'd seen John at the Sunset. Unless Allen and John were in on it together. If they could alibi each other, that could cause trouble. But all Stephen would have to do would be to catch one of them in a lie, and that would be it. They would never make it to court, he would make sure of that.

If it wasn't them, he didn't know who it was. Natalie had motive, but no means. It could be Matt, but why would he strike now, after all these years?

The memory of the man in the coat and glasses crossed his mind. Stephen would never forgive himself if he had been given the opportunity to stop this but let it happen anyway.

"I hate to interrupt you," one of the investigators said, "but I don't think that an investigation will be necessary."

"Why not?" Stephen asked angrily, turning to face the baby-faced investigator. I kept his feet planted to the ground, lest he strike the boy.

"W-well…" the man stuttered. "It's j-just that this w-w-was obviously a s-s-s-suicide."

Stephen's eyesight went fun-house. His head felt like it had just been filled with lead weights. He needed sleep, but I knew there was no chance of that happening soon. Unless I could somehow wrestle complete control from him, sleep would be a long time coming today.

"What do you mean, suicide?" Ariadne asked.

"W-w-w-w-well," the young investigator started to speak, but the older one cut him off, emerging from the bathroom with a grim look on his face.

"There's an open bottle of Vicodin and an empty glass of wine on the sink," the man said. "We'll have to wait 'till the tox screen comes back, but I'll bet you my retirement fund she's loaded to the brim with Vicodin."

"So what?" Stephen asked, blinking his tired eyes hard, trying to sweep the need for sleep away, needing to be alert. You've got to be quicker, his father had told him.

"Well," the man said, "in my professional opinion: The woman decides she's had enough, waits for the kid to leave, pours herself a bath, washes down a mouthful of pills with that Cabernet Sauvignon, climbs into the tub and goes to sleep underwater. With her nervous system impaired by the drugs and alcohol, her urge to surface would have been suppressed."

I'm never going to make it out, Olivia had told Stephen.

The entire world seemed like a bad dream that he could not wake up from; his vision was as unsteady as if he were falling-down drunk. Sound came to him as though he were under water. His body felt weightless, his head a ton of steel. Yet, as far as he could tell, all of it was real.

"And there's no way that this could have been an accidental drowning?" Ariadne asked hopefully.

The man studied her face for a second, reading on it the hope for Stephen's sake that this was not an intentional act of self-destruction. "There is a chance that she might have had a seizure. She had a history of them, and if her body seized while she was in the bath, she could have swallowed the water unintentionally into her lungs." Taking a professional throat-clearing-second of contemplation, the investigator said, calmly and clearly, "But it's doubtful. There are no signs of violence or struggle."

"Are there…" Stephen wet his lips, the inside of his mouth as dry as desert sand. "Are there any signs that someone besides Allen has been here?"

The man shook his head gravely. "We'll keep looking for you," he said, "but unless…" He didn't seem to be able to find the words to fill the rest of the sentence, so he turned to the baby-faced investigator and ordered him back to work. To Ariadne and Stephen he said, "I'm sorry. We're doing all we can do."

"Thank you," I said. Stephen seemed on the verge of going catatonic; I kept him on his feet.

"Come on," Ariadne said, taking his wrist again. I let her pull us out of the bathroom, down the stairs to the dark living room. The room felt very small and constrictive to Stephen; stuffy, claustrophobic. He preferred the lightness and the openness of the bathroom, where Olivia looked up at him. But the living room for me was a quiet relief. I felt that if Stephen was able, he would climb back up the stairs and fall into the tub next to Olivia, join her in her aquatic sarcophagus. But here, in the darkness of the living room, that's where I was comfortable.

"Stephen…" The name left Ariadne's mouth and hung in the air. I didn't respond to it; neither did Stephen.

"I have to find him," Stephen told her.

"Find who?" Ariadne asked. "Allen? William?"

"The person who did this."

Ariadne shook her head. "Stephen, Olivia…she did this to herself."

Stephen, Olivia had said. Let me go.

"No," Stephen told her. "The man with the coat and the glasses did this to her…" and I didn't stop him, he wanted to say.

Ariadne put her hands on his shoulder. "Stephen, look me in the eyes." I felt her palm on my left cheek, pushing down the unshaved stubble, her pointer finger and thumb compressing my earlobe. "Sometimes, there are bad guys in the world. Sometimes, there are monsters that we have to go out and conquer. But this is not one of those times. Olivia committed suicide. She wasn't murdered."

Stephen tried to shake his head, tried to move away, but she held us fast.

"Sometimes, women fill their pockets with weight and jump into a lake because they're attempting to escape from a paternalistic society that suppresses their potential. Sometimes they swim until their strength gives out because they find themselves trapped into a life they are unprepared to handle or aren't content with. Sometimes, women stick their heads in the oven because they're depressed beyond the ability of medicine to help.

"You have to listen to me now, because what I'm going to tell you will be painful. I know what Olivia represented to you. I've asked around about you, and while I don't know the whole story, I do know that you and she didn't end well. And you've been carrying this around with you for a decade. But she wasn't just some symbol of a different life. She was a complicated woman, with flaws and virtues, and hopes and dreams. And when she died, she went out on her own terms. So please—for once in your life—please don't make this about you."

Stephen's hand flew upwards, striking Ariadne's wrist with a whack. Ariadne jerked backward.

"I'm sorry," Stephen muttered.

As she rubbed her wrist, Ariadne's eyes, which had been soft and caring just a minute ago, grew sharp and distrusting, though a second later softened again to a cautious distance.

There's something broken inside of me, Olivia had said.

Allen opened the front door and entered, coffee tray first. He glanced between Stephen and Ariadne, sensing that something had happened. "Hey, guys." The words were somber, but his voice was strong. Stronger than Stephen's. Ariadne greeted him. Stephen just stood and stared. Allen handed Ariadne her coffee, then handed Stephen his coffee, then took the final cup in his hands and downed the last of the liquid it contained.

"I appreciate the coffee, kid," Ariadne said, "but don't you think you should get some sleep?"

Allen walked to the kitchen and tossed the empty cup into the trashcan. Then he took the tray and flung it like a Frisbee, making it curve upward into the air then corkscrew back down into the trash. He said, "I'll sleep later," and walked back over to us, forming a triangle.

Absolutely brilliant, Olivia had said.

If there was any change in Allen's demeanor, it was that he was suddenly darker. He seemed to move with more concentration, more deliberation, as though struggling with himself. His arms didn't twist or swing but moved in marching formation. His eyes, which had been unremarkable, even lazy the night before, were now cut from diamonds. What a difference between pot and coffee, Stephen thought abstractedly.

What? I thought. I could see the thought pattern emerge in Stephen's mind: That Allen had smoked when we saw him last night and taken caffeine just now would explain the change in him. His stiffness could be a sign of jittery muscles, of course. But I knew that he was blaming Stephen behind those eyes; I knew that he was mourning his lover behind those diamonds; so why didn't Stephen see that was why Allen was acting so strong and in charge?

I dove deeper into Allen's mind, going deeper than I had ever attempted into someone who was not Stephen. But all we could think about at that moment was Olivia. The coffee revealed a memory of Olivia; Allen uncovered thoughts of Olivia; all trains of thought now ran the same track; all of the trains crashed, wrecked violently, into Olivia. She was a train stalled on an active track.

"How are you holding up?" Ariadne asked Allen.

Allen exhaled all the air in his lungs and raised an eyebrow at her. He didn't say anything, but Ariadne reached out and took his wrist, consoling him silently. His lips tightened into the grimace of a smile, which disappeared as quickly as it had come.

The older investigator came down the staircase and stuck his head into the living room. "Can I uh…can I get you guys to step outside so they can come in and collect the body?" Stephen laughed the macabre to himself at that word. "Collect." They were only going to "collect" the "body." It was clinical speech, sharp as a scalpel, impersonal and sterile.

"Let's go," Ariadne said, jerking her head in the direction of the door. "We can go sit at the cafe until your class," she told Allen. "Then you and I can go get the police report," she told Stephen.

Stephen opened the door and ushered everyone out.

They followed the same path that Stephen had taken last night, with Allen on point. He had made this walk before in the cold of winter; in the warmth of summer. He knew the landscape of this journey as well as Stephen knew the path between Olivia's old apartment and his.

They arrived at the cafe, which was empty, save for a janitor doing the floors of the dining area. The doors were open, though, so they by-passed the red table and sat down in the cafe area. It was cold inside, but it was clean and well-lit.

"How's the coffee?" Allen asked. "I wasn't sure how you two liked it."

"Bitter," Stephen said. "Just what I need right now. Thanks, kid."

"Fine," Ariadne answered. "Honestly, as many times as I've had to drink over-extracted swill on a stake-out, this is, in comparison, amazing." Stephen agreed, remembering, oddly for all that was on his mind, the coffee he'd once shared with a partner outside a gas station in Maryland. The coffee had been brimming with coffee grinds. "Where'd you get it?"

"The cafe at the corner of Main. They're open twenty-four hours while school is in session." He ran his fingers through his hair and said, "It's where I met Olivia. It's my favorite place in Hazelwood." He looked down, his thoughts going toward the darkness that awaited his last memories of Olivia.

Ariadne shook her head. "Come on, Allen. Don't do that."

Do what? Olivia had asked.

"I'm... I'm fine," Allen lied, poorly.

"You're a punk," I said.

"Whatever, old man," Allen retorted.

"Watch who you're calling old," Ariadne said.

The tension seemed to lessen among the three of them. But Allen still looked at Stephen with that quiet, hidden anger. There was a disturbing depth to the anger and the calm silence that surrounded it. I realized that Allen was a young man accustomed to wearing a mask. Something in his past had caused him to adopt this stillness, and he had almost perfected it. It was the practiced dissociation of abused children and Vietnam veterans.

No one would ever know that anything was wrong, but something always was.

I guess I was always right about you, Olivia had said.

I pushed the cup of coffee toward Allen. "I can't drink anymore." Allen took the cup and drank what remained, then lined up his shot and tossed it like a basketball into the nearest trash can.

You're all talk, she'd told him.

"Stephen?" Ariadne asked.

Stephen tried to answer. "I think…" I'm never going to make it out. "I just need to…" Go home, Lover Boy.

"Stephen," Ariadne said, moving closer to him, reaching out to him.

"Ariadne," Stephen said, taking her hand in his. "Please."

A fine mist settled over the windows, and all that remained outside was the darkness of the morning and the storm. We all sat at the round table, attempting to make a connection with one another, to keep the others sane; but we faced an invisible boundary. It kept us apart like the glass separating the inside from the outside. I knew that Stephen could never let anyone in ever again, no matter how much Ariadne tried, no matter how much Natalie wished; he was as lost to them as Olivia was to him.

I took over, squeezing Ariadne's hand. She nodded and withdrew it. "I need to go see Natalie," I said.

"Alright," she said. "I'll give you a call when I get the report."

"Thanks," I said, heading for the exit.

I was in the darkness, and the mist was swirling around me as I stumbled away from the cafe. I knew the route home. I just had to follow the road past the book store, and I'd be there. A car came down the road toward me, its headlights growing large, filling my vision with light until I couldn't see, then passed, throwing me back into darkness. The mist swirled in shapes that seemed impossible, and the smell of gasoline filled my nostrils as I wandered, lost in the darkness. I was leading Stephen, the blind leading the blind into whatever ditch might be around the corner. Stephen was lost because his anchor was gone; I was just plain lost. I had never walked this street alone before. I had never traversed any darkness by myself. Yet here I was now, alone, in charge, and on a road to nowhere.

And then, just like that, we were by the house. The porch light shone, bringing us in.

I wanted to go to Natalie. But for some reason I didn't. I walked over and sat down on the porch, where Allen had sat a couple nights ago, where Stephen had sat many years ago. The past haunted Stephen. It was beginning to haunt me. And I knew in that moment that I was becoming the past as well. Stephen was disappearing, and I was growing stronger.

For the first time in my life, I was on the verge of becoming the dominant personality. I had wanted this for so long, I had wanted the power, the responsibility. I had wanted Natalie. And for the first time in my life, I was scared. I was scared to act, scared to talk, scared to do anything. I didn't know if I could make it without Stephen.

I pulled my legs against my chest and pulled myself into a shadow. Could I do it? I wondered. Could I survive as Stephen?

I heard a train going down the track, passing by the school where Ariadne and Allen sat. As it approached the town, the horn blew, and I jumped. It was stupid. I knew it was stupid to jump at that sound, as stupid as if I had shrunk from a lightning strike in the distance. But I'd done it inadvertently, and now I felt my cheeks burn. I couldn't do it. I couldn't become me as Stephen. I wasn't strong enough. Or maybe I didn't want to.

Natalie came out on the porch, wrapped in her kimono, holding a mug of wonderful-smelling, freshly brewed coffee. She looked out into the early morning darkness, sipping lightly. The smell of it, along with the chemical swirl of her perfume, was strong in the air. She put her hand on her hip and sighed. Her breath was a cloud in the porch light. She ran her toes along the edge of the porch, then backed away slowly and stepped onto the welcome mat. I imagined how cold her feet must have gotten. The concrete was freezing at this hour.

She turned on the ball of her foot and reentered the house, closing the door behind her. I didn't feel so much as a stir from Stephen.

I counted to six hundred, then stood and walked down the road. I was heading in the direction of Mastern, though I knew I would never make it there on foot. I just wanted to walk. To walk and walk until I couldn't walk anymore. I wanted my feet to be bruised and bloody. I wanted my body to break down. I wanted to suffer. I supposed the reason why might eventually come to me.

I turned right at the emergency light, heading into the eastern outskirts of town, tracing the town limits. I walked along the side of the road, looking in windows and watching the town come to life.

At the corner of Spicewood Springs, I turned back toward the university instead of continuing to Mastern. Cars came rolling along and the sun came bouncing up, and I was still walking, following the shape of the hills. My head was filled with darkness and I didn't know what to do about it. I watched the false dawn light up the horizon. But the darkness inside me didn't fade. I climbed the hill back up to the cafe, groaning, fighting against my fatigue.

The others were still sitting there when I came in.

"How's Natalie?" Ariadne asked.

"Alright," I answered, with a wave of my hand. "Did you know that Olivia was dead before the dispatch called you?"

Her eyes grew wide. "What do you...?"

"You did. Who told you?"

"I... I..."

"Leave her alone, Stephen," Allen ordered.

"Was it Sandra?" I asked. Her hand flew to her mouth. "How did Sandra know?"

"I... I..."

"Stephen, stop."

I glared at Allen and after a moment of fire in his eyes he looked away.

"Stephen," Ariadne said, swallowing visibly. "I understand that you're having a hard time dealing with this death, but you're taking paranoia to a bad place. First, this whole thing about a guy in a coat, now this? Did you even see Natalie when you went home?"

"I just want to know the truth," I told her. "I want to know what's real. And if you're going to hide that from me, then..." I couldn't finish the sentence, because I didn't know what I'd do.

"Stephen," she said again. It made me angry momentarily, but then I remembered that she had no way of knowing who I was. She was just trying to humanize her opponent, to remind him of his identity, to personalize the relationship. If I was Stephen, it might even be nice to hear my name at this time. "As a friend, just please, let it go."

I shook my head slowly, then turned away and left.

I walked north, past my old apartment to the barn. The smell of ribs, chili and dumplings permeated the air surrounding the restaurant which would not be open for several hours.

I turned east and walked down to the strip-mall off Main. None of the shops were open. I walked along the windows, watching my reflection in the glass. I sat down on one of the benches, lay down and rested my head against the arm.

When I moved, I felt the darkness in my head shift as well. I waited there for about an hour, watching the sun rise, then I got up and started walking again.

I walked south to the other cafe, the one where Allen had met Olivia, and got myself a caramel macchiato. I had never understood why Stephen insisted on drinking the bitter stuff when there was something as delicious as this around. I got a large cup, a bottle of water and a muffin, then headed back up Main.

I cut behind the supermarket and wandered along the hills until I hit the road that led to the theater. The morning shows were just starting, so I bought a ticket for the earliest one and went in. Once inside, I pulled out my bottle of water and muffin. The theater was empty, save a young couple making out in the back row. Once the movie began, I put my feet up on the chair in front of me and drifted off to sleep.

I had the dream about the white room again. As the world crashed down around me, I looked at the shadow in the doorway, the lights in the theater came on and I was awake. But I thought I'd recognized the shadow, now that I had seen it again. Somehow, seeing the dream again seemed to make it more real, and I had the sense that if I could just see it one more time the mystery would be revealed. I could buy another ticket, go back to sleep and try to dream the dream.

Instead, I headed northeast. I walked up to the city park and along the red dirt trail. Dave jogged past, waving politely at me. "Hey, Stephen," he said. He stopped to catch his breath, leaning down on his haunches. "What are you doing out here?"

"Just trying to clear my head," I answered.

"Oh yeah, I know the feeling," he said. "Hey, you have any plans for lunch?" I shook my head no. "Come on, man. You can eat at the restaurant, on me."

"I couldn't accept another free meal," I told him. "I'll pay for it this time."

"You feeling alright?" he asked, putting the back of his hand on my forehead like he was searching for a fever. "You don't feel sick, but you're talking crazy. You're family, Stephen; the food's on me." I went to protest again, but it was no use. He was insistent. "Come on man, where'd you park at?"

"I walked here," I admitted.

His eyes grew wide again. "From the other corner of Hazelwood?" I nodded. "Come on, Stephen, what's going on?"

"Olivia's dead," I admitted.

"What?" He looked shocked. "I...I'm sorry," he stuttered. Then he put his hand on my shoulder. "Come on. I'll give you a ride."

I needed to be like Dave. In control.

The steaks that Dave's chef prepared were juicy and tender. I couldn't remember the last time I ate, so I quickly devoured it. Between bites, I explained what had happened that morning since Natalie had gotten the phone call from Ariadne until I had left Ariadne and Allen at the cafe.

"So how are you holding up?" Dave asked.

"With bubble gum and duct tape, mostly," I answered, trying to be funny.

"I mean it," Dave said. "How are you?"

"Alive," I sighed. "I just...I don't know...my head is filled with..." I wiped my face with my palm. Dave nodded, and didn't say anything. He was waiting for me to talk, but I didn't have anything to say. I didn't know how I felt; I didn't know how to pretend what Stephen might have felt; I didn't know what to say, so I just sat there.

"Have you just been walking around all day?" he asked.

"Yeah," I said. "Well, I went to a movie." Confusion crossed his face. "I slept," I explained feebly.

"Stephen," Dave sighed. "I know you're having a bit of trouble with this whole thing, but you can't…you can't run away from reality."

"Yeah," I said, closing my eyes. My head suddenly hurt very much.

"Why don't you go home to Natalie for a while? I bet she's worried sick about you."

I smiled and nodded my head. "I think I probably should."

"Let me give you a ride," Dave said.

"No," I insisted. "I'll be fine on my own."

He opened his mouth to protest, then closed it again. "Alright. But if you need me, I'm only a phone call away. You know that, right?"

"I know," I told him, holding my hand out to him. He shook it once.

"Be safe. I know you've been gone for a while, but the knights still need you."

I left the restaurant and headed east into the poor district. The sun was shining brightly now, cutting through weak clouds melting away in the heat of the day. I began to feel the darkness in my mind disappearing like the clouds. The wind flowed calmly against my face. It felt a little easier to breathe, even though the humidity pressed on my lungs like a wet vest. I felt dehydrated. Mostly, it seemed like I was halfway between life and death, between the light and the darkness, and I didn't know how to find my way to either.

There was a chicken place across from the town church where the road met Watertower. I stopped and got a sweet tea. An older man sat outside the front door, his beard grizzled, his eyes tired, a tattered hat sitting at his feet. I took my change and placed it in the hat. "Bless you, sir," he said to me. I tried to smile, but my lips wouldn't pull away from my teeth.

I walked up Watertower past trailer parks and economy housing. Each structure I passed stood still and dead, like tombstones. Old rusted cars that shouldn't run but somehow did. Houses that shouldn't be standing, wood splintering, paint peeling. A truck drove past me, the driver waved politely. I raised my hand back and kept walking. The subsidized apartments at the end of Watertower marked the end of the city limits, so I turned west, back into town. Three men came out of one of the apartments and watched me walk. As I turned the corner, I saw handguns tucked into their waistbands. I reached under my coat and patted mine, just to make sure it was still there.

Hours passed. I had just arrived at Main Street when my phone went off. It was Ariadne. "Stephen," she started off. I felt tempted to flip the phone closed as Stephen had often done, but didn't. "I just left the police department. I've got the report if you'd like to see it."

"Was it suicide?" Stephen asked.

There was a pause, a catch in Ariadne's breath, and then she said, "It looks like it."

"Have you eaten dinner yet?" I asked.

"Like, lunch dinner or supper dinner?"

"Supper dinner," I said.

"Not yet," she answered.

"Bring your car down to Papa Burn's."

I bought a picnic basket and a gallon of lemonade before she got there. The college girl behind the counter seemed to be afraid of me. I guess I must have looked a mess at that point: covered in sweat, my face red. I had money and I was polite; still, her eyes scanned me suspiciously.

Ariadne and I drove northwest, past the barn, out into the peach blossom orchards. The small pink and white flowers were only just beginning to unfurl, caught in the middle between the small green buds of just a day or two ago and the splash of color they would become. I showed Ariadne a parking spot, and we hiked out to a place where the peach blossoms hung over a small pond. I put the picnic basket down on a concrete bench and gave Ariadne a sandwich. "I'm sorry, about this morning."

"What do you mean?" she asked cautiously.

"You know, the whole slapping your hand thing. And calling you out in front of Allen. It was rude, and I shouldn't have done it."

I looked over at her. Her eyes were filling with tears, while her lips were twisted in a weird half-smile. Several emotions were trying to come out at the same time, and none were making it.

"Thank you," she said, wiping her eyes with a napkin. "I'm sorry about lying to you."

"Yeah," I said.

"Neilson told me you would find out, and that you'd be angry when you did. I just…I didn't know what else to do. I can't tell anybody the truth without betraying a friend."

I put my hand on her shoulder. Reaching across her chest, she put her hand on mine.

"It's terrible, how we live," I said. "We're all…we're haunted by a past that can't help but affect us. We all become a part of that past, living parodies of love and lust, and we fuck up the people that come after us just as much as our parents fucked us up. We create this damnable drama, and we use it as a weapon to cut ourselves off from the people we love. We're all isolated by our own hearts, and all that remains is this darkness."

She squeezed my fingers.

"Light will find a way," she said.

"I hope so."

The sun lowered, hovering serenely above the tree line. We sat there, eating and watching it slowly sink and disappear until the air cooled, and the fading light filtered weakly through the trees. The cold night air seeped in and around us as the moon slowly emerged in the sky.

"I need to head back to Mastern before it gets too late. Do you want a ride back to your house?" she asked.

"No," I said. "I'll walk a little bit more."

"Don't leave Natalie waiting too long," she told me. And then she was gone.

I walked down into the farmlands to the house where Olivia's mother once lived. There was someone living there now, their silhouettes casting shadows through the window. A truck and a car sat in the long driveway. A man came out of the door and walked to the truck, slowly opening the door. A minute later, I saw a lit cigarette bobbing through the air. I watched him for a few seconds, then walked on, toward the town.

I eventually reached Stephen's mother's house. Her death was what brought us back to this devil town, yet we hadn't even come by this place. All of it was to be handled by Neilson and his people. I closed my eyes and shook my head. I felt somehow that the darkness in my mind was Stephen's darkness; I thought that if his heart was not as dark as a coal mine, then perhaps I could think without having to fight this shadow in my head.

I found the spare key and walked in, but once inside I was blind. I wandered around with my fingertips, maneuvering around furniture until I stumbled upon his mother's old rocking chair. I sat down in it and rocked myself back and forth, absorbing the darkness. I listened to the house groan as the foundation responded to my weight shifting across the old floors. I think I might have slept without dreaming.

When I opened my eyes I could make out the shapes around me. There was a chair, there was a coffee table, there was a lamp. I wandered upstairs. In Stephen's mother's room was a full-length mirror that captured my image when I opened the door. Except it wasn't my image; it was Stephen's.

He took the gun from the holster at his chest, released the safety and lifted it. Cocking the hammer, he stared into his own eyes and fired.

The top of the mirror shattered, mirrored glass exploding, the wooden base splintering outward. He lowered the gun to the middle and fired through what would be his heart. More glass, more wood. Then he put his back against the wall and slid down until he was sitting, looking into the only glass that remained. One more shot; no more reflection.

He put the safety back on and holstered the gun. And then, without warning, Stephen whispered, "Take control."

For a moment, I thought he was talking to himself. But the more I waited, the more I became aware that he had spoken the words to me.

"I know you're there," he said. "Take control."

How long had he known I was there? Hours? Days?

"I can't," I said. "I'm not strong enough."

"You're stronger than me," he said. Which was true, in some ways, and I couldn't argue with him about that.

"But I don't know what I'm doing!" I told him. "What if I mess up? What if I lose Natalie? What if I get fired?"

"I don't know what I'm doing any more than you do."

"You gave me life, Stephen. Show me how to live."

We sat silently in the darkness.

"I don't know how to live," he said. "You have control now. Just... hell, I don't know. Use your time better than I used mine."

And then he was gone, and whether I liked it or not, I was in control. I didn't have anywhere else to go, so I went home.

Natalie was asleep on the couch. I sat down on the edge of the seat and combed my fingers through her hair. She gently stirred and looked up at me. I bent down to kiss her, but she put her hand on my chest and pushed me away. "Where have you been?" she asked.

I didn't know what to say. "I just, I had to clear my head," I said.

"You've been gone all day. You couldn't call?" she asked.

What could I tell her? I saw you this morning. I watched you walk along the porch in your kimono, drinking coffee from your mug. "I've wanted to come home all day, I just didn't know how. I'm sorry," I said.

She frowned and tilted her eyes, trying to read my face. "I've been worried about you all day."

I swallowed hard and nodded. She sat up, stood, and paced around the living room, her arms crossed. She refused to look at me. "I worried about you. All day. And you tell me sorry?" I just looked at her. "Remember the last time you were gone all day?" she asked. I shook my head no. "We had a fight. A stupid fight, too. I made you buy expensive tickets to a gala at the Smithsonian, and then I decided it was too cold to go out and asked if we could stay home instead. And you got mad at me for changing my mind and said you were going to go even if I wasn't, because it would be a waste of money to just not go. And I got mad at you for going without me. But I could have gotten over it, except that you never came home that night. And you didn't come home again until the next night. I didn't know where you were, I didn't know if you were safe. You just stayed gone the entire day and never once let me know where you were. You're a shit."

I remembered that night. It was shortly after I was born. I woke up and we were at the gala. Stephen was talking to Dobbs about something, giving him space in case Dobbs had one of his coughing fits. There was a girl in a red dress hitting on Stephen mercilessly. At first he was talking to her just because he couldn't get away; but the more she talked, the more I focused on her. I wanted her. And I had her. And when Stephen woke up the next morning with her on his arm, he thought he was no better than Natalie was when she cheated on Matt. But it was me. It had been me.

"I thought you might have finally given up on us. I thought you were gone for good. I thought you might be lying in a ditch somewhere dead. I thought you might have gotten mugged. I thought that so many bad things might have happened to you, and then when you finally came home, you smiled at me, and kissed me, and talked to me like nothing had ever happened. And now you hear Olivia is dead and you go running off like a love-sick teenager, and I thought all those things again."

She sat down on the couch. She put one hand on my shoulder, the other on my cheek, and looked into my eyes. "Stephen, I can't do this again. You hear me?"

I nodded slowly, my head burning. "I…I…"

"Don't say it again," she said. "I heard you the first time. Stephen…" She paused and looked away, then looked back. "You want to be with me, right?"

"Natalie, yes," I said, reaching out, taking hold of her hips. "I want to be with you. More than anything else in the world."

She put her forehead to mine and looked me in the eyes.

"Prove it," she said.

I kissed her. I kissed her with all the love and passion I had inside me. I kissed her until I felt like my lips would fall off. I kissed her like I would die if I didn't. I kissed her like she would die if I didn't. And when she pulled away and looked at me, her eyes filled with shock and surprise, I thought that she might die of happiness.

"I'm an asshole," I told her. "I don't know how to prove to you how I feel. But I'm going to do my best."

She smiled slightly awkwardly, betraying a look of relief mixed with peace and forgiveness as well as disbelief and caution. She finally broke the stare and put her head on my shoulder.

"Let's go to bed," I said.

"Can we talk more in the morning?" she asked.

"Maybe," I said, kissing her. "I have to go to Mastern tomorrow. But if you want, we can talk when I get back."

"Why do you have to go to Mastern?"

"I think I know where William Mincks is," I told her.

She looked up at me, eyes wide. Then she nodded. "Alright," she said. She might have been saying "Alright, Stephen, go chase your wind-mill." But I wanted to believe she meant "Alright, my love, I'm on your side." Either way, she let me carry her to the bedroom, then fell asleep snuggled against me for the first time.

Chapter 7
Injustice

Thursday, March 3, 2011

I woke up before Natalie and logged onto her computer. Her password challenged me, as Stephen had never learned it from her. I stared at the computer screen for a long time, tapping the keys in random, wondering to myself what her password could be. Then I remembered the other day when we were in the park. She had always wanted her father's attention, but she could never get it from him. She loved her father and blamed her mother for the fact that the two of them had never connected. So I typed in her father's first-name. It didn't work. I tried her father's first and middle names. The database opened like a secret treasure chest.

I searched William Mincks. It was less information than I already had: He had disappeared when he was young, no leads.

Then I searched Darryl Phoenix. There was a false hit with Pastor Darryl Phoenix, from one of those fundamentalist groups in Oklahoma. I excluded that hit. As I'd expected, the name didn't exist in any formal capacity. He didn't have a birth certificate; he didn't have a social security number; he didn't have a driver's license issued in his name. He was a ghost, an apparition, creeping up slowly into existence until nobody questioned that he was real. Just as I'd expected. I checked his first appearance on the grid. He had simply appeared at the age of eighteen, no previous work experience, no school records, no medical records. He didn't exist; then he did.

That was it, I thought. I woke Natalie to tell her I was leaving, kissing her tenderly. She looked up at me and smiled.

"There's something different about you," she said.

I laughed, kissing her again. "Different how?" I asked, running my fingers through her hair, kissing her cheek.

"I don't know," she sighed into a slight smile. "Just…different." Squeezing her tight, I hugged her until I couldn't feel my arms. "You're more affectionate…" I pulled her on top of me and began to kiss her neck, pushing her kimono down her shoulder, licking and sucking until a dark purple hickey formed at the base of her neck. "It's like you're in high school. It's like you're young again."

"You never knew me in high school," I reminded her. I kissed the newly formed hickey, looking up into her eyes. We were together for the first time, looking into each other's minds. I stood at my window, looking into hers; she stood at her window, looking into mine.

"Can I come with you?" she asked.

"Could I stop you if I wanted to?" I asked. "Get dressed; we're wasting daylight."

When we got into the car, she began to talk excitedly. I had never seen her so animated before, waving her hands in front of her as she told me about her trip to the Hub with Helen. Helen had found a chic bohemian head wrap that she tried on, posing excitedly as she danced around. She had made Natalie try it on, but Natalie didn't look as good in it. Helen said she was too modern, "très moderne," that living up north had spoiled her from the past. Natalie had laughed, but she was starting to think Helen was right. "Are we too modern?" she asked.

"Us? No, we're perfect."

"I just feel like somewhere along the lines we lost touch with our pasts. I mean, I hadn't said a word about my father to anybody since I left Hazelwood, and I had almost forgotten about all the people from college. I kind of feel like I was trying to run away from my past, you know?"

"I understand running," I said.

"You don't think that we aren't in touch with our pasts?"

"I don't know how it would be possible to forget your past while you are at the same time consumed by it." The look she gave me was one that I couldn't read.

She told me about how she was nervous when I told her we had to come back to Hazelwood for my, or rather Stephen's, mother's funeral. She was afraid that I, Stephen, was going to fall back in love with Olivia and run away with her, leaving Natalie alone in the world. She didn't have any family left to help her, and if she did, she wouldn't have sought them out. She would have to go back to Virginia and face all her friends alone and tell them what happened. When I, when Stephen, left Sunday night, or rather Monday morning, she was sure she had lost me. But then I came back. And when I went off Tuesday night, or Wednesday morning, by myself, and didn't come home all day, she again didn't know what to think and was getting sick of the whole thing.

I squeezed her knee. "I didn't mean to worry you. I just had to clear my head."

"I know that now," she said. "And I didn't want to call you while you were doing your whole lone-wolf man-thing. But I was still scared."

She told me about the book she was reading, *The Crying of Lot 49*. She said she couldn't understand whether it was meant to be a comedy or a tragedy. I said, "Maybe it's both. A comagedy, maybe?"

"A tragicomedy," she corrected. "I don't know. There's some really tragic stuff, like Oedipa losing everyone in her life that she cares about, but at the same time it almost seems like she's supposed to realize that she's stronger without them. And she is, but she doesn't realize it because she's too busy trying to unravel this mystery that she's found herself in. She wants certainty but never finds it, and in the end she doesn't really need it."

"Kind of like real life," I said.

"Yeah!" She laughed.

She said I didn't seem to be working through Olivia's death. "Are you sure you're alright?"

"I'm…yeah, I'm sad that she's gone," I told her. "But I'm not going to let it take me down."

"Well, I know that she was your fairy tale girl."

Her face was full of sadness. For the last ten years she had been with Stephen despite knowing he was in love with another woman. I reached out and took her hand in mine, interweaving my fingers between hers. She smiled tentatively.

"She wasn't a fairy tale," I said. "I just couldn't bring myself to realize that until now."

We arrived at the apartment a little later than I expected, but when I knocked at the door I could hear Darryl moving inside. I remembered him from only a few days before, the way he stared at Stephen from behind those mirrored sunglasses. He opened the door slowly, his blue eyes open wide as he looked through his reading glasses at us.

"Stephen," he said with a mixture of fear and surprise resonating from his vocal cords. "Briseis. Good morning."

"My name's Natalie, actually."

Such an odd thing, a person's identity, I thought. "May we come in?" I asked.

"Of course," he said, stepping to the side. His apartment was messy, books and clothes forming piles and puddles along the path to his living room, his kitchen filled with empty bottles and pizza boxes. He had two couches in the living room sitting on adjacent walls opposite a television in the corner. His laptop sat open on the floor, a blank word document staring up at us.

"Writer's block?" I asked.

He nodded. "Unfortunately. Can I get the two of you a glass of water or something?"

"No thanks. We won't stay long."

"Please, have a seat." Natalie and I sat down on one of the couches. She reclined and looked around, assessing Darryl's bohemian lifestyle. Darryl leaned forward, elbows on knees. "Can I ask what this is about?"

I mirrored his pose, gripping my hands in front of me. I tried to emulate Stephen's mannerisms, tried to match his tone of voice, tried to convince Darryl, Natalie and myself that I was Stephen. "Ten years ago, I met a girl one night. She was headstrong and intelligent. She was erratic and interesting. She was wild and wanton. I was in love with her."

Darryl turned his eyes from me. "What does that have to do with me?" he asked.

"She had a brother who'd gone missing: William, who was just as headstrong, intelligent, erratic, wanton. Her parents were, shall I say, conservative. And they drove William to run away." Darryl's lungs deflated as he exhaled. He lay back on the sofa, staring at the ceiling. His hands, almost as if by their own accord, found his silver cigarette case and lighter and held them tight. "William was smart enough, his friends loyal enough, to cover his tracks as he ran. But he didn't get very far; just far enough to avoid his parents' search for him while maintaining a relationship with the people he loved."

Now Darryl began to speak. "He bought himself a new identity. It was his first taste of freedom in the world. He had to work day in and day out at meaningless, low-paying jobs to afford a small apartment with too many roommates, but he had freedom. He had to lie about his identity, his name, his history, but he could finally be himself. His first real boyfriend, his first real girlfriend, his first job, his first road trip, the first time he discovered who he was and what he wanted to be in life." He took a cigarette from his case and lit it, inhaling the burning tobacco smoke deep into his lungs. "Only by giving up his birth identity was he able to discover the identity of his heart."

I sat silently.

"How did you find out?" he asked.

"I saw you Tuesday night. I didn't recognize you then because the coat hid the shape of your body and you weren't wearing your glasses. But as I was wandering around yesterday, thinking and trying to clear my head, I started to put the pieces together. Allison, your parents, Olivia—it all started to make sense."

"I just wanted to see her," he said.

"You've been following her for weeks," I pointed out.

"I didn't know how to approach her. Every time she saw me, she got scared. But then Tuesday night it was like, like it didn't matter. She just invited me in. She seemed like she was in a daze, like nothing was real, like I...like I wasn't real." He observed the cherry in his cigarette for a second. "I guess I'm not real, in a way. But then again, who is, right?"

"You are real," Natalie said. "You're one of the most real people I've ever met."

He laughed stiffly, smoke puffing out of his mouth.

"What did Olivia say that night?" I asked.

"She said it was good to see me again. Asked where I'd been. When I told her I'd been in Mastern, she laughed and said of course. 'Of course you've been in Mastern.' She poured me a glass of wine, a uh, Cabernet, and asked why I'd been following her. I told her that now that Mom and Dad were gone, I thought we could have, I don't know, a relationship. She said she didn't think that was going to be an option." He sniffled. "I uh, I asked why, and she said that Mastern was so far away. But if I was ever back in Hazelwood, I should stop by and see her. I was so confused, but I guess it makes sense now." He stamped his cigarette out in his ashtray and covered his face with his palm. "I swear, if I had known what she was planning…"

He started to sob. Natalie jumped from her spot on the couch and wrapped her arms around Darryl, holding him while he cried against her shoulder.

I had never cried, and would never cry, so the act always struck me as strange, but in that moment it occurred to me how fragile people were. In the past three days Stephen had cried, Natalie had cried and now Darryl was crying. Olivia hadn't cried, and now she was gone. Maybe that's what people needed when the going got too tough. To just cry and have somebody there to hold them until there weren't any more tears. But then why couldn't I cry? Was it because I wasn't an actual person? Would I eventually break like Olivia had? The possibility scared me.

Eventually he calmed down. His arm was still around Natalie's waist.

"I just…I left, and then after awhile I came back. The door was unlocked and she was in the bathtub, and she wasn't breathing, just looking up at me with those blue eyes… I called Ariadne and she told me to leave, that she would take care of me."

"You locked the door on the way out?" I asked.

"Yeah."

"I want you to know that Ariadne wouldn't give you up. Even when I called her on it, she protected you."

He smiled weakly. "She's a good friend."

"I know," I said.

Natalie's eyes flicked to me, suspicious as she looked me up and down.

"So what now?" Darryl asked.

"Nothing," I said.

He was confused. "What do you mean?"

"I mean, as far as I'm concerned, you haven't done anything worth either one of us arresting you. And if we did have grounds to arrest you, we would have to arrest Ariadne, Allison and Sandra for hindering an investigation and harboring a fugitive. What do you think, Natalie?"

"As far as I'm concerned, William Mincks is still missing. We never found him."

Darryl ran his hand up Natalie's waist. I think I winced, because Natalie pulled away and rose to her feet.

"I appreciate that, guys. Really," Darryl said.

Darryl's cell phone rang. "Hey, Ariadne," he said, and she was talking rapidly into his ear. He went to speak but was talked over. He had fear and concern in his eyes. "What..." Something was happening. "When..." Something that scared him. "Where..." And then his eyes went blank. "I've got Stephen and Natalie here with me. We're leaving the apartment now." Ending the call, he forced the phone into his pocket and said "We need to take your car over to the Cityscape building."

"What's wrong?" Natalie asked as all rose.

"Ryan Gathers took Sandra and Matt Graycraft hostage and holed himself up in the Cityscape building."

"What? Why?" I asked.

"Hell if I know. If Sandra wasn't there, Ariadne wouldn't have bothered to call."

A perimeter of police cars surrounded the building, the cops all poised to take their guns to Ryan, to put him down like a rabid dog. We found Neilson, Ariadne and Allison among the cops. Ariadne in her armor—full police uniform and bulletproof vest—was arguing animatedly with one of the men in a black uniform, SWAT printed in yellow across his back. "I'm sorry, Detective Stahl," he said, "but you're not authorized to make that kind of decision."

"I've dealt with Ryan Gathers before. I know his strengths and weaknesses. There's no point in risking Matt and Sandra's lives when I can talk him down."

"Excuse me for saying this, Detective Stahl, but you're too close to this. He's not going to talk to the cop who arrested him."

"And you think he's going to talk to the cop holding a gun to his head?"

The SWAT guy stepped forward, leaning in close to Ariadne's face as he said, "You're not needed here, Detective Stahl. Go home."

"I don't respond to intimidation, Thomas. And I don't suppose you'd be doing this if Kurt were here."

"Kurt's not here, and you shouldn't be either. Go. Home."

"I can talk to him," I said. The sound of my own voice surprised me but not as much as the eyes of everybody suddenly staring at me.

"We can talk to him," Natalie said, pulling her badge from her inner pocket. I pulled mine out too, flashing it at the SWAT officer.

"This isn't your investigation!" the officer stated firmly. "What are the feds even doing here?"

"I called them," Neilson said. "They're investigating cybercrimes and illegal business practices by Matthew Graycraft and Ryan Gathers, as well as the disappearance of William Mincks and the death of his sister, Olivia Mincks."

"White collar investigators, that's all I need," the SWAT officer sneered. "Our negotiator happens to be MIA at the moment, so we could actually use your help, but I can only authorize one of you going in at a time. Which one of you is going in?"

"I am," I told him.

"What are your names?" We told him. "Get Detective Stahl to find you a vest while I talk to my men. When I send you in, you'll have one hour. If you can't get him to release one of the hostages in that time, then I'm going to cut the power and send my men in. If you're in there when my men come in, try to disarm the suspect or get the hostages to the ground. As far as we can tell, he's got a Winchester repeating rifle with fifteen rounds per magazine; something he inherited from his rich father or something. It's not very fast, but he's got .44 cartridges, so I'm authorizing lethal force if necessary. You've got five minutes to get ready. Leave your gun with Ariadne."

Ariadne had her fingers around my wrist and was pulling me away from Natalie. She stopped a guy that was about my size and demanded his vest.

"Fill me in on the situation, Ariadne," I said.

"It's a powder-keg," she said. "Yesterday, Matt launched a hostile takeover of Ryan's company. The Gathers Corporation was so entwined with Cityscape, it took only a matter of hours for Matt to depose Ryan like a latter day Bolingbroke and absorb his corporation. Then, to add insult to injury, Kate left him after she found out."

She handed me the vest and took my jacket. "Sandra went to talk to Matt this morning about forming a truce or partnership, possibly helping to maintain the Gardens, when Ryan entered the building through Matt's secret entrance. An entrance we still haven't found, I might add. Be aware that he might have an escape route."

I got the vest on and let Ariadne adjust it so that it was tight against my body. "This is a Type III ballistic vest. It should stop the bullet if he decides to shoot you, but you know how well these things work at point blank range. So do me a favor." She took my hand and squeezed it. "Don't get shot."

I handed her my gun and we ran back toward the group. Natalie stood there looking stoic. Her eyes were filled with worry. She thought she had lost me and had only gotten me back several hours ago. And now I was riding into battle again. "I'll be back in an hour," I told her.

"You better come back to me," she said, "or I'll kill you."

I smiled. "One hour."

As I moved toward the door, Neilson slapped me once on the back. "Go get 'em, kid." Allison reached out and took my hand. "Please, bring her back to me." Ariadne opened the door to let me in. "One hour," she said.

I looked carefully into the lobby. My steps echoing against the walls were the only sound in the suffocating room. I walked slowly, turned down the hall and saw Ryan Gathers standing in the elevator doorway.

"Ah, Stephen. Our mutual friend, Tommy, said you were on your way. I was wondering how long it would take you to swallow your fear and come talk to me." He took his cell from his pocket and threw it to the floor at my feet. It shattered like a glass. "I'm going back up to Matt's office. Follow me when you can."

The doors closed on Ryan, and I watched the numbers above the elevator rise to the top floor, to Matt's office fifty stories up, where it stopped. Then the number was falling back down. I wished I had my gun.

The doors slid open and I stared into the elevator. I was suddenly overcome by the fear that I couldn't do it. I couldn't step into the elevator, I couldn't take down Ryan, I couldn't save anybody. I wasn't a hero. I needed Stephen.

"You can do this," I heard Stephen whispering in the back of my mind.

"I can't do this," I said. "I'm not like you."

"You have to," Stephen said. "Sandra's counting on you. Matthew is counting on you. You have to save them."

"I can't save anybody."

"It was you who caught Stringfield, not me," Stephen reminded me. "You can do this."

I stepped across the threshold and pressed the penthouse button. "I hope you know what you're talking about."

The journey from the ground to the office seemed to last ten years. My mind ran unrestricted through various scenarios of failure. Every floor seemed a mile, every second an eternity; I counted every breath, every heartbeat, every twitch at my temple. Ten years or ten seconds later the door opened. There was no inrush of air, no elevator ding, nothing to announce my arrival except for the sterile silence that filled Matt's office.

Against the window, hands tied behind their backs, were Matthew Graycraft and Sandra Blanche. Standing between them, rifle leveled at my head, was Ryan Gathers.

"Come in, Stephen," Ryan ordered, jerking the gun in a quick motion. I stepped across the threshold, and the doors of the elevator closed behind me. On the south wall of the office was an opening where an abstract painting usually hung. It now leaned against the wall, starbursts of fiery red against a backdrop of black. I didn't know where the opening led, but if the painting was any indication, I wouldn't want to go that way.

"Is everybody safe?" I asked.

Sandra looked at me confused. It appeared that she didn't know who I was.

"That's Stephen Lanford," Matthew said, noting her confusion. "Come to play hero, just as he always does."

"She and Stephen are acquainted," Ryan said.

"Your eyes are different, Achilles," she insisted.

"Is this woman crazy?" Matthew asked Ryan.

"She's sick," said Ryan. "It's her lifestyle."

"Matthew, shut up," I ordered.

"Stephen's here to save you, Matt," Ryan mocked.

"And he's doing an excellent job of it, too," Matt said sarcastically.

"Achilles," Sandra mumbled from her position on the floor.

"Shut up," Matt demanded.

"Now, Matt, let the girl speak her mind." Ryan said in a falsely kind voice. "She won't be able to much longer."

"Achilles," Sandra repeated, "he's got a knife in the shoulder stock."

Ryan reached out and back-handed Sandra across the face. "While I appreciate your right to free speech," Ryan said, "I'm afraid we all have to learn sooner or later that everything we say comes with consequences."

"Ryan," I said.

Ryan brought the shoulder stock up to his arm, leveled the rifle at me and fired. Pain exploded in my chest and I fell back against the door, slid down to the floor. I couldn't breathe. I couldn't feel my feet. And then I couldn't see. Everything was going black.

When I opened my eyes, Sandra was still sitting where she had been, but her hands were unbound and she was smiling. Ryan was gone. Where Matthew had just been sitting, I was sitting instead. Or rather, Stephen was sitting.

Stephen stood up and moved to Matt's desk, then sat down in the chair. "Achilles," he said.

"Not you, too," I pleaded.

He clasped his hands in front of him and placed his elbows on the table. "What would you like me to call you?"

I shook my head. "I guess I don't really have a name."

Sandra stood up and moved to the desk. A second chair appeared and she sat down next to Stephen. "Do you not like the name Achilles? How about Patroclus? He was Achilles' closest friend, and they were raised together by Chiron, the greatest of the centaurs. Or any of Chiron's other disciples: Asclepius or Jason, for example."

"I'm not a great warrior, like Patroclus was. I don't feel like a great healer, like Asclepius was. I don't feel like a hero, like Jason was. I feel like Aeneas. I feel as though fate or the powers that be have decided to drag me through the fire against my will, and right now I feel like I'm failing."

"Aeneas' greatest virtue was piety. He was a good man who was placed into an extraordinary situation. But when it came to getting his hands dirty, he did what he had to do. Can you do what you need to do?"

I shook my head. "I don't know," I admitted. "I did once."

Stephen and Sandra began to speak in unison, as though both of their consciences were one. I would realize later that they were, that this was all happening in my head, and so they were nothing but two representations of the same thoughts. But at the time, it seemed very much as though I had stepped into the den of two oracles linked together by the possession of some ancient god or goddess. Was I dreaming? Was I unconscious? Confusion reigned.

"Aeneas, what are you doing?" they asked.

"I'm trying to talk Ryan down."

"You aren't acting like it. You're acting like you are scared to move, scared to speak, scared to even attempt to do your duty."

"He shot me!"

"And you gave him that chance."

I stood silent.

"Do you have nothing to say for yourself, Aeneas?"

I thought about what I wanted to say. Had I nothing to say for myself? I had a lot to say for myself. I had everything to say for myself. But what could I possibly say to them? Words were useless in this dimension; thoughts were useless in this dimension. "Send me back," I told them. "Send me back to Matt's office." It was the only thing they would listen to.

"Send you back?" They laughed. "Why on earth would we do that?"

"I have to save Sandra. I have to save Matthew."

"You can only save one of them," they told me.

"Then I choose Sandra," I said without hesitation.

They turned their heads to look at each other, then back at me. "If that is what you've decided to be your mission, know that you can only save one, and we cannot help you in this matter. The final decision rests entirely with Ryan Gathers. Your chosen mission is not going to be easy. Nothing worth doing in life will ever be easy. And you will have to choose your own missions from now on. There will never be a stable meaning to your life, as you will always have to adjust to new missions, new circumstances, new people. We won't ever be able to help you from this point forward. You are on your own, completely and entirely, in a world that is constantly changing where you will never receive everything you want or need. Do you accept this awful responsibility?"

"I do," I vowed.

"Then open your eyes."

"My eyes are open," I said.

"No," Sandra told me. "They aren't."

"Good luck, Aeneas," Stephen told me. "You're going to need it."

When I opened my eyes, smoke was rising from the barrel of the rifle. It had to have been less than a second since he had fired a bullet into my chest plate, a bullet that knocked the wind out of me and crashed me against the wall.

"That ought to take the fight out of you," Ryan said.

"What the hell are you doing?!" Matthew shouted. "You could have killed him!"

Ryan turned and placed the hot barrel of the gun to Matthew's cheek. Matt pulled back, slamming his head against the glass of the window as his skin cooked. "That may still be an option, Matthew. But if I had to throw my vote in the hat, I would say that you'll be out before he will. Or maybe," he swung the barrel to Sandra's shoulder, pressing the heated metal down into her skin until she screamed, "maybe the little pest who's been bogging down my legal team with action group after political interest group after action group, costing me money and ruining my reputation."

"Ryan," I said, stumbling to my feet.

He swung the barrel back to me. "Stephen, I swear that if you come any closer to me, I'll put a bullet through your skull."

"I'm staying right here," I said, putting my hands in the air. "You've got all the power here. I'm just here to try to make sure everyone gets out of this alright."

"And what exactly do you mean by 'alright?' I'm not 'alright.' Matthew's not 'alright.' This little whore over here isn't 'alright.'" He laughed suddenly. "You certainly aren't 'alright.'"

"My name is Sandra," she informed him.

"How exactly is the big celebrity Stephen Lanford going to make everything alright?" Ryan asked.

"I can't right now…"

"Big surprise."

"But if you talk to me, tell me your story, then maybe we can come to some form of alright. Nobody has to die here today, Ryan."

Through the iron sight at the top of the rifle, I could see Ryan sizing me up, trying to decide if it was worth speaking to me, if it was worth attempting to come to a compromise. Finally, after several seconds of looking at me from that sight, Ryan dropped the barrel of the gun to the desk.

"Do you see this gun?" he asked. I nodded. "My father gave me this gun. My father wasn't born rich, like Mr. Graycraft. My father was the son of a mechanic, who lassoed the stars with his bootstraps and pulled himself up inch by inch. This rifle was his symbol of strength and civilization. It represented man's victory over the animals. It represented the West's victory over the natives. It represented control over the world.

"He never made it up to Graycraft's level, but he got us up higher than your old man. He made enough to start his own company, to put me through school, to leave me with a legacy. You see, though, my father left me everything. Matt was left enough. Enough to get started, to go to school. But he needed my help, my company, to launch him to where he is now. And he was happy to take me with him while I was an asset. Until yesterday, when Matt decided that my company, the company that he had used as a launching board for his own ambitions, was his property, and not mine.

"So now, I'm going to take my father's old hunting rifle, his ultimate symbol of strength and civilization, and I'm going to show Matthew Graycraft what victory looks like."

Ryan took the barrel and stepped over so that it was pointed at Matthew's nose. Matt shrank from it.

"Ryan, come on, that's not victory," I said. Ryan looked back at me as

I continued. "You aren't gaining anything by killing somebody, you're throwing your life away. You kill the hostages and that's it, they'll come in with their flash-bangs and automatic weapons, and they'll put you down like a dog. That's not strength, that's not civilization, that's not victory."

Ryan chewed the inside of his mouth as he contemplated my words. "I guess you would be the expert in this matter," he finally said. "So what would be victory?"

I quietly exhaled the breath I'd been holding and began to list the options. "I'll call our buddy, Tommy. I'll tell him that you're surrendering yourself, right? I'm going to tell him that everybody is okay, that both the hostages are safe and that you've acted in the best interest of all parties involved. You haven't hurt anybody, so you won't be in any real trouble once we get out of this."

Ryan sneered. "For as much celebrity as you have, I have to say, I'm fairly disappointed, Lanford. For someone like you to think in your wildest imagination that surrender could be victory." He stepped around the table and raised the rifle at me again. He walked forward, coming closer. I turned my body to make myself a smaller target and raised my hand. If he got close enough, I could disarm him. Then, around the halfway mark of the length of the office, he stopped. "Have they found the secret entrance yet?"

"Yes," I lied. "They have a team watching it for an escape attempt."

Ryan smiled. "You're lying," he said. "You have a tell, Stephen. I saw it all those years ago when we were playing poker, and I see it on you now. You're not like most people. Most people try to hide their lies, to cover their mouth or think about what they're about to say. You answer quickly. Your brain selects the best answer, and you blurt it out without stopping to consider it. Most people would think you were honest. But I know that you're lying, and I know that they haven't found Matt's secret entrance yet.

So here's my solution to the problem. I'm going to leave, and you're going to stay here, and we're never going to cross paths ever again."

"Ryan," I said, "If you run, they will kill you. Face the consequences of your actions. That's strength. That's civilization. That's victory."

Ryan fired once. The glass of the window shattered, the wind rushing in with the sound of a freight train. He fired again, and the bottle of scotch on the desk exploded, alcohol and glass painting the two cowering hostages. He shot once more, then ran to the secret entrance and climbed inside.

I ran to the window and knelt down at Sandra's side, trying to cover the blood that was pouring from her inner thigh. He'd hit the femoral artery and she was bleeding badly. I stretched her out, stripped her jacket off, tied a tourniquet above the wound. But the crimson puddle formed beneath her, mixing with the alcohol like a sanguine wine. "Achilles," she whispered.

"Sandra."

She ran her fingers through my hair and whispered one word. "Love." And then she was gone, her green eyes fading to black as her soul departed. I kissed the tips of my pointer and middle fingers and placed them to her lips. Then I closed her eyes with those same fingers.

I felt as though I might die here with her, make her funeral pyre my own. But still, I could not cry.

"Is she dead?" Matt asked shakily.

I whirled on my feet and grabbed him from the floor, pushing him up against the wall beside the window. If I wanted to, I could have thrown him out. "Matthew," I said, gazing into his frightened eyes. "Look what you've done."

"I...I didn't," he stammered. "It was Ryan."

"It was you who did this," I told him, pointing at Sandra's lifeless body. "You manipulated, you smothered, you kicked him and used him like a pet for your own personal gain. You fed him just enough to keep him happy, and then when you stopped feeding him he bit the neighbor. You are responsible for this."

"No!" he cried. "It wasn't me."

"This is what happens when you use other people for your own benefit. This is what happens when money is more important to you than people. Your hand might not have held the gun, but as far as I'm concerned, you're just as guilty as Ryan."

Tears were streaming down his face. He whimpered softly, pathetically.

"I'm going after Ryan now," I told him, pulling my phone from my pocket and placing it in his hands. "I need you to call Ariadne, the first number in the call history, and tell her what happened. Can you do that?"

He sniffled loudly, then nodded his head. "Yeah. Yeah, I think, I think I can do that."

"Good," I said. I slapped my hand down on his shoulder like Stephen had done to John, to Columbus, to Allen. It was a sign of friendship, but Matt seemed to flinch from it as though I was attempting to hurt him. "Peace, Matt," I said softly. I ran to the secret entrance and stepped through.

Chapter 8
Pursuit

Thursday, March 3, 2011

A square metal staircase descended into darkness. I ran down it, skipping as many steps as I possibly could without losing my footing. I could hear Ryan's footsteps rattling below me. He could hear my footsteps booming above him. And so we became hunter and prey.

And then the sound of another gunshot echoed through the wall, splitting my eardrum as though the bullet had passed through my tympanic membrane, reverberating through my head with an insect buzz I would hear forever. I ran faster, jumped downward, tripped on the metal as I spun around the rails, downward, downward, ever toward the earth.

At the bottom of the stairs was another body, arms spread out, the dark blood reflecting what little light there was in the hall. I felt the neck for a pulse and found none. Turning the body over, I saw William Mincks. Or Darryl Phoenix. I wondered in death which he would rather be.

I closed his eyelids slowly. Then I rose and started for a door to the left. I tripped over something and tumbled to the ground. Reaching behind me, I found the rifle that had been Ryan's. His father's before him. It had been his symbol of civilization. I had seen his version of civilization, and I didn't want anything to do with it. In his world, there was no room for people like Sandra; in his world, there was no room for people like me. As I gripped the stock of the handle, I felt that the shoulder had a hollow hiding spot in the butt. It was empty.

He's got a knife in the shoulder stock, Sandra had told me.

I dropped the rifle and ran after him.

I followed the dark tunnel, an open exit letting light pour inside. From that outlet, I could hear the sound of distant music. As I drew closer, I could hear the steady thump of drums. I followed the sound of a guitar and voices, many voices singing.

As I exited the tunnel, I thought I saw Sandra standing there, welcoming me back to the light. But once my eyes adjusted, I realized that I was in the Gardens. Looking behind me, I saw what appeared to be a tool shed, filed against the corner of the fence. The Gardens and the Cityscape building were connected by a secret tunnel, one that nobody would ever suspect was there. Why was it there?

I looked around, trying to find which way Ryan had gone. He could be anywhere: into the crowd; through the east gate toward the river; through the west gate toward the interstate; through the north gate toward downtown; through the south gate to the parking lot. Then I saw him running, Natalie pursuing close behind. Where was her gun? Why didn't she have her gun out?

I followed them through the crowd toward the parking lot. As Ryan passed the fountain, he turned and bolted east to the river. Natalie lost a few seconds as she circumvented the fountain, but I was able to gain a few, putting us almost on a level. She was faster than me, so she quickly gained on Ryan, until Ryan turned around and fired a weapon—Natalie's I could now see. We ducked, people panicked, the path between us and him obscured with bystanders.

"Are you okay?" I asked.

"Ryan shot Darryl!" she shouted back. She had a cut on her left cheek, a deep one, bleeding down her face in red teardrops.

I reached out to wipe the blood from her cheek, but she jerked her face away from me, leapt to her feet and began to shoulder her way through the crowd. I followed.

Outside the east gate, we searched but saw no sign of Ryan. "Where could he have gone?" Natalie asked.

"Anywhere," I told her.

"You're the genius!" she yelled at me. "Where would he have gone?"

"It depends," I told her, "He could be going to his home, but he probably realizes the cops will be there waiting for him, in which case he'll probably be going to someone that he trusts, someone he's sure won't turn him in."

"He doesn't have anyone like that," Natalie said. "His closest friend was Matt, and his wife left him. He's alone."

"Call Tommy, get him to send a security detail to Kate, in case Ryan does go after her. Let's assume he's not going after her, though. He's alone, so he'd be going somewhere that nobody would find him, a safe house or an apartment that only he knows about."

"Close to here?"

"As long as he's on foot, we can catch up with him. He might have transportation stashed somewhere around…"

"The river!" Natalie shouted, running past me. I ran after her.

As we approached the fence that separated the road from the river, we saw where somebody had used wire-cutters to make themselves a portal between the two worlds. Natalie jumped through, landed hard, then rose and bolted south down the riverside. I climbed through and followed.

We ran until we couldn't run anymore, never once catching sight of Ryan. There was no way to know if he had followed the river south or sailed against it. There was no way to know if he was even on the river. There was no way to know anything.

Natalie took her cell phone and called Tommy, telling him that we lost Gathers. I could hear him yelling at her, but she kept on talking, told him that Kate needed protection in case Ryan came after her. He stopped yelling, and she continued telling him we were calling Dobbs to see if he knew. With any luck, we could have a welcoming party waiting for him when he got there. She hung up on him before he could yell at her again.

She threw her arms around my neck and hugged me for a minute. I held her as well as I could. The vest, my armor, disrupted any feeling of her hug. She ran her hand over my chest, feeling where the bullet had slammed into me. I gasped.

"Are Matt and Sandra alright?" she asked.

I exhaled sharply as her fingers pushed down on the bruise. Then I shook my head, avoiding her eyes.

"Stephen?" she asked.

"Ryan's beyond redemption," I told her. "This wasn't an act of passion, he planned this. There was never any talking him down."

Natalie bit her lip. "Both of them?" she asked.

I shook my head again. "Just Sandra."

Her eyes filled with anger, pain and sadness. She walked away from me, back toward the hole in the fence. I followed a ways behind her.

She called Dobbs and told him what had happened, then shut her phone. "How long?" she asked.

"How long what?"

"How long have you known that Darryl Phoenix was William Mincks?"

"Just since yesterday," I told her. "Just since Ariadne and I talked."

"Alright, hold that thought, because I'm going to come back to it in a second. If you just found out that Darryl is William, or William is Darryl, then why did you ask Dobbs about it on Monday?"

I didn't know what to say. That hadn't even been me. "I just wanted information about William. I didn't make the connection until yesterday."

"And when did you talk to Ariadne about William yesterday?"

"At breakfast. At dinner."

"Uh huh…" she said. "So you couldn't come home and see me while you were on your little walkabout, but you had time to eat breakfast—and dinner—with Ariadne fucking Stahl."

"Natalie, please."

"No, Stephen. Not right now. I need to clear my head." She stormed away from me. I followed behind her. "Please stop following me. You are not going to follow me around like a lovesick puppy."

"The car is this way," I told her. "Where the hell am I supposed to go?"

"Go get a ride from…" She paused for effect, and snarled the name. "Ariadne."

"Matt has my cell phone," I said.

"Not my problem," she retorted.

I stopped and let her walk ahead until she was out of sight. Then I walked the long way up the road and down toward the Cityscape building. Thomas and Ariadne met me on the road. Ariadne hugged me. "Where's Natalie?" she asked.

"I don't know," I said. Then added, "I think she's got Ryan's scent. She's got a bloodlust for him. Is my car here?"

Thomas stepped between the two of us and put his hand on my shoulder. "You got lucky this time. Matthew Graycraft has friends in high places, and one of them just told me that as much as I'd like to chew you to pieces and make sure you never get a chance to wear that badge again, you've got immunity in this situation.

"However, if you ever step foot in my city again, you better not so much as change lanes without signaling or I will nail your ass to the wall. I will shoot you down like a fighter jet, and ask questions later, do you understand me?" His words might have been taken as though they were angry, but I knew that wasn't true. He wasn't angry; he understood perfectly the risks of sending me into the Cityscape building. But no cop can stand an agent pulling jurisdiction, especially when the situation spoils. Nothing I did, before, during or after my time in the Cityscape building would have changed his attitude because the simple fact was that I was on his territory, and he was going to do everything in his power to scare me out.

I let him rant, thankful that Matthew was covering my back in what was a spectacularly uncharacteristic move. "Yes," I told him. "I understand you perfectly."

"Good." He stormed off as well.

I stood there facing Ariadne. I didn't want to look her in the eye, but she put her hand on my cheek and tilted my head back. "I don't blame you," she said.

"You should," I told her. "If I had never gone in there…"

"Then Ryan would have killed Matt and Sandra and escaped without a word. You put up a fight, and you saved Matt's life."

"I didn't save Matt's life," I told her. "I traded Darryl's life for his."

She looked at me with the condescending air of someone who sees the bigger picture while you're still struggling with a minor detail. "Darryl was dying. He had only a few months left before the cancer would flood his cells and take him from us."

I stammered. "I…I'm sorry. I didn't know."

"Now you do," she said. "And even though I wish you could have saved Sandra, I don't blame you for her death. The same thing would have happened if the SWAT team had stormed in. The same thing would have happened if I had gone in myself. You did everything you could."

My mouth was so dry, I felt if I spoke, my tongue would break off.

"Stephen…" She sighed.

"Please don't call me that," I blurted out without thinking.

Her eyes grew wide as she looked me up and down. Then she laughed once, as though I were joking. Her left eye twitched as her brain worked out what my words must have meant. And then she spoke.

"Your voice," she said. "Your eyes. The way you've been acting." I closed my eyes as my breath caught in my lungs. I thought I was going to suffocate. "You…" she said. And then she was silent for a moment. "Does Natalie know?"

I shook my head. "Are you one, too?"

"Yes," she said. "What do I call you?"

"I don't know. Sandra called me Achilles. And Aeneas. I think…I don't even know anymore."

"Achilles? Aeneas? Yeah that sounds like Sandra. Sorry, I don't think I can call you either of those."

"Yeah, I know. Those are both weird names."

"No, I mean with Aeneas, Achilles, Ariadne, people are going to start thinking we're in mythological Greece." I smiled. "Come on, Lanford," she said, "let's go get a couple burgers for lunch, then I have to take you down to the station to get debriefed, and afterward I'll arrange a ride out to Hazelwood for you."

I sighed in relief. "That sounds nice. Thank you."

We drove to an old diner near the boardwalk and sat across from each other as we ate our burgers and fries. "So, yeah," Ariadne said. "I'm going to tell you that I've seen a lot of weird stuff in my days here in Mastern, and before, in Hazelwood, but this is probably the most surreal thing I've ever done."

"Yeah. I've got to tell you, it's a strange experience just being out. Up until yesterday I'd never even spent more than a few hours in control. Now I'm the dominant personality. It's something of a change for me."

"I should have known. Your first day on the job is never easy."

I laughed. "Was yours this bad?" I asked.

"Not quite this bad. I had about fifteen years as a dominant personality before I went dark for a decade. But get this: My first night out after the blackout, my first night as a police officer, Matthew Graycraft threw a fit in the middle of a university function. Vegas night, I think. Assaulted a woman. Got the snot beaten out of him by two students, though. Real chivalrous guys, the knights of Hazelwood."

"Sorry," I said, running my hands through my hair. "I, uh…Stephen kind of manufactured that whole scene."

"I'm not exactly surprised by that revelation. Seems like Stephen liked to shake things up everywhere he went. You're not like that, are you, Lanford?"

"I…I don't know, to tell you the truth. Let's go knock over a bank and then you can ask me again." She laughed. "Honestly, I don't think I'm cut out for this lifestyle," I added. "I've been sitting behind Stephen's eyes, watching things happen for so long I don't think I'm really the best person to be running around like this. He's the man of action. I don't think I am."

She smiled with a look of understanding. "Thinking of changing things up?"

"Maybe. I'll jump off that bridge when I come to it, I guess."

She checked the time on her phone and said, "Come on. You'll have plenty of time to think about that while they're debriefing you."

The debriefing was boring, as it always is. I sat in a chair for several hours while Tommy and an officer asked me to tell and retell the story. I told my side until it sounded like an old joke, stale and well-rehearsed. What did Ryan say? What did Matt say? What did Sandra say? What had I said? I told them several times everything I knew. They told me as much as they thought I needed to know. It didn't really matter now; I had only one question, and neither of the men circling me could answer it.

Ariadne was waiting with a cup of coffee when I came out of the precinct. "Come on," she said. "Walk to the river district with me."

I should probably be getting back to Natalie, I thought. At least I could call. I patted my pockets. "Matt has my cell phone," I said.

"No he doesn't," Ariadne told me, pulling my phone from her own pocket. I took it, asking how she'd ended up with it. "Matthew gave it to me. Whatever you said to him up in that tower, it definitely got under his skin. He seems like a brand new person." She paused and joked, "You don't think he could be an alternate personality, too, do you?"

I faked a laugh and dialed Natalie's number. It rang a couple times, then went to voice mail. She had clicked the red button because she didn't want to talk to me.

"Yeah," I said. "Let's go."

We walked down to the river district. I didn't know where I was going, so Ariadne led the way to a sports bar on the corner. It was empty aside from Allison Weston and Neilson. Ariadne gave Neilson a hug, then moved on to Allison.

Neilson slapped my shoulder and said, "Tough brake, kid." Allison didn't say anything. She just stared off into space, smoked her cigarette and watched the smoke corkscrew in front of her.

"Detective Stahl!" the bartender smiled. "What can I get for you tonight?"

"Something strong for me and my friends," Ariadne told her.

"Do you smoke?" Neilson solemnly asked me. I told him I didn't. He handed me a black cigarette and said, "You do tonight." I took a matchbook from the bar, the name Interference Sports Bar printed in red against the black. Neilson handed a cigarette to Ariadne as I struck the match, then lit both my cigarette and hers. "Seven bars in the river district, seven cigarettes, seven shots," Neilson said. "When I was a kid in New Orleans, we'd have this mourning tradition. When something tragic happened, we'd go to every bar along Bourbon Street and do a shot at each one. Mastern, unfortunately doesn't have a Bourbon Street. So tonight, we're making the river district our stomping ground. Understand?" I nodded. "When tragedies happen, people need to do something. They need a way to cleanse themselves of the evils of the world. They need a way to diffuse the emotions that would otherwise poison them. And what better way than to get drunk with friends?"

The bartender poured four kamikaze shots. Ariadne paid, then raised her glass. "What are we toasting to?"

"To Mastern City," Neilson said. "It's not perfect, but without it we would never have had Sandra. She was a rose growing through the concrete." We shot.

I felt the heat rise to my face almost immediately. I yawned.

"Are you gonna make it, Lanford?" Ariadne asked. I told her I thought I would, but that I couldn't promise anything. "Good," she said. We smoked our cigarettes together in silence until they burned to the filter. She took my arm in her fingers and pulled me away from Allison and Neilson. Not far, but far enough to have some privacy.

"You ever been here before?" she asked. I just looked at her. "Sorry," she said. "I just don't know what to talk about with someone who's only, what, a day old?"

I rolled my eyes. "Actually, I was born on the day that we caught Stringfield. I guess I'm almost three years old by now."

"I'm not sure you're old enough to be drinking," she joked. "Or smoking. Should you even be in this bar?"

"Oh, you're a stitch," I told her.

"I'm a cop," she said, "I've got a million bad jokes, I suck at interpersonal relationships, and I flirt like an awkward penguin." She smiled at me. "I bet you just want to drop everything and date me now, don't you?"

I coughed, stifling my laughter under the back of my hand. "I thought you and Neilson were a thing."

"Us? No, I'd never go down that path," she told me. "He and I are old friends, and while I love him like a brother, I'm not interested in him romantically."

"So, the other day in the park?"

"Just two friends," she laughed. "You didn't think…?"

"I don't know what I thought," I told her. "I guess, yeah."

"You know for someone so smart…"

"I sure can be awfully stupid," I finished. "Yeah, I know."

"So you know at least one thing about yourself," she said. "Come on. That's one bar down and six to go."

We formed into a group and left as a unit. The night was beginning to fall as we made our way downriver, away from the Interference to a new bar with a new bartender and a new drink. The humidity gathered around us, pulling the sweat out of us as we made our way into The Corner Lounge. There were more people in this bar.

"Four kamikaze shots," Neilson ordered and paid. "What are we shooting to?"

Ariadne said, "To Hazelwood, without whose constraints we would never have had the pleasure of Darryl's company, nor the genius of his writing." We shot again.

Time began to lose meaning for me as the alcohol from the second shot hit my brain. There were fans hanging from the ceiling, spinning slowly. I watched one of the fans for a second, admiring the way the blades cut the light like a strobe.

"It's kind of cute watching someone who's never drank before," she said. "You look like you're having a good time."

I licked my lips and yawned again. "I don't get it. Stephen used to drink all the time. Whiskey, wine, beer. Shouldn't we share the same liver? Shouldn't we have the same tolerance?"

"Maybe," she said. "I wish I could give you an answer, but your situation is unique."

"I wonder if it is, though," I told her. "How many people out there have Dissociative Identity Disorder that don't ever get diagnosed, that don't ever come forward to their family or friends? How many people out there are like me?"

"That's a question," she said. She took two cigarettes from Neilson and handed one to me. I produced the matchbook and lit both cigarettes. "Maybe there are lots of people like you out there. Maybe you're one of the few. Which would you prefer?"

"To not be alone," I told her. "But I don't know. I almost wish there were only a few of us. How sad it would be if there were many of us out there, all living in the shadows of a dominant personality."

"Why should that bother you?" she asked. "There are people all over the world without multiple personalities who are in the same boat. Women live in the shadows of the patriarchy; minorities live in the shadows of white supremacy; people with alternate sexualities live in the shadows of the kyriarchy. Would it really be such a tragedy if you found out you had something in common with ninety-nine percent of the world population?"

"I don't know. I guess the fact that anybody should live in the shadow of anyone else seems to me a tragedy."

"Tell me about it," she muttered. "I'm the first female detective in Mastern, in the heart of the south. Think about how many people wanted me to fail. Think about how long I had to struggle, how much harder I had to fight than any detective before or since. Maybe you're not so unique, after all."

"Well, just steal my thunder then," I joked.

The four of us walked along to the Red Fox, Ariadne and I hanging off to the side as Neilson and Allison talked. Another bar, another cigarette, another shot. Three down, four to go.

"To Sandra," Allison somberly toasted. "The love of my life."

We all raised our glasses, threw them back. I was getting better, but I still felt the alcohol harder than Stephen ever had. It warmed my face and made the room move.

I tried to offer my condolences to Allison, but she ignored me. Ariadne pulled me away a few seconds later and challenged me to a game of pool. I thought it was a fine idea until she sank shot after shot, and I didn't get to play. She laughed at me when I finally got a chance, and the balls went everywhere but where I wanted them to.

"Never played pool before, have you?" she asked.

"I guess not," I answered. "Like, I understand how it should work, and I've seen Stephen do it enough to know that it can work, but my hands and my body won't do what my mind wants them to. You know?"

"I think I do," she said. "It'll just take practice. Nobody does it perfectly their first time. Especially not if they only get one shot the entire game."

She came up beside me and leaned over the table, showing me how I should position my body in order to aim, explaining where on the cue ball

I would need to hit in order to make my shot. I followed her advice and sank one.

"Good job," she said. "Let's rack up and we can try again."

She taught me how to rack, then told me to break. "Now when you open, move the cue ball a little to the side, and aim right here," she pointed at the space between the first and second balls, "Then shoot it just how I taught you." She leaned over the table, giving me a perfect view of her cleavage as I tried to line up my shot. "Make sure you don't pull back. Follow through your shot with as much force as you can."

I shot. The cue ball ricocheted off the three and landed in the corner pocket.

She laughed hard. "Let's try that again, shall we?"

The next game was better. The more I worked, the more control I had over the cue stick, and the more Ariadne coached me, the better I was at making the balls go where I wanted them to. It didn't help that Ariadne kept walking around to the opposite side of the table from me, leaning forward so that all I could think about was the gleam of the light off the skin of her chest and the lace of her red bra. She beat me, of course. She was more experienced, and she had better control than I did, but I was still able to play a decent game.

"You'll do better next time," she said, taking me by the hand.

We left the Red Fox and wandered down the street. Allison and Neilson walked ahead. "There's something I've been wondering," I told Ariadne. "A couple things actually."

"Well, start with the first one and then we'll move on to the second one." We clambered inside the Blind Pig Speakeasy, the fourth bar on our way downriver. "It's your turn to toast, by the way."

The bartender put four shots on the bar, I paid. "To Darryl Phoenix. He taught me more about identity in the two meetings I had with him than anyone I've known my entire life." We shot. "Why was there a secret passageway connecting the Gardens and the Cityscape building?"

"I'm surprised you don't know," Ariadne said. "It was your father, or Stephen's father, that used to run that passageway."

"My father?"

"Yeah. We never knew exactly where the tunnel was, but it was Eric Lanford who used to run drugs and moonshine up and down those tunnels and stairwells for the elder Graycraft." I tried to light our cigarettes, but the match slipped from my hand, landing in the ashtray. Ariadne took the matchbook from my shaking hands and lit it, using it for my cigarette, then her own. "You really didn't know? Eric Lanford and Matthew's father were in business together. Eric ran the criminal underground, Matthew's dad ran the business world, Ryan's father ran the politicians. Together they controlled Mastern, right up until your father moved your family out to Hazelwood and retired. That's when the gang wars started up. You didn't know any of this?"

I shook my head. "I knew about the moonshine, and I knew that my father worked for Matthew's father but none of this other stuff."

"It makes sense why Stephen turned out the way he did, of course," Ariadne mused. "They say that criminals and cops have similar personalities. Good cops are able to think like criminals; good criminals are able to think like cops."

"I guess it does all make sense." The band began to play. The drums and the standing bass came in first, the piano joining them a few notes in. Two distinct chords worked together to create an informal, almost lazy run, before the trumpet came in atop the others. I recognized it as an old Miles Davis song. "'So What,'" I said.

Ariadne shrugged. "I don't think anything of it. The sins of the father aren't any concern of mine."

"No," I laughed. "That's the name of the song they're playing. It's by Miles Davis."

"Oh," she laughed. "I don't listen to a lot of jazz. Do you like modern music?"

I shrugged.

"I'm going up to see the Kingdom Goes Blind in Virginia next month," she continued.

I shook my head.

"They're kind of indie like The Dear Hunter but more artsy-progressive like The Mars Volta. But they also have more structured songs like My Morning Jacket, or Portugal the Man."

I shook my head again.

"You have absolutely no idea what I'm talking about, huh?"

I smiled.

"You should come with me," she said. "It'll be good for you."

"That actually sounds really nice."

We left the Blind Pig and walked toward the Daedalus Pub, stop number five on our journey downriver. It was filled with people, but we were able to find four spots at the end of the bar where we could sit and talk to each other. However, because we were pressed together, Ariadne and I couldn't speak with the intimacy that we had in the other bars. We ordered a new round.

"To Olivia," Neilson said. "As a teacher and as a person, she touched countless lives." We all drank.

"What was the second thing?" Ariadne asked.

"What's your real name?"

She and Neilson both laughed. Allison didn't; just lit another cigarette and went to work turning it to ash. We all followed suit.

"Actually, I have something of a...procedure? Custom?" she

searched the smoke in front of her for the correct word. "Ritual. For when people want to learn my name. You see, there can't be more than ten people in Mastern who know my real name. Of those people, I'm including my boss, the person who signs my paychecks, and the manager at the bank. Allison knows it, but that's only because she knew me before I became Ariadne. Neilson doesn't know it at all. So if you want to know my name, there's something I'm going to need from you, and I can't take what I need from you yet."

"So you might tell me what your real name is sometime in the future?" I asked.

She thought about it for a moment, then said, "Let's just say, I'm not saying I won't."

Neilson laughed as he stamped out his cigarette. "I've been asking her for years, kid. I was going to look it up on my own reconnaissance, but Ariadne asked me not to."

"When Sandra named me Ariadne, I became Ariadne," she said, "just like William became Darryl. My real name is no longer important because it no longer describes who I am. But if you really want to know, Lanford," she smiled at me, "I'm sure you'll find out eventually."

Allison put her arm around Neilson's shoulder as she tried to stand, using him as a crutch for her rise. Neilson put his arm around her waist and helped her. Ariadne and I followed them toward the door.

The room was beginning to dance, and it was now impossible for any of us to walk a straight line.

The sixth bar on our stop was the Primitive Times Tavern. It shifted left and right as I stumbled up to it, opened the door and ushered everybody inside. The place was smoky and crowded. We slowly bobbed and weaved through the swarming people until we found a circular booth along the far wall. The cocktail waitress appeared like an apparition.

Ariadne took my arm and placed it around her shoulder, leaning close to me, her warm breath on my earlobe as she whispered, "Since Sandra named me Ariadne, nobody has learned my name without first having given me something in return. Something very valuable to me, though they may be given freely enough by men like Stephen. I hope it's something very valuable to you, too. Because even if I want it very bad, if you don't value it, there would be no point in your giving it to me. If you don't value it, it would be meaningless for me to receive it."

"What is it?" I asked.

"A kiss," she replied.

I couldn't give one to her, not now. Natalie was at home, possibly waiting for me. Natalie's lips were the only ones that I wanted to kiss right now. Natalie was the only girl I wanted snuggled up against me as Ariadne was right now. But why was I letting her get so close to me?

"I can't," I told her.

"Good," she replied.

The waitress returned and placed the shots on the table. "To the future," Ariadne said. "Behind us lie both good days and bad days; now let's look forward to those days we have not seen." We shot.

As we lit our cigarettes, the smoke that we made joined with the smoke around us. We became a part of the bar, part of the collective that had gathered. We were one; we were a community. The lines between us blurred, the walls that separate us fell. Though our physical walls were still as solid as the table and the booth, our spiritual walls seemed to mesh and mix like the smoke. In that moment, I felt we were united. Against what, or whom, I didn't know. I was very drunk.

Neilson had Allison under his arm, consoling her as she grieved. I had my arm around Ariadne. I couldn't say why. Maybe she was holding me up. But we were together, and we were alive, and we were friends.

That's what Allison needed in that moment. That's what I needed in that moment. And the best thing I could do was to follow this through to the end.

We rose, we left, and headed toward our final destination, the Fountain of Gold. But when we approached the doors, we found them barred against us. The Fountain of Gold was closed, the doors locked. We could not complete our funeral march, our healing ritual.

Allison walked to the door, placed her forehead to the applewood, breathed in as deeply as she could, and sobbed. Her clenched fist pounded on the wood, her sneakers kicked it, her cries ricocheted off it.

Neilson looked to me, I looked to Ariadne, Ariadne looked back at us.

Then Allison turned on me, pointing her finger in my chest, pushing me backward into the road. "This, this is your fault!" she shouted.

"Allison." Ariadne put her hand on the girl's shoulder. Allison shrugged it off.

"Why couldn't you have let Matt die?! He's a bastard, a sad example of a man, and you let him live!"

"I'm sorry…"

"Sorry? You're sorry you let my Sandra get shot, die, you let Ryan take her from me, and you're sorry? You let Ryan take my William, my Darryl, you let my best friend get shot and die, and you're sorry? You let Olivia take her own life, and you're sorry. I'll say you're sorry. A sorry excuse for a human being." She wobbled off. Neilson followed her.

I stood there in the street for several minutes, watching her go. Then a car came by, and I had to move. Ariadne took my arm in her hand, put her chin on my shoulder. "She doesn't mean it," Ariadne whispered. "She's just upset." I nodded slowly. "This evening was supposed to be an—epiclesis. A rite of spiritual transformation," she said.

"No, I understand," I told her. "I just wish there was something I could do."

She kissed my cheek. "Life draws us bad cards sometimes. We just have to play the hands we're dealt. It's not the individual hands that matter, though. It's how you come to the table, how you play the game and what you take away. Don't get too caught up on one bad hand, Lanford. It'll drive you crazy."

I smiled. "Thanks, Ariadne."

She called me a cab and sat with me while I waited.

"Have you thought anything more about what we were talking about at the diner?" she asked.

"I haven't made a decision yet," I told her. "It's weird, having to make my own decisions. I've been watching Stephen make poor decisions, criticizing him as he went through life, but I never knew how hard it would be when I was the one playing the game."

"Are you going to be alright? Playing the game, I mean."

"I'll have to learn sometime," I told her. "I'm a smart guy. I'm sure I'll learn it eventually. Like playing pool."

"I'm sure you will," she said.

It was a long ride back to Hazelwood. I admired the trees shining in the moonlight and the roll of the road in the circles of the headlights. Though I had seen this road through Stephen's eyes many times, every inch of road between Mastern and Hazelwood seemed newly formed, as it was the day after being poured and crafted.

Was the world somehow younger now? Was I somehow different? In the darkness of the moment, I almost imagined that I was twenty-one, and this world was ripe for my harvest. I realized, as soon it entered my mind, it was an incomplete thought, a false thought, and that I should not allow it to take over. Nevertheless, the thought remained, like a burr clinging tight to the coils of my consciousness.

The bedroom light was on and the door was unlocked when I arrived at the house. A suitcase sat next to the couch. I walked through the dark living room to the bedroom, where Natalie sat on the bed with her laptop and a pile of papers before her. Her hair was pulled into a pony tail and she wore her work clothing. A long, pale bandage hid the scar on her cheek. She didn't seem to notice me.

I climbed onto the bed and leaned in to kiss her. She shrugged me away and glared. "Stephen," she said, "I'm leaving."

My heart stopped. "What?"

"I've got a plane out of Mastern to Chicago, then Seattle. I think that Ryan is heading to China. He's got a small production company there, Minola Incorporated, where I think he's stashing a small fortune in corporate assets and enough money to live on. He also has two American fronts from which he can secure a plane, assuming he has friends willing to help him run. Depending on where he's going and how lucky he gets, he can be out of America before sundown tomorrow. I'm betting he's heading to his office in Washington state, so I've gotten in touch with Dobbs and I'm going to try to cut Ryan off before he leaves."

"So…"

"You're not coming with me," she told me. "Finish up here and head back to Virginia."

"Natalie," I pleaded. "Please don't do this."

"I have a mission now, Stephen. And I know that it's not as important as your missions are, but it's mine, and I have to pursue it."

"What are you talking about?" I asked. "I don't have any problem with you going after Ryan, but I don't want to lose you. I want to marry you. I love you."

She closed her laptop slowly, the latch clasping with a resounding click. I saw the beams of headlights pulling into the driveway shine through the windows. "You smell like alcohol, smoke and perfume. You've already lost me, Stephen" she said. She stood up and slipped her laptop into its case, then carried it and her suitcase out the door, closing it behind her.

Why couldn't I cry?

I fell backward on the bed, kicked my shoes off, swung my feet up onto the blankets.

Olivia's blue eyes looked up at me from the depths of her aquatic sarcophagus. Would I eventually snap as she had done? Would I eventually join her in those dark depths?

I pulled my shirt off, unhooked my belt, removed my socks. I could see Sandra there, looking up at me from her wooden funeral pyre. Love, she whispered. And then William. Darryl. Shot down like a dog on the concrete floor of the tunnel. Only by giving up his birth identity was he able to discover the identity of his heart.

I pulled the covers up, lay my head down on the pillow. I could see Stringfield there, staring up into space. Do me a favor, he said. Show people what is real. Show them what is true. Don't let the illusion win. My head pounded hard.

And then I was lying in a field, the tall grass wafting above my head as I watched clouds float through the brilliant blue of the sky. What field? I wondered. Where? I stood and walked to where a small creek passed by a tall tree. I sat down, my back against the tree, and watched the water flow south. On the other side of the river I could see the shadowy specter, sitting lotus position. It picked a dandelion from the ground beside it and blew a cloud of florets across the river to me. I took one of the florets in my hand. It sprouted a white rose from my palm.

I spun it in the air. It hovered, a small helicopter. I blew lightly on the flower and it floated back to the shadow. The shadow took it, placed it to its nose. Then, both the specter and the flower began to dissolve into the air, particles sparkling in the sunlight, diamond dust rising into the heavens. Then it was just me, the golden sunlight, the smell of the river, and the cool wind against my face.

That was the first night I would ever sleep alone. I would spend many more nights alone, but I would always remember that particular night.

Andrew Massie

Chapter 9
A Retrospection

Friday, March 4, 2011

By the time a banging at the front door roused me, the sun had begun to fall to the west. I considered very strongly ignoring it, of staying under the covers until it was time to return to Manassas. But I had a headache, and the pounding was exacerbating the pain. I pulled my shirt on and wandered through the house to the door.

Columbus stood at the door, his nostrils flaring as I got closer. "Come on, man," he said, waving his hand in front of his nose. "I know you've had a bad few days, but take care of yourself."

"Sorry," I said, ushering him inside. "I didn't expect to have company."

He walked in and jumped onto the couch, resting his head against the pillow at the far end. "Why don't you go get cleaned up?"

I nodded and went to the bathroom. There was a bloody washcloth draped over the shower curtain rod. Natalie must have used it to clean the blood from her cheek the night before. I tossed it in the trash, then took a fresh one from beneath the sink. I took a short shower, washing away the grime of the night before.

"I saw your escapades from yesterday on the news this morning," Columbus said when the water stopped. "I was going to come by before school, but Gilbert had to get out to work, so he dropped me off early."

"How is the news painting me this time?"

Columbus chuckled lightly. "It depends on which station you turn to. Local Eight paints you as a hero cop shot in the line of duty. They cite your public service, your FBI career, and your bestselling book to show that you did all you could against an enemy that could not be contained. Local Five paints you as a federal vigilante who got two innocent people killed when you stuck your nose into a local operation. Your man Thomas Mackia backed that story. The national networks haven't picked up either yet."

"Thank heaven for small favors." I pulled on a new shirt and started brushing my teeth.

"You really know how to make an impression everywhere you go, don't you? Do they like you this much in Virginia?"

I spat. "You don't know the half of it." In the bedroom, I slipped into a clean pair of jeans before returning to the living room. "Let's just say I don't get invited to too many parties."

Columbus moved so he could see me as I collapsed in the recliner. "So, Darryl Phoenix, author, was William Mincks. Didn't see that one coming."

"Is there a reason for this visit?" I asked.

"No need to get defensive, Stephen. I just thought you could use a friend. Like I said, I know you've had a hard week. Monday, your ex has a seizure, then you get into a fight with Ryan Gathers; Tuesday, that same ex commits suicide; Wednesday, you apparently go insane and start wandering the land like a modern day Odysseus; then after everything yesterday…" He paused and looked around. "Where is Natalie, anyway?"

I licked my lips. The roof of my mouth felt like someone had taken a cheese grater to it. I ran my tongue over my freshly brushed teeth. Then I started to laugh. I don't know why. I was looking at his face, thinking about his question when, all of a sudden, I was struck dumb by the absurdity of everything that had happened in the last five days.

"What's so funny?"

"She's gone," I told him, giggling like a moron. "She left last night. Thinks I'm sleeping with Ariadne. Heading north by northwest to catch Ryan Gathers before he escapes to China. Like something out of a freaking spy movie!"

"Wait, wait, wait." He shook his head as though to clear dust from the crevices of his brain, then raised his eyebrows at me. "Start from the beginning, 'cause you aren't making any sense whatsoever right now."

I told him what had happened. I condensed the story, leaving out insignificant details, summarizing wherever possible to give him just the bare facts. I revealed seeing Olivia and John on Sunday; the conversation with Allen on Monday; the meeting in the Gardens and the confrontation with Olivia on Tuesday; the investigation and my meetings with Ariadne on Wednesday. I spent a lot of time telling the story of Thursday morning: confronting Darryl, then the stand-off with Ryan, finally the pub crawl and break with Natalie. The entire time I told the story, all I could think about was how absurd it all was.

"Well," he said when I had finished, "I look forward to your next book."

The sound that came from my throat was a combination of convulsing laughter and pain. I rubbed my eyes, which were sore and watery from my being asleep for so long. "I don't know what to do," I admitted.

"When are you going back to Virginia?" Columbus asked.

I paused. "Sunday morning."

"You'll figure something out," he told me.

"In a day and a half?"

"It doesn't seem to me that the constraints of time hold much sway over you."

There came another knocking at the door. "Come in!" I yelled.

Allen opened the door and stepped inside cautiously, looking around. John stepped in behind him. "Allen Silverman?" Columbus asked, looking the boy up and down.

"Mr. Graffney?" Allen asked in return.

Columbus rose to his feet and took Allen's hand. "I didn't realize this was the Allen from your story, Stephen. It all kind of makes sense now." Columbus reached out and mussed Allen's hair real quickly. "He's a good kid at heart, but he can be a real troublemaker."

"I didn't know you and the old guy knew each other," Allen told Columbus.

"This is Hazelwood, kid," Columbus said. "Everyone knows every-one."

"What are you guys here for?" I asked.

"I just wanted to check on you," Allen said. "I know you've had a rough couple of days. John said he wanted to come, too. I told him he could."

"What did I tell you?" Columbus asked. "A good kid at heart."

"You two are ridiculous," I laughed. "But thanks. I know it can't be easy for you right now, either."

Allen ran his hand through his hair a couple times, apparently return-ing it to the state it held before Columbus had mussed it. He walked across the floor and sat down on the couch. "It hurts," he said.

"I know," I told him.

John shook Columbus' hand and joined Allen on the couch. Columbus sat down in his original spot.

"I really appreciate you guys coming over," I told them. "I wish I'd known beforehand, though. There's not really anything to do here."

"We should call Dave and get him to bring us dinner," Columbus offered.

"I can call Mary and get her to bring drinks when she gets off work," John added.

"I've got a deck of cards," Allen said.

There was another knock at the door. "Come on in!" I called. "Join the party."

Neilson opened the door and peaked in. "Oh, wow. There really is a party going on in here." He stepped inside and walked across the floor to the side of the old coffee table. "What's the topic of discussion?"

"You're not a lawyer in this house," I told him. "What'd you come here for?"

"I just wanted to tell you that Allison felt really bad about what happened yesterday. She wanted me to stop by and tell you that she's sorry."

"Allison Weston?" John asked. "She's not coming here, is she? I don't want her and Mary getting in a fight."

"No," Neilson assured him. "She's staying in Mastern for the day."

"Good," said John.

"You're staying for the party though, right?" Columbus asked.

Neilson thought for a moment and asked, "How old is the kid?"

"Twenty-one." Allen answered automatically.

"Sure, I'll stay," Neilson smiled.

Another knock came at the door. "Come on in!" I shouted. "Might as well leave the door open."

The door swung open, stopping at a wide angle to reveal Matthew Graycraft. He was wearing his work clothes as though he had just come from the office, but everything about his stainless white shirt and suit pants was askew. His tie was missing, his top few buttons were unclasped, his shirt untucked, his cuffs unticked, his face red, his eyes puffy.

"What are you doing here?" Neilson asked. His voice was pointed, so I held a hand up to him.

"I just..." he stated. He clenched and unclenched his hands a few times. When he relaxed his fingers I could see fingernail marks on his palm. "I want..." His teeth dug into his tongue, and he exhaled loudly.

"Spit it out," I said.

"It'll hurt less once it's out in the open," Columbus told him.

Matthew took a deep breath. "I've never before had trouble speaking my mind. For most of my life I've believed that people like you are either my enemies or stepping stones on my path to success. I've always acted in my own best interest, and now that I'm looking back on my life, looking back on the events of the last few days, I realize that I've made very serious mistakes. So I wanted to come talk to you, one man to the other."

"I'm listening," I said.

He looked at Columbus, Allen, John and Neilson, then back to me. "I've been an idiot," he said. "I have always assumed that I was just a bastard, and that I couldn't change, but now I don't know. I feel like I don't have anything stable in my life to hold on to."

"What's changed?" I asked.

He looked me in the eyes and said, "Sandra is dead, Ryan is gone, and Edna is pregnant."

There was silence in the room for a long while as we all just looked at him. I leaned back in the chair, placing my fingers to my temple the way that Stephen used to. It didn't help me focus. Then Neilson rose, took a step toward Matt and stuck his hand out. "Congratulations," he said.

Matthew took the old man's hand and shook it once.

"I'm so sorry for everything I've done," Matt said.

I stood up and crossed the floor, sticking out my own hand. Matthew took it as well, shaking it firmly.

"Then change," I told him, slapping his shoulder, "before your kid gets here. You can't screw this one up."

Matt swallowed hard. "I don't know if I…I don't know if I can do it. Edna and I talked earlier. She says if I make some major changes, I could still keep her. But can I really change that much?"

"Yes," I told him. "We all can."

"Where do I start?"

"You already have. Dave will be at the party later," I told him. "Why don't you continue with him?" He nodded.

I pulled him inside and pointed at a free spot on the floor beside Neilson. As he walked over, Columbus and John both congratulated him. Allen introduced himself. "Oh yes," Matt said. "Olivia told me a little about you."

"She told me a bit about you, too," Allen said.

"I'm sure her reviews of me weren't as favorable as they were of you."

"She said you were the devil."

Matt winced. "Just one example." He put his hands on the table, looked up at Allen and said, "I'm trying real hard to be a good man now."

"Oh great," Allen said sarcastically. "After all the hurt you've caused, it's nice that, after all this time, you've finally decided to come to the light."

Folding his hands in front of him, Matt looked down into his lap. "You would honestly deny me redemption?"

Allen sighed. "Of course not," he said.

"Redemption isn't a tabula rasa," I told Matt. "It's hard work. Nobody is going to just forget that you created Ryan Gathers and set him onto his path. Just remember your responsibility from now on. Every time you look at Edna, every time you look at your kid, every single time you look at your house, and your job, and every person under you, remember that you're not just responsible for yourself. You're responsible for every single one of them."

"I'm going to try," he stated shakily.

"Don't try," Allen said. "Do."

Matt nodded.

I turned to Columbus. "Go ahead and call Dave. Gilbert too. I'm going to go pick up a pizza real quick, so we have something to munch on until Dave gets here with some real food." I turned to John. "If you don't mind getting Mary to bring us some drinks, I'll stop on my way home and get some mixers."

"Let me come with you," Neilson said.

We were on the road and down the street before Neilson scratched his nose and asked, "So how are you holding up?"

I chewed on my tongue for a few seconds. "I'm afraid I'm cracking," I admitted. "I was talking to Columbus earlier and started laughing, and couldn't stop. I hear Sandra and Olivia talking to me when I think about them. I see William's blue eyes looking at me when my own eyelids close. I don't know what I'm going to do."

Neilson nodded. "You know the last time I heard you say those words? You know the last time I had to ask you that question?" I shook my head. "It was just after your parents divorced. You were young, tongue-tied around girls, socially awkward, failing a couple classes and struggling with therapy. Your mom came in one day with you after school and left you there while she ran out to do chores, and I asked you, 'How are you holding up, kiddo?' You told me that you felt like the world was pointless.

You felt like crawling into bed and sleeping forever. You said you didn't know what you were going to do."

"What did you say to me?" I asked.

"I didn't say anything to you. I took you into my office and you sat and talked to me for over an hour while I worked. I listened to you tell me about your father, and how he was so stubborn and mean that you two always fought. And your mother: how she worried so much about you that you two always got into it and about how you didn't have any real friends. I heard that you and your girlfriend had just broken up, about how you hated your homeroom teacher because she always made you stay after class, and it was making you late to your other classes which was starting to affect your grades, and about how you didn't feel like your therapist was helping you with your anger. I just sat there and listened to you talk."

He coughed into his hand and continued. "About a week later, your mom brought you back. Things had gotten a little bit better, but now you had a new set of problems. Again, I just sat and listened. Then every week until I had finished your mother's affairs. Each week things were a little bit better, and you had a new set of problems. But you always got past your problems, and life always went on."

I smiled as I pulled the car into the pizza shop. "Thanks for being there for me. It was nice having someone to talk to."

"Don't forget that you always have someone to talk to if you need it. You don't always have to go it alone, you know?"

"I forget sometimes," I admitted again.

"Well, don't. If you ever feel that way again, like you just want to crawl into bed and sleep forever, why don't you give me a call? I can listen to you, even while I'm working."

"I know. I will," I told him. "I promise. You can listen to me while you're typing away, and keep me marveling at it."

He smiled. "One more thing, too, kiddo," he said. "If you break Ariadne's heart, I will personally come to Virginia and kick your ass."

I laughed. "She's too young for you, old man."

"You've been hanging out with that Silverman kid for far too long," Neilson said.

"You just don't understand us young folks."

"I invite you to look in the mirror sometime, Stephen. You're not a young man yourself anymore."

Younger than you think. "Silverman won't let me forget it," I told him.

We got the pizza and drinks and drove back to my house. I half expected Matthew to have left, but he was still there, conversing fairly pleasantly with John and Columbus. Static crackled in the air between them, but it wasn't as strong as the cosmic dissonance which would have once roiled around them. Allen sat on the floor in front of the couch, listening intently as the older guests talked. He didn't seem to be interested in adding to the conversation, but he was definitely attentive. I wondered if years from that night he would look back and remember those conversations the way that I still remembered Stephen's conversations, playing them backward and forward in my head, discerning what Stephen had done right and what he'd done wrong. Or maybe like at Matt's office, wondering what Stephen would have done.

We munched on pizza and played poker until Dave showed with a box full of party food and began unpacking it in my kitchen: paczki balls and beignets; wonton cups stuffed with crab and shrimp; apricots topped with Amaretto cream cheese; bacon-cheeseburger sliders topped with horseradish and honey barbecue sauce; chocolate, white chocolate, and dark chocolate wine truffles.

"Dave?!" I cried. "Who do you think you're feeding?"

"The knights of Hazelwood, obviously," Neilson said, popping a beignet into his mouth.

Mary showed up an hour or so later, asking for help with an ice-chest filled to the brim with beers, vodkas, gins, whiskeys, rums, tequilas, white and red wines, various schnapps, fruit juices and sodas.

"You guys realize this is a small party, right?" I asked her.

"Hey," Mary winked at me, "Here in Hazelwood the rule is you go hard."

By the time Edna showed up, people were coming in that I had never seen before in my life. They all called me Stephen and shook my hand, told me how much they liked my book, said how much of a tragedy it was about Olivia, or Sandra, or both. They gave me their condolences on Natalie leaving me. News traveled quickly in Hazelwood, and I smiled as genially as I could, even at the occasional disingenuous condescension and judgment in their eyes.

When Ariadne got there, my party guests were pumping dance music from my stereo system and had already clumped into conversation groups. Edna was in the living room talking to one of her friends, Matt stood on the porch. I wandered outside. From his vantage point he could look through my kitchen window at Mary and John making out against my fridge.

"Feeling a little voyeuristic?" I asked.

He jumped, then relaxed. "I just...I was never like that. I was wondering what it's like."

"Why don't you try it some time? I know Edna wouldn't mind."

"Did anything ever happen between you and Edna, way back when?"

"No," I told him.

"Good," he said.

"Have you talked to Dave yet?" I asked.

"Yeah," he responded. "We're working on getting his Mastern project funded. He thinks that with my support, he can turn it into an avant-garde meets old-fashioned dinner-and-a-show type establishment. Something bigger than he'd ever be able to do by himself. He's real excited about it."

"And you're not?"

"I'm afraid I'll lose money on it."

"Would you rather lose money, or lose Edna?"

"Yeah, that's the rub," he admitted.

Ariadne came walking up the driveway. "Hey, guys," she said, not recognizing Matt. She put her arm around me, and I put my arm around her. Then she looked up and saw who it was I was talking to. "What are you doing here?" she asked.

Matt looked at me, then said, "Nothing. Sorry." He walked inside, probably to find Edna.

"What's he doing here?" she asked me.

"He came to apologize," I told her. "I think he's one of us now."

"Just like that?" she asked.

"He was one of us in the beginning. He just needed to find his way back," I told her. Then, "Natalie's gone."

"How are you dealing with that?" she asked.

"I don't know," I told her.

"Thanks," she whispered.

"For what?" I asked.

"For not lying to me."

"Thank you," I whispered back.

"What for?" she asked softly.

"For not making me have to."

We were so close in that moment, my arm around her waist, her arm around mine. I could smell her soft perfume, could feel the beating of her heart, could almost taste her lipstick. And yet, as close as I felt to her, I realized then that we still had a ways to go.

"Let's go for a walk, Lanford," she whispered.

We went down the road, toward town and the bookstore on the corner, toward the university, toward the heart of Hazelwood. Until we reached the circle of the light, we could hear the sound of music coming from the house, beats blasting through the night.

"How are you?" I asked.

"I feel like I swallowed a bundle of razor wire," she told me. "I can feel it running between my teeth, cutting into my throat, winding down my esophagus through my heart, my lungs, all the way down to my stomach. I keep thinking about Sandra and Darryl. I can't stop myself. I keep thinking that I can call them up anytime I want, and then I remember that they won't be there. They won't ever be there ever again. And when I remember that, I feel like that razor wire is wrapping around my stomach like a snake. It feels like I'm dying."

I kissed her hair and hugged her close. She took my hand and pulled me back toward the house.

"When did Natalie leave?" she asked.

"Last night, just after I got home. She thinks you and I were sleeping with each other."

"You can't really blame her, can you? After all, Stephen had been running around with Olivia for the past week."

I stopped walking. "How did you know that?"

She shook her head. "They didn't make me a detective because I'm pretty." She took my hand again and pulled me along after her. "Also, Neilson told me."

"Did he now?"

"There are no secrets in Hazelwood," she told me. "In case you'd forgotten."

Allen stood outside lighting a cigarette as we came up the sidewalk. He smiled and waved at Ariadne. She reached into her jacket and produced the pack of cigarettes we'd been smoking from the night before.

"Hold on one second," I told her. I walked inside and maneuvered my way through the crowd to the side table, where I grabbed Eric Lanford's bottle of moonshine. I found plastic shot glasses that Mary had brought and grabbed Neilson, jerking my head toward the door.

I put the shot glasses on the hood of my car and poured the rest of the moonshine among the four receptacles. Ariadne lit a cigarette and handed it to me, then lit one for herself, handing the rest of the pack to Neilson. Neilson took one and lit it up.

"What are we drinking to?" Ariadne asked.

"It's Allison's turn," Neilson said, "which I guess means that it's actually Stephen's turn."

"Let Allen have it," I said. "I got one last night, he hasn't had one yet."

Allen smoked his cigarette. "Give me a minute," he said.

"So far we've toasted to Mastern, Hazelwood, Sandra, Olivia, Darryl, and the future," I told him.

"Well then there's only one thing to toast to," Allen said. He raised his shot glass into the air and said "'A requiem for flowers, sung in secret from rolling hills, buried in the crimson coda that is winter, unheard in city streets, the shadow of a black rose plucked without reason. To all the people that this world systematically destroys, our hearts go out to you.'"

"That's beautiful," Ariadne said. "What's it from?"

"A poem. One by Darryl Phoenix."

There was a moment of silence, before Neilson held his glass out. "Cheers," he said.

We shot. We smoked.

The words hung in the air, filling everyone; and who knew if they were right, or if they were meaningful, or if they were pretentious? They were there in that moment, and then they were gone. And then Allen was gone, and then Neilson was gone, and finally Ariadne and I were alone. Except my house was still filled with strangers and the sounds of a party.

I went to the shed in the back yard for the extension ladder, set it against the house and climbed to the roof. Ariadne said, "One second," and walked inside. When she returned she had two plastic cups that she held in one hand as she climbed up to sit beside me on the sandpaper shingles. I leaned up and took a drink of the nectar from the cup, a citrus drink with an apple aftertaste. She snuggled up against me.

"Ambrosia," she whispered in my ear.

I touched my cup to hers and together we drank, holding each other and looking up into the sky. A shooting star passed overhead. Lady Luna looked down on us, smiling sweetly as she did on all lovers. As I drifted off to sleep, time began to slip away again as it did when Ariadne was there, Ariadne who was like me. I didn't know how, but she made me pull up my anchor and drift away into the night sky, floating serenely between the divine light of the stars, not quite of this earth.

Andrew Massie

Chapter 10
The Spring Festival

Saturday, March 5, 2011

Helen and James came that morning to find our friends passed out around my house like corpses on a battlefield. My guests had fought spirits the night before, and it was easy to tell who won.

When they found the ladder, James and Helen climbed up to sit next to us, looking up at the morning sunlight shining through the tree branches. Ariadne and I slowly stirred, joining the world of the living. Shielding our eyes with our hands, we all watched the sun rise. I imagined Helios standing in his chariot, urging his solar steeds upward into the sky. The time had come to light the day again. Then I remembered that it was the earth that circled the sun, and not the other way around, and I tried to imagine Helios and his solar steeds pulling the earth through space into an elliptical orbit around the sun, but the image was somewhat less pleasing, so I let it go.

My back ached and my skin itched from the shingles, but I had slept better that night than the night before. Maybe when I got back to Manassas I would have a restful night's sleep.

In the lazy sag of the morning, my eyes pained, my skin like a burlap cover, I almost expected the day to limp along as lethargically as I felt. But Helen, leaning on one arm like an aristocratic oil-painting, looked over at me and said, "I told you she was trouble."

"You surely did," I admitted.

"I'm sorry to hear Natalie is gone," James said. I gave a grunting approximation of yes. He nodded to Ariadne on the other side of me. "Will Ariadne be joining us at the festival tonight then?"

"Crap," I said, putting my pointer finger to my temple. "I completely forgot about the festival."

"Told you," James said, looking to Helen.

"He's had a hard week," Helen responded.

James slapped my shoulder and said, "He doesn't seem much the worse for wear. The love of his life is gone, and he's still going strong."

"Which one are you talking about?" Helen asked. "The classical one or the modern one?"

"You know I am sitting right here?" I asked.

"I am, too," Ariadne pointed out.

"Yeah," Helen said, "We know."

"We're your family," James said. "And I don't know Ariadne that well, but it seems like she's in it with us, too. So we get to bust your chops. I mean, it's not like you don't deserve it."

"Thanks," I muttered, lying back.

"Don't take it personally," James said. "What are friends for if not to make us better than we are by ourselves?"

"Don't answer that," Helen ordered, raising her finger into the air like a mother bossing her children around.

Ariadne stretched her muscles tight and lay down on the roof, snuggling her head against my side. "I think I might be going crazy," she said. "I've never slept on a roof before. I don't even know you two, and all of a sudden we're family."

"You didn't know me a week ago, either," I pointed out to her.

"You didn't grow up in Hazelwood, did you?" James asked. Ariadne said that she hadn't.

"This is our life," Helen said. "It's not linear, it's not rational, and even if we don't live happily ever after, there are still enough happy moments scattered throughout to make it worth it, don't you think?" Ariadne smiled and nodded.

"Besides," James said, "Strange people are more fun."

We sat silently, watching the sun rise into the sky. Then, after a while, we went in. Ariadne didn't have any clothes for the funeral, so Helen took her to the store to find something to wear. James and I stayed at the house, waking and nursemaiding the guests from last night, offering them water and aspirin for their hangovers. Many had left the night before: A fight had broken out between guests, though between whom, nobody could or would say. We were able to get the house cleared out before Helen and Ariadne returned with clothes and a bouquet of flowers for the service.

Helen and James went to my room to change while Ariadne and I sat in the living room on the couch. There was a distance between us that hadn't been there the night before, as she sat on one end, resting her head against the pillow, while I sat on the other end, watching her rest.

"Have you made up your mind what you're going to do?" she asked.

I sat up and put my hand down across her knuckles. "I have an idea," I told her. "But it's crazy. I don't know if it'll work. I need to think about it some more."

"Will it make you happy?" she asked.

"I think so," I answered.

"You can always go after Natalie, you know," she said. "I wouldn't blame you for it. It'd be the safe bet."

"I could," I told her. "But I won't. I've hurt her badly enough. Now someone else deserves a chance."

She smiled. "You don't miss her?"

"I do. But there's no point in going back. I learned a lot from my time with her; now it's time to move forward. Besides, after Stephen, she could never trust me."

"Stephen never saw her for what she was. His mind reduced her to a symbol, a puzzle, just like it did every woman he ever knew. She shouldn't have trusted him." She moved over and put her head on my shoulder. "Can I trust you?" I folded my arm around her. After a few minutes I felt her body relax as she drifted away into sleep. When Helen and James emerged from the bedroom, dressed in mourning suits with faces to match, I felt her body tighten as she awoke, rising away from me.

We entered my bedroom and closed the door. There was a tense confusion for a moment as we both wondered what was going to happen. Then Ariadne stepped up to me, and began to pull the shirt up over my head. I raised my arms to make it easy for her, then I grabbed the bottom of her shirt at her hips and began to pull it off as well. She ran one of her hands over my chest, looking up into my eyes, her breathing visibly deepening. Then she unbuttoned and unzipped my jeans, letting them fall down my hips. I stepped out of them and guided her down onto the bed and pulled her tight jeans down and off, running my hands gently up and down her hard muscles and soft skin. She took her socked foot and gently put pressure on my shoulder, pushing me away. I took it, and kissed her ankle, looking down at her.

She got up off the bed and walked over to the dresser where the bag of her new clothes lay. I watched her ass move under her black panties as she drew out the skirt from her bag, bent over, stepping into it one foot at a time, then pulled it up, zipping it at the side. She pulled a silver tank top on over her head, then a black shirt down over that. She removed the white socks and asked, "You like what you see, Lanford?"

I swallowed hard. "I'd like to see more," I admitted.

She smiled. "Get dressed. We don't want to be late." I dressed, she took my hand, and together we left. But before we were out the door, she stopped and asked, "Do you have a couple of thick blankets?" I told her I did, and showed her where to get them. "Why?"

She nodded, but didn't say anything.

It was raining when we got to the church by the interstate. I sat between Ariadne and Helen, with James at Helen's right, while we watched the folks pour into the church to pay their respects to the dearly departed. There were nearly enough people to fill the enormity of the church. Despite her problems, Olivia had lived a decent life, touching the hearts of students, of her fellow teachers, and the friends she'd made in Hazelwood throughout the years. And she was so young. All of us filing into the cold church together, sitting together, made the room warm as the preacher walked in to begin the service.

"There are two passages that I would like to discuss today," he began. "If you will all turn to First Corinthians, book fifteen, passage fifty-one." He turned his own pages as the rest of his congregation flipped through their books, searching, then he read aloud over the finishing sounds of search. "'Behold, I show you a mystery!'" He spoke with such conviction, barely looking at his book, that for a second I thought he might be channeling it, acting as medium for a force bigger and older than any of us.

He spoke for a long time from the two passages, made many grand remarks about Olivia and her service. We sat patiently.

After the ceremony, we were invited to walk by her casket, to say a few words to her before she was closed off from us forever. She looked like a porcelain doll, painted with care and beauty. Her eyes were closed. I wanted to open them, to look into those blue irises, deep and empty as the deepest ocean trench. Then, feeling my body move by itself, I leaned forward and kissed her lips softly, and my mouth spoke Stephen's words, "I'll always love you, Olivia. Goodbye, Lover Girl." And then I was floating dreamlike back to my seat as someone else walked behind me to visit with the empty husk.

I saw Allen in the line, watching me. I nodded at him and raised my hand.

As we sat in the outdoor patio of the Sunset, eating Papa Burn's sandwiches and watching workers assembling wet tents for the festival, I felt very meditative and serene, as though nothing at all had happened. Today seemed to me like any other day. I wondered for a moment if I had learned anything from the past week, or if I was just unfeeling. I couldn't tell, but then again, I could hardly remember myself from a week before. I wasn't anybody then, and now I was someone. I had no voice, no identity, no property, no family. In a single week, everything had changed. And the clincher was, there would never be a point in my life where I would stop changing.

Allen sat down at the table with us. He removed his jacket, loosened his tie and unbuttoned his cuffs, pushing them up his arm. "What now?" he asked.

"We keep moving," I answered. "That's all we can do."

"But what's the point?" Allen asked. "I've been asking everyone I know that question and not one person has been able to tell me. Not my teachers, not my parents, not the priest. What's the point?"

"Allen," I said, refusing to adopt Stephen's mannerisms, but trying my best to project the confidence that came so naturally to him. "I know that your life hasn't been easy. I know that this isn't the first tragedy you've gone through; it won't be the last, either. But people like you and me, we've got advantages that others don't. People like Olivia, and Darryl, and Sandra. You may feel like the world has it out for you, but you can't deny that it had it out for them. So I can't tell you what the point is. Maybe there is one, and maybe there isn't. But if you have any strength within you, you keep moving. Because we can protect them when they can't protect themselves from us. I don't know if we can choose to become something that we're not. But we can refuse to be like Matthew, and Ryan, and Darryl's parents. We owe it to the people we've lost to be better. We have to be better. It's our duty as the knights of Hazelwood."

Allen looked up at me suddenly, and I knew that even if he didn't believe me, my words had hit him somewhere deep inside. "Are you making me a knight now?" he asked.

"Seems so, kid," I told him.

The five of us went to the barn, but we were all in our nice clothing, so we couldn't eat their barbecue ribs like we had back in college. We ate pulled pork sandwiches instead, covering ourselves in napkins in case we dripped. However, we did get barbecue sauce all over our faces, which made all of us laugh. It was like old times, when Stephen was still in control. At the same time it was different. Time had gone by, and circumstances had forced us to change. Yet we were still enjoying the nostalgia. The old and the new blended together within us, creating new tastes that were just as pleasant and enjoyable as the old ones.

The weather cleared up in the afternoon, and the spring festival started on time. It seemed as though the entire county had shown up to celebrate with us. Ariadne and I were there; so were Helen and James; so was Allen.

We walked the tents and attractions, playing games alongside everyone else. I picked up one of the old-fashioned shooting games and popped three balloons, winning a stuffed pony for Ariadne. "You've still got the shot," Ariadne told me.

"I've actually been thinking about handing in my gun," I told her, lowering the toy rifle to the ground. "I think I'm going to ask Dobbs to put me on a desk job when I get back to Virginia."

"Because of Sandra?" James asked.

"Maybe," I answered. "I think maybe I've just outgrown it. Or maybe it was never really for me. I didn't even have the urge to put my gun on this morning. I don't think I've thought about it for a single second all day, to be honest. It's like a toy you have when you're a kid, and you hold onto it as long as you can, because for you it represents security."

Allen watched my mouth moving, listening to every word I said.

We ate popcorn and funnel cake and apples dipped in chocolate and caramel with peanut pieces sprinkled on top of them.

"There he is," someone said from behind a stand, pointing at me. "That asshole hotshot."

We had lemonade and tea, and we laughed and joked as we walked through the festival grounds.

"I think I want to start writing," I thought aloud. "I want to take over where Darryl left off. I want to show people what's real. I want to show people the truth."

"What's your pseudonym going to be?" Ariadne asked.

"I don't know," I answered. "Sandra called me Achilles and Aeneas, but I was looking for something… I don't know, different."

"How about Ulysses?" Allen offered.

I shook my head. "I'd prefer something new, more modern, I guess."

"Très moderne," Helen quietly mocked.

"How about Casey," James suggested. "It's relatively modern."

"I like it," Ariadne said. "It reminds me of Cassandra, who could see the future and was powerless to stop it."

"If it's truth you want," Helen said, "why don't you add in the word Aletheia. It's the Greek word for truth."

"Casey Aletheia Phoenix," I mused. "Casey A. Phoenix. That sounds…" I searched for the word, and came up with "right."

We wandered to the center of the festival grounds where a band was about to play. The female singer at the front of the stage waved at Allen, and he waved back. "Are we ready to go?" the male singer asked into the microphone, then turned to the drummer and nodded. The drummer counted off and the band played. We watched them for a while, listening to their songs about plastic people living inside a boxy world and lovers torn apart by the pitfalls of modern life. The last song we heard before leaving was about returning home after a long time to find the lights still on and being amazed at the sight of your own personal lighthouse leading you home.

By the time we emerged at the other end of the festival grounds, the music was a distant hum like a church hymn in the distance.

I hugged Helen and James. "It was good seeing you both," I said.

"Come back soon," Helen said. "I don't want it to be another ten years before I see you."

"Promise," I said.

As they drove off, I turned to Allen, who held his hand out to me. I shook it strongly, looking him in the eyes. There was a new fire behind them that had not been there this morning. I felt that the rain of the day had fallen over him and washed away all of the fear; I hoped that the fire would grow in my absence. Of course, no teacher really knows what happens when their students go off on their own, but I felt confident that Allen had the ability and drive to make his own way in this world. Olivia must have had that same confidence in him.

"What now?" I asked.

He smiled. "I'll keep moving. Thanks, old man."

"Punk," I said, smiling back at him. And then he was off as well, walking into the falling dark.

Ariadne and I were alone then, all of our responsibilities for the day fulfilled. I wasn't sure what we were going to do now. But she wrapped her arm around my hip and took the keys from my belt-loop. "Come on," she said.

I got into the passenger seat and watched her adjust the seat and the mirrors, molding the car so that she was able to sit comfortably before turning the key and bringing the car to life.

We drove north, then west, then northwest past the barn. I realized then where we were headed, the hill that overlooked the pond beside the peach blossom trees, flowering so madly with the early signs of spring. We parked, she handed a blanket to me, and we climbed the hill to the spot where just a couple days ago we'd eaten dinner together.

As we lay down on the blankets and looked up at the stars, she gasped. "You can see so much more clearly out here, can't you?" Lady Luna was beginning to rise in the sky, bathing us in her light, dimming the stars. I could see every one of Ariadne's features, gilded in silver like a goddess.

"Yeah," I said, brushing the hair from her face.

"So…" She sighed pleasantly. "What have you decided?"

I kissed her. I kissed her lips with all the love my soul could muster. She kissed me. She kissed my lips so that I felt I might break if she stopped. And when she did pull away from me, I thought I might die. I felt as though I had no more breath in my body, but as she twisted my head and kissed my cheek, and softly whispered that single word, "Sophia," I was resuscitated by a power I had never felt before.

"Casey," I whispered back. We kissed again.

"Casey," she moaned between kisses.

"Sophia," I whispered back.

I was undressing her, and she was undressing me. The next moment, her shirt was off, and so was mine, and my mouth was tracing her skin, my lips molding themselves to the curves of her dress as I pushed her bra to the side. The crickets chirped to life, an orchestra to accompany our music. She began to sing a melody that filled the night. Mist began to rise from the pond, and the cold of the night began to fall around us. Her song reached a crescendo. The stars popped into existence as though they had been created to frame us.

I rolled off of her, pulling her atop me, pillowing her warm cheek against my chest. She kissed me, rubbing her legs up against mine.

"Did you see it?" she asked.

"See what?" The light had filled my mind and body, had crossed every fiber of muscle below every tissue of skin, had soaked into my brain. I had seen it. But could she see what had passed through me?

"The light," she said, looking in my eyes. "The reason we came out here tonight."

I nodded. "I saw it," I told her. She smiled.

"I told you," she teased, glowing brightly in the darkness, "if you just open yourself to it, the light will find a way."

About the Author

Andrew Massie was born in Belleville, Illinois and grew up on military bases around the world. He earned a BA in English from Louisiana Tech University and an MA in the Humanities from the University of Chicago. He currently works in higher education in Louisville, Kentucky.

Author website at http://awmwrites.tumblr.com

If you enjoyed *In the Shadows of My Mind,* consider these other fine books from Savant Books and Publications:

Essay, Essay, Essay by Yasuo Kobachi
Aloha from Coffee Island by Walter Miyanari
Footprints, Smiles and Little White Lies by Daniel S. Janik
The Illustrated Middle Earth by Daniel S. Janik
Last and Final Harvest by Daniel S. Janik
A Whale's Tale by Daniel S. Janik
Tropic of California by R. Page Kaufman
Tropic of California (the companion music CD) by R. Page Kaufman
The Village Curtain by Tony Tame
Dare to Love in Oz by William Maltese
The Interzone by Tatsuyuki Kobayashi
Today I Am a Man by Larry Rodness
The Bahrain Conspiracy by Bentley Gates
Called Home by Gloria Schumann
Kanaka Blues by Mike Farris
First Breath edited by Z. M. Oliver
Poor Rich by Jean Blasiar
The Jumper Chronicles by W. C. Peever
William Maltese's Flicker by William Maltese
My Unborn Child by Orest Stocco
Last Song of the Whales by Four Arrows
Perilous Panacea by Ronald Klueh
Falling but Fulfilled by Zachary M. Oliver
Mythical Voyage by Robin Ymer
Hello, Norma Jean by Sue Dolleris
Richer by Jean Blasiar
Manifest Intent by Mike Farris
Charlie No Face by David B. Seaburn
Number One Bestseller by Brian Morley
My Two Wives and Three Husbands by S. Stanley Gordon
In Dire Straits by Jim Currie
Wretched Land by Mila Komarnisky
Chan Kim by Ilan Herman
Who's Killing All the Lawyers? by A. G. Hayes
Ammon's Horn by G. Amati
Wavelengths edited by Zachary M. Oliver
Almost Paradise by Laurie Hanan
Communion by Jean Blasiar and Jonathan Marcantoni
The Oil Man by Leon Puissegur
Random Views of Asia from the Mid-Pacific by William E. Sharp
The Isla Vista Crucible by Reilly Ridgell
Blood Money by Scott Mastro
In the Himalayan Nights by Anoop Chandola
On My Behalf by Helen Doan